S0-BRB-780

WITHDRAWN

THE BLOOD OF OTHERS

Each of us is responsible for everything and to every human being.

DOSTOYEVSKY

SIMONE DE BEAUVOIR

The Blood of Others

TRANSLATED FROM THE FRENCH

BY ROGER SENHOUSE & YVONNE MOYSE

INDIANA STATE
T.C. LIBRARY

NEW YORK   ALFRED A. KNOPF

1948

PQ
2603
.E362S33

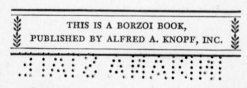

THIS IS A BORZOI BOOK,
PUBLISHED BY ALFRED A. KNOPF, INC.

Copyright 1948 by Roger Senhouse and Yvonne Moyse. All rights
reserved. No part of this book may be reproduced in any form
without permission in writing from the publisher, except by a re-
viewer who may quote brief passages in a review to be printed in
a magazine or newspaper. Manufactured in the United States of
America.

FIRST AMERICAN EDITION

Originally published in France as LE SANG DES AUTRES; copyright
by Librairie Gallimard 1945.

TO

NATHALIE SOROKINE

31 Aug 73 JA

138060

THE BLOOD OF OTHERS

WHEN he opened the door, their eyes turned toward him.

"What do you want?" he asked.

Laurent was sitting astride a chair in front of the fire. "I must know whether or not you've decided that it's to be done tomorrow morning."

Tomorrow. He looked about him. The room smelt of soapsuds and cabbage soup. Madeleine was smoking, her elbows on the tablecloth; a book was in front of Denise. They were alive: for them this night would have an end; there would be a dawn.

Laurent looked at him.

"We can't delay," he said gently. "I must leave at eight o'clock to get there — if I am to go." He pronounced his words carefully, as though he were speaking to an invalid.

"Of course." He knew that he must answer and he could not answer. "Listen, come and see me when you wake up; just knock — I must think things over."

"All right, I'll knock at about six o'clock," said Laurent.

"How is she?" asked Denise.

"For the time being, she's asleep," he answered, and walked toward the door.

"Call out if you want anything," said Madeleine. "Laurent is going to lie down, but we'll be here all night."

"Thanks." He closed the door.

He must decide. Her eyes are shut, each breath labors between her lips; the sheets rise and fall. They rise too often; the effort of living is too obvious, too noisy; she is struggling, her light is failing; at dawn it will be out. Because of me — first Jacques and now Hélène. Because I did not love her and because I loved her; because she came so close to me and because she remained so far apart. Because I exist and she, free, solitary, and eternal, is bound to my existence, unable to avoid the brutal fact of my existence, fettered to the mechanical sequence of her life; and at this last link of the fatal chain, her very heart struck by the blind steel, by the hard presence of the metal, by my presence — her death. Because I was there, solid, inevitable, for no apparent reason. I should never have existed. First Jacques, now Hélène.

Outside, the night has fallen, a night without street lamps, without stars, without voices. A patrol went by some time ago; now no one is abroad, the streets are deserted. In front of the big hotels and the ministries the sentries are on guard. Nothing is happening. But here something is happening: she is dying. "First Jacques" — again those icy words. But in the slow passing of the night, through other words and scenes from out the past, the original evil unfolds its story. It has deliberately assumed the shape of a story, as if anything else might have been possible, as if everything had not been predestined since my birth: the utter rottenness hidden in the womb of all human destiny. Entirely posited at my birth, entirely present in the odor and the shadow of the death room, present at every moment and throughout eternity. Today and for all time I am present. I was always present. Before that, there was no time. Since time was, I am, forever, and even beyond my own death.

He was present, but at first he did not know it. I see him now, leaning against a window in the gallery. But he did not know it; he thought that only the world was present. He was looking at the begrimed skylights

[4]

through which the smell of ink and dust rose in gusts, the smell of other people's work; sunlight flooded the old oak furniture, while the people below were stifling in the dull light of green-shaded lamps; throughout the afternoon the machines purred monotonously. Sometimes he fled; sometimes he remained motionless for hours, allowing the sense of guilt to enter into him through eyes, and ears, and nostrils. At ground level, under the dirty panes, boredom stagnated, and in the long room with light-colored walls the sense of guilt eddied out in sickly spirals. He did not know that through the fanlight, when they raised their heads, the workmen could see the solemn, fresh face of a middle-class child.

The blue upholstery velvet was soft to his cheeks, the kitchen, gleaming with copper, exuded a good smell of melted fat and caramel; from the drawing-room came a murmur of silk-smooth voices. But in the scent of summer flowers, in the crackling flames of a cozy winter, tirelessly stalked a sense of guilt. When he went away for the holidays he left it behind him. With no sense of guilt, stars shot across the sky, apples were crisp to the tooth, cool water bathed his naked feet. But as soon as he returned to the flat, embalmed under white dust sheets, as soon as he shook the naphthalene-larded curtains, he found it again, patient and intact. Season succeeded season, the countryside changed, new adventure stories were published in books with gilt edges, but nothing changed the even murmur of the machines.

From the dark ground floor the odor of guilt insinuated itself into the whole house. "One day it will be your house." On the front of the building there were letters engraved in the stonework: "Blomart & Sons, Printers." With unhurried step his father would come upstairs from the workshops and into the big apartment; unmoved, he would breathe the thick air that stagnated on the staircase. Nor did Elisabeth and Suzon suspect anything; they hung pictures on the walls of their rooms and arranged cushions on their divan beds. But he was sure his mother knew this uneasiness which dulled the brilliance of the sunniest days; for her too, through the shining parquet floor, through the hangings of silk and the deep pile carpets, seeped the sense of guilt.

Perhaps she had also met it somewhere else, in unknown shapes; she carried it with her everywhere, under her fur coats, under the dresses gleaming with sequins, which clung to her little rounded body. That was probably why she always seemed to be making excuses for herself; she spoke apologetically to the servants and to the tradespeople, she walked with small hurried steps, all huddled together, as though to reduce even more the amount of space that she required on the earth. He would have liked to ask her about it, but he never quite knew what words to use. One day he tried to talk about the workmen, but she said quickly in a smooth voice: "Oh no, they don't mind so very much — they're used to it. And then, in life, we all have to do things we dislike." He had not questioned her further; what she said did not carry much weight, she always gave the impression of speaking in the presence of an exacting and influential witness who must not be shocked. But when she feverishly cut out a layette for the cook's child, which she could have bought quite easily at the Bon Marché, when she spent her nights repairing the housemaid's clumsy darns, he seemed to understand her. "It's silly, there's no need for you to do it," scolded Suzon and Elisabeth. She did not try to justify herself, but from morning to night she flew all over the place in an endless flight, spending hours pushing the old paralyzed governess's wheel-chair, talking in deaf and dumb language to her deaf cousin. She liked neither the old governess nor her cousin: it was not for their sakes that she spent herself. It was because of that joyless odor which seeped into the house.

Sometimes she took Jean to see her poor — to Christmas trees and tea parties given to well-scrubbed children, who politely gave thanks for the beautiful plush bear or the clean little overalls — they did not seem unhappy. The beggars in rags who crouched on the pavements did not worry him either; with their white eyeballs, their stumps, and the metal flutes that they played by blowing through their noses, they took their place as naturally in the street scene as a camel in the desert or pigtailed Chinese in China. And the stories he was told about these poetic vagabonds and touching little orphans always ended in tears of joy, handshakes, clean clothes, and crusty loaves. Poverty only seemed to exist to be relieved, to give rich little boys the pleasure of giving: it did not worry Jean. But he knew there was something else, something that the books with gilt edges did not mention, that Mme. Blomart did not mention. Perhaps one was forbidden to speak about it.

I was eight years old when for the first time I came face to face with the original evil. I was reading in the gallery; my mother came in with an expression on her face that we often noticed, an expression full of guilt and apology, and she said: "Louise's baby is dead."

Once again I see the twisted staircase, the stone corridor with those many doors, all alike; Mother told me that behind every door there was a room in which a whole family lived. We went in. Louise took me in her arms, her cheeks were flabby and wet; Mother sat on the bed beside her and began to talk to her in a low

[7]

voice. In the cradle was a white-faced baby with closed eyes. I looked at the red tiles, at the bare walls, at the gas ring, and I began to cry. I was crying, Mother was talking, and the baby remained dead. In vain could I empty my money-box and Mother could sit up for nights together: it would always be just as dead.

"What's the matter with that child?" asked my father.

"He went with me to see Louise," my mother answered.

She had already told them the story, but now, with words, she tried to make them feel it: meningitis, the night of agony, and in the morning the little stiff body. Father listened as he swallowed his soup. I could not eat. Over there Louise was crying, she was not eating; nothing would ever give the child back to her — no, not ever. Nothing would blot out that unhappiness which fouled the world.

"Come now, drink your soup," said my father. "Everyone's finished."

"I'm not hungry."

"Do try a little, darling," said Mother.

I lifted the spoon to my lips and put it back on the plate with a kind of hiccup. "I can't!"

"Listen," said my father, "it's very sad that Louise's baby is dead, I'm deeply grieved for her, but not all our life are we going to mourn it. Now, just you hurry up!"

I drank. In a trice the hard voice had loosened the tightness about my throat. I felt the lukewarm liquid slip down my throat, and with each mouthful something flowed into me that was far more nauseating than the smell of the printing works. But the tightness was relieved. Not all our life.

Tonight, until the dawn and perhaps for a few more days — but not all our life — after all, it is her sorrow,

[8]

*not ours. It is her death. They had laid him on the
bench with his torn collar and the blood caked on his
face; his blood, not mine. "I'll never forget it." Marcel
too cried in his heart. "Never, oh little one, my little
pony, my good little boy — never will I forget your
laughter and your living eyes." And his death is deep
in our lives, peaceful and strange, and we who live remember; we live to remember it now that it no longer
exists, any more than it existed for him who is dead.
Not all our life — not even for a few days — not even
for a minute. You are alone on that bed, and I can only
hear the labored breath that comes from your lips,
which you cannot hear.*

He had drunk his soup and eaten all his dinner. Now
he was crouching under the grand piano; the crystal
chandelier shone with many fires; the crystallized fruits
sparkled under their sugary casings; soft and tinted
like sugar cakes, the lovely ladies smiled at each other.
He looked at his mother: she did not look like those
scented, fairylike beings; a black gown bared her
shoulders; her hair, dark as her gown, was twisted
smoothly round her head like a band of watered silk,
but in her presence he did not think of flowers or
splendid cakes, or of seashells, or of blue-tinted shingle
on the beach. She was a human presence, no more. She
hurried from one end of the drawing-room to the other
in her tiny satin slippers, the heels of which were far
too high, and she smiled too — even she. A short time
ago her face had been distressed, her low, intense voice
had whispered in Louise's ear; now she smiled. "Not
all our life." He had dug his nails into the carpet.
Louise's baby is dead. He forced himself to visualize
the scene: Louise sitting on the edge of the bed, crying.
He had stopped crying and at this very moment he was
even looking through the motionless, transparent pic-

[9]

ture at the mauve, green, and pink dresses, and desires once more rose within him — a desire to bite those creamy arms, to thrust his face into that hair, to crumple those light silks like a petal. Louise's baby is dead. In vain; it is not my sorrow.

It is not my death. I close my eyes, I remain motionless, but I am remembering things about myself, and her death enters into my life, but I do not enter into her death.

I slipped out from under the piano, and in bed I cried myself to sleep because of that thing which had poured into my throat with the tepid soup — more bitter than the sense of guilt — my sin. The sin of smiling while Louise was weeping, the sin of shedding my own tears and not hers. The sin of being another being.

But he was too young to understand. He thought that the sin had entered into him unawares, because his clenched fingers had opened, because his throat had been loosened. He did not guess that it was in the very air that fills my lungs, in the blood that courses through my veins, in the glow of my vitality. He thought that if he tried hard enough, he would never again know that foul taste. He tried hard. He sat at his schoolboy's desk, and his innocent eyes looked fondly at the smooth page, which had no past and was as virginal as the future.

Empty page, empty canvas, pure and icy earth that shines far beyond the revolutions to come. Marcel has thrown away his paintbrush — that blood on Jacques's face — that blood that streams for every drop that we have spared and for every drop that we have spilled. Your blood: red on the white cottonwool and on the gauze, so lazily heavy in your swollen veins. "She will not last the night." No flowers, no hearse: we will hide you in the earth.

The mud on my hands, the mud on our souls, that

was the future of the good little boy so innocently trac-
ing his pothooks and hangers. He could not guess, he
did not know the weight of his own presence. Trans-
lucent and innocent in front of the blank page, he
smiled at a fair, rational future.

My mother spoke so rationally, as though she never
made small fluttering movements, as though she never
walked with little, reticent steps. She said that poverty
and slavery and armies and wars, as well as devouring
passions and tragic misunderstandings, were simply
due to the stupidity, the abysmal stupidity, of mankind. If they had not wanted it, everything could have
been quite different. I was indignant at their folly; I
thought we should have taken each other by the hand
and gone through the town, she trotting on her little
high-heeled shoes and I dragging her forward with my
childish enthusiasm; we would have stopped the
passers-by in the squares, we would have gone into the
cafés, we would have made speeches to the crowds. It
did not seem so very impossible. On the feverish morning of a *coup d'état* in an arcaded street of Seville,
panic-stricken people had suddenly begun to run.
Obediently following the crowd, Father ran, dragging
Elisabeth and Suzon with him. She had stopped dead
and, in order to stem the foolish onrush, she had spread
out her little arms; I was convinced that if Father had
not seized her, if he too had stretched out his great
masculine arms, the crowd, quelled, would have returned to its unhurried pace.

But my father did not think of stopping the blind
progress of the world; in a dignified manner he ran
with the crowd, and exhortations failed to arrest his
obstinate pace. When I innocently began to ask him
questions, he smiled at first; later he did not smile, he
spoke with bitter pride of his hard-working and ab-

stemious life. His right to the luxuries that surrounded him seemed to be all the more positive since he did not trouble to enjoy them. He worked all day, and at night he read big books and made notes as he went along. He did not like entertaining, he almost never went out. He ate and drank with indifference. It seemed as if he considered that his cigars, his Burgundy, and his armagnac 1893 were honorable distinctions, necessary only to the peace of his conscience.

"Equalization merely reduces everything to its lowest level," he would explain to me. "You'll never raise the masses; all you'll succeed in doing is to abolish the élite." His voice was cutting, unanswerable, but deep in his eyes was a kind of angry fear. I was silent, but little by little I sensed the truth: voluptuously, as if it were incense, he breathed the corrupt odor of the world. For it was not only in the house, it infested the whole town, the whole earth. At night, in the subway, it was the same anguish that choked me. The men had placed their hands palm-down on their knees, the women's eyes were lifeless, and the swaying of the journey mingled their sweat and their sorrows with the heavy atmosphere. The train passed through a tiled station in which multicolored posters reflected the daily face of the outside world, with its slow-combustion stoves and its tins of *foie gras;* then it plunged into the black tunnel. It seemed to me that this summed up the entire fate of the weary crowd, and it saddened me. I thought of a film that I had seen with my friend Marcel: of a town buried in the bowels of the earth, where men wasted away in suffering and in darkness, while on white terraces above, an arrogant race enjoyed the splendor of the sun. The story ended with a flood, a rebellion, and, amid a tremendous wreckage of alembics, with a luminous reconciliation. And I asked myself: "Why don't these people rise up?" Often on a Sunday I dragged Marcel to Aubervilliers, to Pantin. For hours we would walk along endless blank walls, among gasometers, factory chimneys, and houses of blackened brick. Whole lives were spent there. From morning until night the same weary gesture: only one Sunday in the week. "They're used to it." If they really were used to it, that only made it worse.

When I used the word "revolution" to her, she flushed. "You're only a child! You don't know what you're saying!" I tried to argue, but she stopped me, her body shaken with passionate horror. It was senseless to try to change anything in the world or in life; things were bad enough even if one did not meddle with them. Everything that her heart and her mind condemned she rabidly defended — my father, marriage, capitalism. Because the wrong lay not in the institutions, but in the depths of our being. We must huddle in a corner and make ourselves as small as possible. Better to accept everything than to make an abortive effort, doomed in advance to failure. That prudence! That senseless prudence! As if there were a means of escape!

Keep the door shut, your lips shut — but my silence shouts orders. "If you don't answer me, I'll go," or else, "If you don't answer me, I won't go." My presence in itself is a spoken word. Go on, go forward into the mud of the night. Decide. I decided your death and I am not quit of it. Again! I would cry mercy, but there is no mercy. Oh, ill beloved! Had I earlier cast off the snares of prudence, I should have opened my door, I should have opened my arms and my heart. Silent, rigid. "I would not lift a finger to cause the death of a human being" — and bearing down meantime upon the earth with the whole of my motionless weight.

[13]

You are dying. Others are dying by inches, their bodies striped with weals, the skin stuck to their bones. Two million prisoners shiver behind barbed wire. Little Rosa threw herself out of the window. They found him in his cell, he had strangled himself with his underclothes.

Senseless! He hated that prudence. He raised his hand, he raised his whole arm; he looked angrily at his mother. "We will change the world." That imprudence! That senseless imprudence! He wanted to speak, to act.

And there is Jacques, lying on the bench, his shirt open, the blood clotted on his face, and his eyes shut.

But it all seemed so simple then; poor, innocent, good young man. He raised his clenched fist; he chorused: "Tomorrow, the International will be the human race." No more war, no more unemployment, no more servile work, no more poverty. Death to men of ill will and joy on earth. In his imagination he pulverized the old world and built up a new universe with its pieces, as a child rearranges the pieces of a Meccano set.

"It's done! I've joined the party!" I proclaimed in a loud voice as I came into Marcel's studio.

Marcel put down his paintbrush and turned his easel to the wall. All his canvases were turned to the wall, one never saw anything but their rough backs.

"Of course," he said, "it was bound to end like that."

"If we don't lift a finger, do you think the world will change by itself?" I asked.

Marcel shook his head, "There's nothing to expect from the present world; the dough is sour. I prefer to make a new one altogether."

"But yours only exists on canvases."

He laughed mysteriously. "We'll see."

He did see — but at that time he was young too, and although he doubted, he still hoped. Nearly every day I knocked at his door. Sometimes he greeted me cheerfully, sometimes with indifference. He greeted me — fiercely, he should have shut his door in my face. But he knew this no more than I did, or perhaps he knew that one can never keep a door shut. I used to go in. Jacques would be sitting at a little table, working; he was like his brother, but his features were more delicately molded, not rugged. Marcel would be putting a bottle of cheap brandy on the table laden with cacti, shells, mandragora roots, and the queer mosaics he amused himself by making out of stones, nails, matches, and pieces of string; and in a glass jar, a hippocampus, a little spiny black crook supporting the noble head of a horse. We would light our cigarettes and we would talk. I liked to talk; I chose my words with care: they were to lead Marcel to that purified world toward which I was hastening — and it was Jacques who heard them. He would raise his head.

"Fight at the side of the proletariat!" he would say. "How could we? We don't belong to them."

"But since we want the same thing as they do —"

"That's the point: we don't. A worker wants *his* freedom; you'll never want anything else but other people's freedom."

"That doesn't matter. The main point is to get the same result."

"But it's impossible to disassociate the result from the struggle that leads up to it. Hegel explains it so well; you ought to read him."

"I haven't time."

He annoyed me a little with his philosophic subtleties. I thought that he was only talking; and all the time he was passionately living every moment.

"Of course, if you want a thing, you must agitate to get it," he would say, "but as for actually getting what you've asked for — to get a something that I didn't want can be of no advantage to me, it doesn't belong to me at all. That is what the Fascists cannot understand. I admire Marx because he asks mankind to take and not to receive. Only you and I have nothing to take; we're not that sort. No, you can't *make* yourself a Communist."

"Then what must we do?"

He shrugged his shoulders in distress. "I don't know."

I would smile. He was only a schoolboy; I oughtn't to have smiled: he at least knew that he took up space on earth and that he would never extend beyond the opacity of his own presence. I still did not know this; my eyes were fixed on those future horizons upon which no sense of guilt would stalk.

And then one day I saw myself. I saw myself, solid and opaque, at the family table, on which an omelet was steaming, full light focused on my well-cut suit and on my well-kept hands; I saw myself as Jacques saw me, as the workmen saw me when I went through the shops — as I really was: old Blomart's son. Under their dumbfounded gaze — four pairs of scandalized eyes staring at my swollen cheek — I became aware of myself, nor did I lack proofs.

The cheek had swollen still more during the morning. "What on earth can I tell them?" Before going to the dining-room, he dabbed his face for a long time with a damp towel. The eye was almost closed.

"Good morning, Mother; good morning, Father," he said airily.

He bent to kiss his mother.

"Good heavens! What has happened to you?" Mme Blomart was horrified.

"Oh, what a face!" said Suzon.

He sat down without answering and unfolded his table napkin.

"Your mother is asking what has happened to you," said M. Blomart dryly.

"Oh, it's nothing," said Jean. He crumbled a piece of bread between his fingers. "Last night I went to a Montmartre bar with some friends and there was a riot."

"Which friends?" asked his mother. Her color had risen a little, as it did when she was annoyed.

"Marcel and Jacques Ledru," replied Jean. He, too, was afraid of blushing; he did not like lying to her.

"So you stopped someone's fist?" said M. Blomart slowly. Behind his pince-nez his eyes gleamed shrewdly.

"Yes," he answered, and passed his hand over his swollen face.

"The fellow must have had a powerful fist, a fist like a policeman's club," said M. Blomart. There was a hard expression on his face as he looked at his son. "What were you doing at midnight in front of Bullier with a lot of lunatics who were howling the *Internationale*?"

Blood rose to Jean's cheeks; he swallowed painfully. "I was coming out of a meeting."

"What's this fine story?" said Mme Blomart.

"The story," said M. Blomart in measured tones, "is this: the police superintendent telephoned me this morning to inform me that your son was nearly charged with insulting behavior and assaulting an officer of the law. Luckily Perrun is a decent fellow; he had him released at once when he heard the name."

A lifetime of work and honor. . . . Jean stared at

[17]

the purple capillaries which striated his father's cheeks — apoplectic cheeks. M. Blomart's calm was evidence of a command of himself difficult to overcome. Whatever Jean might do, in spite of the mottling and the gray goatee, he was intimidated by that virtuous countenance.

"They attacked us without provocation," he said, "under the plea that we were causing a disturbance and obstructing a public thoroughfare. They beat us up and took us to the police station."

"I conclude that the police did their duty," said M. Blomart, "but what I should like to know is how you came to be at a Communist meeting."

There was a deathly silence. Jean's fingers kneaded a pellet of bread.

"You know that on that subject I have never agreed with you," he said.

"So you are a Communist?" said M. Blomart.

"Yes," answered Jean.

"Jean," implored his mother. It was as if she were begging him to retract an indecent statement.

M. Blomart caught his breath; with a sweeping gesture he indicated the well-spread table.

"Then what are you doing here, at the table of an abominable capitalist?" He laughed derisively as he considered Jean.

Then suddenly he saw himself. He had looked almost wildly at the big dining-room, at the cupboard full of old wines, at the cheese omelet; he was there with those others. He rose, he left the room. My flat, my house; a human body takes up so little space, it displaces the atmosphere so little — this enormous shell engulfing so small an animal. And in his wardrobe all those clothes made of choice materials tailored specially for him: old Blomart's son.

He banged the door behind him and he walked for a long time. It was a fine autumn day. Fresh and vital, a few flowers that had mistaken the season swayed in the rusty foliage of the chestnut trees. He walked along in his good shoes and his well-cut suit. Old Blomart's son: he was taking up space on the earth, a space he had not chosen to occupy. He did not know what to do with himself, but it did not worry him too much: surely everything could be adjusted; surely there was a way of living. How could he have guessed that he was dangerous?

Dangerous as the tree that unconsciously spreads its light shadow round the bend of the road; dangerous as that hard black toy which Jacques looked at, smiling. It seemed so harmless to walk along with one's hands in one's pockets, sniffing the rusty aroma of the trees. He was kicking a chestnut, which shot along the asphalt, and the air he breathed was not stolen from anyone. He thought: "Old Blomart's son will cease to exist." He could soon learn the trade, two years' apprenticeship at the most; after that, the bread he ate would really be his own. He suddenly felt very happy; he understood why his childhood and his youth had always had a stale taste: it was the rotten sap of the old world that ran in his veins, but now he was going to cut away his roots and make himself a new being.

A smell of fried onions hovered about the landing and he could hear an appetizing sizzling on the other side of the door. He knocked. "Come in," said Marcel. Jacques was bending over a frying-pan, enveloped in a thick pungent vapor. Jean ran his hand through his hair.

"How are you, my good little cook?" He went up to Marcel, who was relaxing on the divan. "Good morning, old man."

"Good morning," said Marcel, stretching out a careless hand. He sat up suddenly. "I say, you've got a face on you! Have you seen it, Jacques?"

Jacques reluctantly turned aside from the steaming frying-pan, where two large sausages were sweating away in their fat with staccato gurgles. "Good heavens," he said, "what hit you?"

"A good clip from a club." Jean touched his cheek.

"They certainly hit hard," marveled Jacques. "Was it last night?"

"Yes, just as we were coming out of Bullier, the cops came down on us."

There was pride in his voice. Idiot, blind, unaware of the danger of his presence, of the trap hidden in every word, in every accent of his complacent voice. And Marcel let me speak, while he smiled his wide cannibal's smile — idiotic and blind too — instead of throwing me downstairs.

"They might have torn you to pieces," said Jacques.

"Don't get excited, little horse," said Marcel, "you can see that he's still intact." He touched Jean's temple. "Shall we offer a libation to it?"

"I'd rather have something to eat," Jean replied.

He looked longingly at the sausages, resplendent on their bed of golden-brown onions; their crusty skins had burst open, their meat oozed out from the gaping slits.

"You had no lunch?" asked Marcel. "Didn't you dare show up at home?"

"Unfortunately, I did show up," said Jean.

"Did it cause a sensation?"

"Just a bit." Jean took a few steps and stood by the empty easel. "Do you know the brainwave I've just had? I'd like to be apprenticed to old Martin as a printer and say nothing to my father; then once I know the trade, I'll clear out of the house."

I ought to have guessed. Jacques's eyes shone with incredulous delight; they were too bright.

"Why?" asked Marcel. "What good will it do you?"

"I don't want to stay in an unjustifiable situation all my life."

"Do you think there are any justifiable situations?" asked Marcel. He cut off a huge piece of sausage in the frying-pan and devoured it. "Let's eat," he said.

"And now," he said when the meal was finished, "clear out: I'm going to work."

"I'm clearing out," I replied. I looked at Jacques; it was such a fine day and I did not feel like being alone. "Are you working too? Won't you come for a walk with me?"

He flushed with astonishment and pleasure. "Won't it bore you?"

"I suggested it."

We went and sat in Montsouris Park, near the lake; a swan was sailing along on the water and we were surrounded by children.

"How lucky you are!" said Jacques. "You always seem to know what you ought to do."

"If you didn't burden yourself with a lot of intellectual scruples —"

"But I am an intellectual," said Jacques.

I shrugged my shoulders. "Then be resigned to your fate. Go on philosophizing."

"To act for the sake of acting would be dishonest," he said, "but perhaps my scruples are also dishonest."

He looked at me in uncertainty. He was so young, so eager — it should have been easy for him to live. He had only to let himself go.

[21]

"You're too timid," I said. "As long as you wonder if the workers' cause is really your own, it won't be. Just say: it is my cause."

"Yes," said Jacques, "but I can't say it without having a reason. I would have to have said it already." For an instant he looked silently at the big white swan and then he smiled. "I'm going to show you something."

"Let's see it."

He hesitated and thrust his hand into a pocket. "It's a poem, my latest poem."

I didn't know much about poetry, but the poem pleased me.

"It seems to me to be a beautiful poem," I said. "In any case, I like it. Have you written many others?"

"A few. I'll show them to you if you like." He looked very happy.

"What does Marcel say about them?"

"Oh, you know, Marcel is my brother," said Jacques in confusion.

I suspected that Marcel considered his brother to be a young genius. Moreover, who was he — this being that I was quietly beginning to murder near the lake on which a swan was sailing, under the placid eyes of children's mothers? What was he *not* to be?

From then onwards I spent all my days in the workshops. "I want to learn the technical side of the work," I said to my father. In my turn, I was saturated in the smell of work and in the dead light of the green-shaded lamps. "The ventilation is insufficient," I said to old Martin. "We ought to install some new ventilators. You should speak to my father about it." He tugged his mustache. "It's always been that way," he said. There were a handful of old workmen who were much more like family retainers than real proletarians. I hated their respectful tones and their obstinate resignation. "It's always been that way." That was the point! All those inert things, which existed without having been chosen, must be destroyed. Seated at the keyboard of the linotype machine, I was choosing a new personality for myself. "I will do it." I touched my gray linen overalls. I will close the door behind me, I will walk in the streets with my head held high. Old Blomart's son will be no more: an honest-to-God, stainless human being will take his place, dependent only on himself. I raised my head and caught the eye of a young workman, who hastily looked away. He had guessed that under my dusty overalls was a light tweed suit; if I had tried to speak to him, he would have taken me for an *agent provocateur*. I was still the boss's son.

"When are you going to make up your mind?" Jacques would ask.

"When I really know the trade."

Two years passed in this way. I had become a good typographer. I knew all the secrets of typesetting and printing. And yet I did not leave.

"When I have found a job."

But I did not look for one. It was because of my mother. She was there, frozen, silent, never asking questions, but ready to tighten her mouth at the first shock, as she had done at that lunch after the meeting at Bullier — as on the day when she found out about Suzon's clandestine rendezvous. We were free, free to soil our souls and wreck our lives; she only allowed herself the liberty of suffering because of it. It was far worse than if she had made demands on us. I could have hated her demands and her upbraiding. But she was there — no more: I grudged her being there, simply because she was there. It was her actual presence that I had to hate. Could I love her and hate her presence? I did not understand and I fought against the truth. *The truth of my love and of your death.* It was not her fault; it was not my fault. And the fault was there between us and we could only escape from each other. Escaping her and escaping the pain I caused her through my fault, and escaping from myself in order not to read in my heart the secret that weighed upon her.

"You've only got to speak to her. She'll understand, in the end."

He went to her one evening. She was sitting in the little drawing-room near the lamp; she was reading. A year ago she had cut her beautiful black hair, which now richly aureoled her head in a short, thick profusion; even her hair was a rich human possession; no animal's mane, no disordered growth, but a woman's hair, brushed and shining, cared for by skilled hands. He looked at it for a long time and then came and sat in front of her. Suddenly he began to speak: "You know, Mother, I'm not going back to the printing works." She listened for a moment, then she spoke in her turn, her chest heaving, both hands pressing against the arms of her chair. "But it's senseless!" Indignation gave her voice a formal tone.

He pleaded. "Please try to understand me; I disapprove of the system; how can you expect me to be willing to benefit from it?"

"But you've already benefited from it; it's your duty that you're refusing to do. Your education, your health — you owe these to your father, and now that he needs you, you are going to leave him alone."

"The benefits I've had up to now I had in spite of myself. I don't consider that I am under any obligation."

She rose; she went toward the piano and arranged some flowers in a vase, then she turned round.

[24]

"Then what are you waiting for? Why don't you tell your father?"

"I wanted to speak to you first."

"That's dishonest. You let him pay for your apprenticeship, and now you eat his bread in comfort while you look for work: it's too easy."

He stared at her angrily. The hesitation and cowardice for which she blamed him were due to her. She stared at him too, her lips tight, her cheekbones flushed. They measured each other up for a moment, each defying in the other the reflection of their mutual weakness.

"All right, I'll speak to him at once."

"There's nothing else left for you to do."

The voice was cutting, harsh. He heard another voice within her, which was begging that he should not speak. "Not yet; give me only a little more time." But neither she nor he could take into account those silent, broken words. He went out of the drawing-room, and as he went, he kicked a little silk hassock. With what zealous, snarling justice did she take sides with that man whom she did not love! Always ready to sacrifice herself first, together with that which she loved most dearly. "She has asked for it. What is more, she is right — I can't do otherwise." He went down to the next floor and knocked at the office door.

"I would like to speak to you."

"Sit down."

He sat down. He spoke without shyness, bluntly, glad to unburden himself. Since he was being compelled to do so, he was only too happy to burn all his bridges behind him; in this way he would be pitched into the fight past recall, he would not differ greatly from an unemployed workman seeking his daily bread. He emptied his wallet on the desk. "I swear you'll never hear from me again."

[25]

"I did it!" He opened his wardrobe and looked with relief at the clothes on their hangers. It was over. He spread out an old number of *L'Humanité* on the bed, a toothbrush, soap, and a razor. He hesitated for a second, then he took a shirt, some handkerchiefs, two pairs of pants and three pairs of socks. It was not a very heavy parcel. "I'll go and see Thierry's, Coutant & Sons, and Faber's."

He tucked the parcel under his arm. "I will do it." And lo! he had actually done it. He repeated: "I have done it." Once again he saw the green lamps, the dusty workshop, he saw himself in his gray overalls, promising: "I will do it." It was so easy then; he had only to decide not to see his mother — not even that, only not to make up his mind to see her, and he did not see her. But while he wrapped up his underclothes, she was there, in the little drawing-room or in her room — somewhere in the apartment. He said angrily: "It's not my fault. I couldn't have done otherwise." "I could not . . ." as if an impersonal and impartial fate had existed outside himself, as if one might have called upon it for help. But the iron had entered into her soul. "I was all she had." She would be alone henceforth, with the satins and the velvets, with a prowling sense of guilt, surrounded by a thousand burning shards that would also pierce her heart. Not a single tear would she shed; she would only stay up even later into the night, bent with icy devotion over Elisabeth's or Suzon's dresses. And yet it was not her fault. "Not her fault, not my fault." Wherein lay the fault? His irritation increased; he thought that it must be somewhere and could be pulled up with both hands, like a weed. "I ought to have broken it gently to her. She ought not to have been obstinate." But we should have always reached

[26]

the same place: my departure, her loneliness, and the unfairness of her suffering. He gave a last look round his room, the room in which he would no longer be. The furniture and the pictures that she had chosen for him would only set off his absence; she would quicken her step as she passed the closed door. He went out of the room. Silence reigned in the corridor. The waxed floorboards creaked under his feet. He walked to the end of the passage and knocked.

"Come in." She was on her knees before a pile of fawn and gray stockings. Deliberately — she was deliberately spoiling her life. But how could he protect her against herself? Sometimes he managed to do so; he alone could do so, and he was going.

"I have just seen Father." She raised her head. "He ordered me to leave the house immediately."

"Immediately?" She remained kneeling, but her hand had let fall the bundle of stockings that it was holding.

"It's only to be expected." He shrugged his shoulders. "You were right: there's nothing left for me to do here."

"Immediately," she repeated. Her lips had parted; they were no longer stiff, but yielded entirely to the welcome heat of her wrath. "What is to become of you?"

"I shall soon find work. Meanwhile, I'll stay with Marcel." He went up to her and touched her shoulder. "I would have liked not to hurt you."

She passed her hand through her hair, revealing her tired forehead.

"Well, you think you're doing the right thing."

He went slowly down the stairs. "It's what I wanted. There's nothing to regret." She remained up there, kneeling in front of the heap of stockings, alone. "I did it — but I also did something else. I didn't want her to suffer."

Ah, I did not want your death! She is there, lying on the bed, her eyelids motionless; her yellow hair on the pillow already looks like a withered plant. Shall I see again her living eyes?

He said: "There's nothing to regret." Senseless! He should have regretted everything; the crime is everywhere, beyond remedy and expiation: the crime of existing. "There's nothing to regret." He wildly invoked that desperate consolation, trying to approve his action, and yet feeling the pull of that weight which dragged him backwards and which was none other than himself — thinking in a wave of anger: "We should have nothing behind us."

"We always have something behind us," said Marcel. "That's why your attempt seems to me to be so arbitrary."

"But I'm not attempting to do anything extraordinary," said Jean. He was sitting on the divan stuffed with crackling wood shavings, with a glass of brandy in his hand. "All I want is to set off in life with no more advantages than other people and to own only those things that a man can earn through his own efforts."

"His own efforts," said Marcel, "that's easily said." He looked Jean up and down.

"Yes," answered Jean, "my father paid for this suit and these shoes; he also paid for my apprenticeship. But no one starts from absolutely nothing."

"That's just what I was saying." Marcel's smile showed his discolored teeth and wrinkled his saurian skin. "If it were only that suit! But your cultural background, your friends, your boyish, well-fed,

[28]

bourgeois health — you can't rid yourself of the past."

"When I've lived for a few months like a real working-class man, it won't weigh on me very heavily."

"There'll always be a gulf between you and a working-class man: you choose freely a condition to which he submits."

"That's true," said Jean, "but I shall, at least, have done everything I could."

Marcel shrugged his shoulders.

It did not seem to me that my efforts were so funny; my life had changed for good and all. I had really blotted out my name and my face, and in the workshops of Coutant & Sons I was a workman just like the others. At eight o'clock I crossed the gray courtyard where bales of paper were piled up under the tarpaulins — every single day. As I passed, the workers did not turn their heads, nor did the foremen smile at me. I settled down at my machine. I looked it over carefully; I was responsible for it. I began to strike the keys. "It's the real thing. I'm going to do it all my life!" When I took off my overalls, I no longer went home to a silken drawing-room, filled with tulips. I rode through the depressing streets of Clichy in a bus. I went back to a room filled with the smell of cooking and laundry, with a gas ring in a corner and a sink by way of a washbasin. "It's not very cheerful," my mother would say. But it pleased me that my dwelling should be reduced to the bare measure of a man: the six surfaces necessary to make a cube, a hole through which to allow the light to enter, another to allow me to enter it myself.

"You must be happy," Jacques used to say to me.

"I am very happy."

He often came to get me when the workshops

closed; we had dinner in a little set-price restaurant. The paper napkins, the clogged salt-cellars, the finger-marked glasses, and even the taste of dubious cooking fat, which henceforth was to be the uniform taste of all the food I ate, to him were full of poetry; we went and sat on the wooden seats of the neighborhood movie houses, we drank red wine in bistros; he would ask me questions:

"Don't you find it rather difficult to adapt yourself? Are you really on an equal footing with the others?"

"I'm even under the impression that I'll quite easily manage to influence them," I would say.

It needed patience. I knew that it was difficult for Communism to get a hold in those small firms; but I was a good speaker, and at the trade-union meetings I held their attention. I hoped I would manage to get myself sent as a delegate to the union's committee; it would be possible to do some good work there.

"I've something to tell you," Jacques said to me.

We were sitting in a little café in the neighborhood of the Clichy Gate, near the window on which was chalked up: "You may bring your own food here." Two plaster-coated masons were drinking a pint of red wine at the next table.

"Is it good news?"

"You can judge for yourself: I'm going to join the party."

"Is that really true? Have you made up your mind?"

I was looking at Jacques with uncertainty, "It's what I wanted." And yet I hesitated. I was beginning to suspect that nothing ever happens in the way one had wanted.

"Yes, I have made up my mind. Does that astonish you?" He smiled proudly.

"But the other evening you were raising so many objections to Marxism?"

Jacques shrugged his shoulders. "The system is not so very important. My problem was to know whether I could act. Then something was loosened — I can." He smiled. "It came to me by watching the way you live."

"I'm glad," I said. I was not glad, I would have preferred Jacques to have convinced himself through rational argument; I felt as if I had trapped him. I added: "I should like to have a better idea of how you came to that decision."

"The other evening, after our talk, I went home on foot. I was thinking about what we had been saying; but I was thinking of you and of me, and suddenly I felt that I could no longer bear to be alive unless my life were to serve some purpose."

"I understand," I said.

My uneasiness did not pass away. Did I serve any purpose? That point did not concern me. I could not carve out a just fate for myself in an unjust world. I wanted justice. For whom did I want it — for others or for myself? You once said hotly to me: "One always fights for oneself." I fought against the guilt and the sin, the sin of being there, my sin. How had I dared to drag into that fight any other being but myself?

I said: "I'm not trying particularly to serve a purpose."

But Jacques did not hear. He too was engaged in a fight that was no one else's.

"Do you think I am too young and that there's nothing I can do?"

I pulled myself together. "The young ones are our strongest asset," I said. I looked at Jacques in the manner that he expected of me, the businesslike manner of a militant Communist, sure of his aims. "Fists and healthy lungs are needed at the moment. I'll introduce you to Bourgade the day after tomorrow."

At that particular time there was work to do for those who wanted to rebuild the world. The walls of Paris were covered with election posters and almost every evening, throughout the city and the suburbs, our friends and our enemies came face to face. Almost every evening Jacques met me and we went together to a hall or a schoolroom filled with a stormy crowd. I liked to watch him beside me, stamping his applause, flushed and happy. Our jeers smothered the fine phrases of reactionary speakers; when ours rose to speak, we kept order with our fists.

"Do you think there'll be a rough-house tonight? A real one?" Jacques asked me.

"You bet! The day before yesterday we didn't let Taittinger open his mouth; they'll certainly try to make things hot for us."

We were all happy that afternoon. Denise was triumphantly happy. Only Marcel's face remained unsmiling. He had had his hair cut for the occasion, but he could never manage to look conventional. With harassed politeness he endured the compliments of the highbrow socialites.

"Braun has had eight offers already," Denise was saying. "He says it's a terrific success. The critic from the *Cahiers d'art* declares that you are the greatest painter of your generation."

Her eyes sparkled; a living rosy flush glowed on her brow and with surprise he suddenly remembered that she was only eighteen; usually he never thought of it. Her voice, her smiles, her make-up, everything about her was so artificial that her very freshness assumed an artificial charm; only her luxuriant red hair gave a hint that under her expensive dresses was a body pulsing with animal vitality. She rescued a lonely petit-four from a plate. "Have some sandwiches," she said; "there's plenty of food left."

Jean bit into a roll filled with *foie gras*; the sweetish taste reminded him of the crystal chandelier and the beautiful, appetizing ladies of his childhood; the carpet was thick under his feet, and in the air, mingled with the smell of oil paintings, was a perfume of aristocratic femininity. Three months had been enough; now with astonishment he found himself once more in that sugary world; the web of his days was made up of the smell of paper, the noise of machines, the taste of badly cooked steaks. "I don't belong to them any more." The women looked as if they were made of spun glass. With shocked amusement he listened to their parrot cries and the lilting of their velvet voices.

He went up to the wall. A moment ago, when he entered this human aviary, the pictures, modestly enclosed in four wooden moldings, remained flat and silent before him; in order to wrest their secret from them, he must believe in them. He wanted to believe in them. He stood in front of one of the canvases. Between two walls, drenched in sunlight, a single hoop rolled toward that point where the parallels meet in infinity. Little by little, as he looked at it, the picture came alive. What it was saying could not be translated into words; it was said in painting, and no other language could have expressed its meaning; but it spoke. He advanced a few paces. Under his attentive gaze, all the pictures came alive. They awoke memories more ancient than the beginning of the world; they evoked the unpredictable face of the earth far beyond the revolutions to come; they exposed the secrets of a jagged coastline, of a desert sprinkled with shells, as they remained solitarily within themselves, protected from any conscience. Statues without faces, men turned to pillars of salt, landscapes scorched by the flames of death, oceans frozen into the immobility of the absolute instant: these were the thousand shapes of absence. And while he looked at this universe devoid of onlookers, it seemed as if he were absent from himself, and that he remained, outside his own personal history, in an empty white eternity. "And yet that dream of purity and absence only existed because I was there to lend it the strength of my life." Marcel knew that.

"Leave it alone," he said. "You'd much better come and have a drink." He dragged Jean toward the long table covered with a white cloth over which Denise was fussing. "Have you nothing to give us but that foul champagne?"

"There's some port," said Denise.

"Grocer's port," said Marcel. "Oh, well, as today is a high day —"

"Don't grumble," said Denise. "It's a beastly bore, but now it's over."

"Over!" exclaimed Marcel. "They're going to stay there for thirty days, hanging on the wall! How could I have let it happen?"

"What's wanted," said Jean, "is another kind of public — a real public."

"What's wanted is that I should not need a public," replied Marcel. He seized a chair with both hands. "My pictures ought to exist like this chair; it is strong, you can sit on it; when we have gone, it will remain there, standing on its four legs."

Denise shrugged her shoulders. "Well, why don't you turn cabinetmaker?" she asked with a touch of irritation.

Marcel let go the chair, which rolled onto the carpet. "But a chair isn't interesting," he said.

"You've got a lot to complain of!" said Denise. "In a month's time you'll be famous!" She smiled artfully. "After all, it's not so bad to be a great painter; quite a number of very nice people have put up with that fate."

No one answered. Denise often used words that had no meaning for us. Neither Jacques nor I could quite understand why Marcel had decided to marry her. He probably loved that dry and intelligent little face, overwhelmed by the heavy mass of hair; and then, he did not attach much importance to what he did with his life. Denise had wished to conquer him and she had conquered; she had persuaded him to agree to this exhibition, and she intended walking at his side along an unobstructed path to fame and happiness. I see again her scarlet smile and her warm glance, in which was reflected the dark gold of her hair. Nothing had ever resisted her; she was a spoiled young thing, a brilliant student, and she went through life with daring and sophisticated ease. For her it was a day of triumph that was coming to an end.

"Are we going straight there, or are we calling at your place first?" said Jacques.

"Let's call at my place, because of the revolvers."

"Do you think we ought to take them?"

"It can't do any harm. On Monday when they started shooting, our boys had nothing to protect themselves with."

Night had fallen; we were passing through the prosperous districts. I felt uncomfortable in them. Among the pedestrians hustling along on the pavements, I was lonelier than an atom lost in the ether; for them I was only an obstructive body and around me I could only

[35]

discern a milling crowd. It was just at the time when the shops were closing; with their noses against the windowpanes, the shopgirls dreamed over their evening's outing. "For you, too, the street lamps had lit up. You had taken the glass jars of candy back into the shop; you were nibbling a piece of chocolate while through the window you watched those happy people who were allowed to go for a walk at night on their own; you thought that it was dull to be so young." But I only saw anonymous young girls behind the shopfronts, whose fate revolved on its own axis, forever separate from mine.

We left the middle-class streets and followed the long avenue teeming with proletarian opulence; we went up to my room. From the wall cupboard that served as my larder I took a hunk of bread and a piece of cheese. "Would you like some sausage?"

"No," said Jacques. "All those iced coffees have spoiled my appetite."

I slipped my hand into a drawer of the dressing-table. Under the handkerchiefs and the shirts were two revolvers, the one that I had bought with my savings, and the one that Jacques had pinched from his father. I tested the safety-catch. I was meticulously careful, I intended to leave nothing to chance.

"Here," I said. "Don't draw it unless you are really threatened. That little gang would be only to pleased if they could do the national funeral stunt all over again."

Jacques weighed the weapon with curiosity. "I'd never have thought that it could kill. It looks just like a toy."

Just like a toy. And didn't I look like a nice harmless young man, sitting among the comrades, stamping and clapping my hands? They were my brothers, Jacques was my brother, we were carried away by the same impulse. Tomorrow, thanks to us, the revolution will be accomplished, and those who jeer at us, we close their mouths with our fists. His shirt open over his chest, his hair falling in long locks over his rosy face, Jacques struggled in the midst of those raised clubs, a smile on his lips, happy to give his life. . . .

"Ruth! Ruth!" She tosses on her bed; she is calling. I do not know whom she is calling. Both of us alone in this room, both of us together in this room, and each of us alone. Ruth — whom does she see? I hear that name, but I see no face. I look at her, for hours I have been looking at her, and behind her closed eyelids I can see nothing; about me press my own memories — it is my own personal history that unfolds.

In the tumult, there is the sound of a shot, then immediately another. "The youngster fired first!"

Murderer! Murderer! I walked in the night, I staggered, I ran, I fled. He had been there, so quiet, in the midst of his poems and his books. I took him by the hand, I gave him a revolver, and I pushed him into the track of the bullets. Murderer. At the top of the stairs, Marcel is there, surrounded with the smell of oil paintings, reading or sleeping, near the motionless hippocampus; he is waiting for Jacques. I climb the stairs; I cannot go up, I cannot go down, time must stop and engulf me, engulf Marcel, engulf the world; and the treads are firm under my feet, each step is in its place; the door is in its place. Behind the door Marcel is waiting for Jacques; and I am there, and I am going to speak. A single word and the thing will exist, it will never cease to exist. A rap on the door, a word, and time is cleft asunder, divided into two fragments that can never again be united. I knock on the door.

First Jacques, now Hélène. And even that is not enough: Laurent's turn will come. The instants pursue their course, driving one another forward, driving me forward without respite. Go forward into the night of the future. Decide. Harried by life, which drives me forward toward new corpses, toward weeping women, toward cell doors that close and open, that open on death. On the walls of Paris, on the white tiles of the subway stations, a newly printed yellow poster, with new names on it. *"Don't go." Then everything will have been in vain, there will have been no reason for your death*. Ah, how can I halt the merciless drive! Go on, go on, decide. Every beat of my heart casts into the world a decision from which there is no recall. Shut the door, shut your eyes: *decide to shut the door, to shut your eyes*.

There is no salvation. Not even the intoxication of despair and blind resolve, since you are there, on that bed, in the fierce light of your own death.

2

THE BICYCLE was still there, brand-new, with its pale-blue frame and its plated handlebars, which sparkled against the dull stone of the wall. It was so lissom, so slender, that even when not in use it seemed to cut through the air. Hélène had never seen such an elegant bicycle. "I'll repaint it dark green, it'll be even more beautiful," she thought. Grudgingly she left the window. What was the use of being there, looking at it, longing for it? For the past week that was all she had been able to do. What a splendid prize! She thought of it all the time, twenty times a day she leaned out of the window to gaze upon it, but she had as yet been unable to lay her hands on it. "I'm getting soft," she thought sadly. When she was a child, she did what she wanted to do, without a moment's hesitation. She wiped her paintbrush on her overalls. That was that: she had come to the end of the day. There would be another day tomorrow and it would be the same thing all over again. She took a piece of cross-ruled cardboard out of her bag: 20 November 1934. She daubed the empty square with gray — gray, black, only two red-letter days since the beginning of the month.

Downstairs the shop bell tinkled and Hélène ran below. Standing in the middle of the shop, a little boy was looking shyly at the jars of candy.

"What would you like?" asked Hélène.

"I'd like that," said the little boy, pointing his forefinger at a chocolate truffle.

Hélène picked up the truffle with a pair of tongs and

wrapped it in tissue paper. "That's just a franc."

She threw the franc into the drawer of the till and through the plate-glass window she gazed after the little boy, who was nibbling his truffle as he went up the road. He was going home; everyone was going home, it was a melancholy time of the day. Night was falling on the chocolate pralines. In her mouth Hélène tasted the usual flavor of congealed fat.

She opened the door that gave onto the courtyard; the handlebars and the mudguards gleamed in the shadow. Hélène went closer. It must be heavenly to sit on that beautiful yellow saddle and grip the handlebars in one's hands! She shot a glance at the concierge lodge. It really seemed as if the concierge had made a point of not leaving the house during these last few days. "Yes, I want it and I must have it," said Hélène. So smooth, so clean, so bright, both delicate and strong with its open wheels and its fat, good-natured tires. She pinched one of the frail spokes between her fingers, she tested the brick-colored tire — it was as hard as iron — how strange to think that it was only a thin tube filled with air! Hélène stood back a little from the bicycle; how proud and free it was! "I'll go everywhere I want. I'll come home late at night. Only a pool of light will go ahead of me in the silent streets, I shall hear the muted sound of that soft, even friction. I'll look after it well; I'll have a little oilcan, like an engineer, and I'll pour oil into its innards." She looked up at the third-floor windows. "If only she doesn't get nervous and take it up to her flat!" Hélène's head was burning, her lips and hands were trembling with desire. "The first time the concierge goes out . . ."

The shop bell tinkled. She rushed back. "Paul! What a happy thought!" she said joyously.

He took her in his arms and pressed his lips to her

cheek; she gave him a fleeting kiss. "You're going to help me shut the shop and then we'll go up to my room. Would you like some chocolate?"

"Not at this hour of the day," said Paul. He opened the door and gathered up into his arms one of the heavy jars aligned on the sidewalk. "You're always astonished that anyone could refuse chocolate!" he said, laughing. "The first time I saw you, you insisted on stuffing me with it."

"It was my only means of seduction," answered Hélène.

"It didn't need that to make me like you," said Paul.

"That's true, your affection has always been disinterested," said Hélène. She smiled. "Are you taking me out to dinner? I've got some spare cash — it's on me."

"Not tonight," said Paul. "I'm dining with a pal."

"Oh!" said Hélène.

"Tomorrow, if you like," said Paul.

Hélène took hold of a jar without replying. These dinners with Paul were not very exciting, but they were better than having dinner with the family, and it so happened that tonight she felt in the mood. Tomorrow . . . well, tomorrow was tomorrow. Without another word they finished bringing in the jars.

"What have you been doing today?" said Paul kindly.

"I've been working. What else did you expect me to do?"

"Show me."

"If you like."

She took him into her room and Paul went up to the table.

"It's awfully pretty," he said.

"You know, Verdier told me that three quarters of the designs they've sold were mine," said Hélène. "But you'll see! That pig of a woman won't give me a penny more for them."

Every time the same thing happened; she greeted Paul with pleasure, and after five minutes she was bored with him. She eyed him critically; he was rather good-looking, with his fair mane of hair and his fresh freckled skin; but under his obstinate forehead, his eyes were too sentimental. The shell was hard, but transparent; perceivable beneath it was an innocent mollusk, just like the one she discovered in herself.

"What are you thinking about?" asked Paul.

"That life is boring," answered Hélène.

"And yet you're lucky," said Paul. "Just think if you had to work eight hours a day in an office or in a factory. . . ."

"Might as well commit suicide," said Hélène. She added aggressively: "I wonder how you always manage to be good-tempered."

"You know, working men haven't time to bother about moods," said Paul a little dryly.

She looked angrily at him; he was annoying when he began to drum working-class virtues into her.

"I know, I'm lower-middle-class, you rub it in enough. And what does that prove? It's ridiculous, always explaining people's behavior by exterior circumstances; it is as if what we think, what we are, doesn't depend on ourselves."

"It depends very much on one's circumstances," said Paul. He smiled. "It's because you are lower-middle-class that you dislike this idea; it's essential for you to think that what happens to you is unique, and that there is no one else exactly like you."

"I'm quite certain of it," said Hélène.

"The whole lower middle class has a mania for not being like other people," said Paul. "They don't understand that it's only another way of being exactly like each other." He chewed over his idea with an obstinate and complacent expression. "A worker doesn't care a damn for being an exception to the rule; on the contrary, it pleases me to feel that I'm the same as my comrades."

"First of all," she retorted, "you are not the same. You're a typographer, you've had some education."

"That makes no difference. A worker is a worker."

"Then according to you," said Hélène, "there are thousands of girls in the world exactly like me?"

Paul laughed, unruffled. "You know, there's a saying that no two leaves are the same on any tree."

Hélène shrugged her shoulders impatiently. "You can mistake them for one another in bulk?"

"In bulk, yes." said Paul, who was still laughing.

"Right," said Hélène. She stood squarely before him. "Then why do you pretend that you love me, and not some other girl?"

"There are also thousands of fellows like me on earth," said Paul, "and that means thousands of people loving like us." He took Hélène by the shoulders and looked at her gaily. "Every Jack has his Jill."

"Then, if it comes to the point, there could be an exchange of Jacks and Jills," said Hélène. She freed herself from his embrace. "It seems to me that when you really love someone, you can't even dream of loving someone else."

"Of course," said Paul. "But that always happens when you're in love; you don't want anything but what you've got."

"Oh, you're mixing me up," said Hélène. She took a step toward him. "Answer me, yes or no, could you love some other girl than me?"

Paul hesitated for a second; what was so terrible

about him was that he took everything so seriously; she did not expect him to answer in good faith.

"Actually, at this moment, it's difficult for me to imagine it, and yet I know quite well that I could. You could love some other fellow, too."

"I never said anything to the contrary," said Hélène. Paul flushed slightly, but the blow had not struck home; he was only embarrassed that she should have lowered herself to wound him. There were moments when she wanted to slap him, so as to shake his preposterous modesty. He did not consider that he was an exceptional person, but in his eyes neither was she, Hélène, exceptional; everyone was ordinary and to love one another was quite ordinary. He was quite certain that she loved him.

"There's not much point in asking oneself such questions," said Paul. "Perhaps there's even no sense in pretending that things might have been different. What is certain is that I love you." He smacked her. "You know that perfectly well, you little devil."

"You frequently mention it," said Hélène.

"Don't be an idiot!" said Paul. He put his arms round her and touched her mouth with his lips; they were good lips, honest and fresh, which she liked to feel against her own. She closed her eyes; she felt utterly comfortable with his strong arm about her, and the warmth in her body, and his tenderness, which enfolded her. She disengaged herself, smiling.

"Well, if you love me, do something for me," she said.

"What?" asked Paul.

"Put off your friend and take me out to dinner with you."

A shadow passed over Paul's face. "I can't."

"Say rather that you won't." Hélène turned her back

on him, took a comb out of her bag, and passed it through her tousled hair. "I bet it's a fellow from the party."

"No," said Paul eagerly, "it's Blomart, you know —"

"Oh, Blomart!" said Hélène. She rolled a curl round her finger. Of all the friends that Paul talked to her about, he was the only one whom she wanted to meet. "Well, don't put him off. Take me with you."

"What an idea!" said Paul.

"Why? Are you ashamed of me?"

"But there's no sense in it. I tell you that we have to have a very serious talk."

"What about?"

"It's of no interest to you."

"It so happens that it does interest me!"

Paul shrugged his shoulders; he looked quite unhappy. "I'm not being kind," thought Hélène, but, hang it all, she had been stewing in her own juice for so long that she needed a change; if she did not look after herself, no one would look after her; that was the rule — each for himself. ✓

"Since I tell you that it interests me," she said, "you might explain things."

"Well, you know that there are a lot of trade-union groups; there are too many of them, we are frittering away our strength; a congress is being held at Toulouse to try to unite them. Blomart is going as a delegate for one of them. I want to persuade him to vote with us."

"Yes," said Hélène. "Is it because you don't both belong to the same group?"

"He used to be a Communist, but he left the party," said Paul deprecatingly. "And now he absolutely refuses to affiliate with the International. He wants to revive the old French trade-unionism: no politics, the unions take their stand on a professional basis. But nowadays the game is being played on a political basis."

He was about to continue; he had no sense of proportion once embarked on these subjects — either he did not speak about them at all or he said too much. Hélène cut him short.

"I won't prevent your talking," she said. "Where are you meeting?"

"At the Port Salut." Paul hesitated for a second. "But I can't take you. It's no business of yours."

"But I want to come," said Hélène sulkily.

"Please," said Paul nicely. "Don't be difficult. We'll go out together tomorrow night."

"I don't want to go tomorrow," said Hélène. Her voice softened. "You say you love me, and when I ask you to do me a wretched little favor . . ."

"It's funny that you won't understand." Paul was slightly annoyed.

"I understand perfectly well: it isn't done." Hélène shrugged her shoulders. "Well, that's just it, when you love someone, you do things that aren't done!"

"Oh, that's the kind of tommy-rot you get from the movies," said Paul.

His unruffled and assertive attitude made Hélène's blood boil. "Is that your last word? You're not taking me?"

Paul shook his head, half smiling. "No."

"Well, then, you might as well go at once: I'm not stopping you!"

She made for the door and opened it.

"Hélène, don't be stupid!"

"Are you taking me or aren't you?"

"Oh, all right!" said Paul. He went out of the door. "See you tomorrow night."

"If I'm in!" she shouted after him angrily.

[46]

She leaned over the banisters; the doorbell t
and the front door closed. "He's gone. He doesn'
if I stay moldering away here, he doesn't care i
angry with him, he's already forgotten about it."
sat down on the stairs. Paul loved her, that was
tain; for three years he had loved her faithfully, devo-
tedly, warmly; but she did not feel that she meant a
very great deal to him; she did not mean a great deal
to anyone. Who at this very moment minded about
her? Here she was, bathed in the aroma of honey and
cocoa that rose from the shop; she might just as well
have been anywhere else, it would have been no better.
As a child, she was neither here nor anywhere else: she
was in the arms of God; He loved her with an eternal
love and she felt eternal like Him; from the refuge of
the shadows she offered Him each beat of her heart,
and the slightest of her sighs took on an infinite sig-
nificance, since God Himself received it. Paul was not
interested in her as God had been, and even if he had
been more so, Paul was not God. Hélène rose to her
feet. "I need no one. I, Hélène, exist; isn't that
enough?"

She went upstairs to her room and stood before the
mirror. "My eyes, my face," she thought with a touch
of fervor. "I. Only I am myself." It was rare that she
could strike such brief sparks from herself; she only
had to touch her own hand as if it were the hand of a
stranger to find herself back at once in the midst of a
hopeless personal intimacy. Hélène threw herself on
the divan bed. Her joy had already evaporated. She
was no longer confronted with anyone; she was entirely shut up in herself; however much she pretended
that she loved herself, that love was nothing better
than a small, weak pulsation inside her shell; and her
boredom, sour and insipid as curdled milk, was part

and parcel of her own flesh, glaucous and flabby and slightly, shiveringly sensitive. Just like an oyster — an oyster must be aware of its existence in exactly this way; my thoughts are the oscillatory cilia; they seem to be stretching out toward something, then they withdraw, they start out again, they retire. Hélène jumped to her feet. "Impossible! There must be something. How do other people manage? They must be better oysters than I am, they do not even suspect that their shell may have an outside to it."

"Mademoiselle Bertrand?"

Hélène leaned over the banisters. "Yes."

"I'm going out for a moment. May I set up the notice-board to tell callers to apply to you?"

"Yes, of course," said Hélène. "How long will you be out?"

"About half an hour," said the concierge. "Many thanks."

"Don't mention it," said Hélène.

She waited for a moment, then charged downstairs. Her heart was beating loudly. It was now or never: a better chance would never recur. She opened the door into the courtyard and slipped along the wall. Windows gleamed like threatening eyes in the dark frontage of the building. Suppose someone saw her? If she ran into her parents or one of the tenants? She was rooted to the ground; her hands were sticky and her legs shaking. "Have I become such a coward?" How she wanted that bicycle! It had become a symbol of her earthly lot, and if she did not find out a way of making it hers, all hope was lost.

"I want it." She seized the handlebars. How light it was! Again she hesitated; the baker's wife would see her pass and so would the pork-butcher, the whole neighborhood would recognize her; she might as well

[48]

leave behind her a signed note: "I took the bicycle."
"Never mind!" she said through set teeth. Wheeling
the bicycle, she walked toward the archway into the
street. Now she was shaking so much that she would
no longer be capable of staying on the saddle. "It's ridiculous," she repeated despairingly. In an hour's time
there would be a fine to-do in the house. "I shall be
accused, and they'll take it away from me." She looked
all around in anguish; already she could not bear to be
separated from it, it was her property, a dear, familiar,
and obedient pet, her friend, her beloved child. "To
run away with it and never come back. . . ." She drew
her hand over her perspiring forehead. "There's one
way, and one way only."

She took the bicycle back to its place and ran
through the courtyard. "Never mind my self-respect;
after all, we haven't really quarreled." She sped like an
arrow down the rue Saint-Jacques and stopped at the
door of the restaurant. "Supposing he won't?" She
took a deep breath; her face was burning; a fog separated her from the outer world, her mind's eye was
still fixed on the bicycle's brilliant plating. "If he refuses, I'll break it off, I'll never see him again." She
pushed the door open; a stove was roaring in the middle of the tiled room; people were sitting at tables
covered with oilcloth. But Paul was nowhere to be
seen.

"What can I do for you?" asked the proprietor. Under the blue apron his belly advanced threateningly.

"I'm looking for someone," murmured Hélène. Her
glance lit on a solitary young man who was sitting at
one of the tables at the back of the room; he was not
eating, he seemed to be waiting for someone, and a
book was open in front of him. She walked up to him.
He looked at her questioningly — he was no longer

quite young, he must be at least thirty. His eyes were not unfriendly.

"Isn't your name Blomart?" she asked.

He smiled. "Yes, that's me."

"Do you know if Paul is coming here soon?"

"Paul Perrier? I'm expecting him any moment now." He was still smiling, a queer kind of repressed smile; it was impossible to tell whether it was friendly or ironical. She hesitated.

"I want to ask him to do something for me." She looked agonizedly at Blomart. "It's very urgent."

"Perhaps I could do it for you instead?"

Hélène's heart began to beat rapidly. He would be even better than Paul; his face was unknown in the neighborhood. She looked him up and down. How far could she trust him?

"I take it that I can't help?"

"Perhaps," said Hélène. "If you would. . . ." She must look silly, shifting from one foot to the other. "It's this: I don't want to go home now because my parents would make me stay to dinner with them and it bores me. But my bicycle is in the courtyard and I need it at once. . . . You couldn't get it out for me? It's only a few steps from here." She looked at the clock — seven thirty-five. The concierge had already been away for twenty minutes.

"I'm willing," said Blomart. "But if anyone sees me take hold of your bike, what will they think?"

"Then you can come and get me here and I'll say that I sent you." She looked at him imploringly. Blomart rose. "It's at 200 rue Saint-Jacques — in the courtyard, the pale-blue bike. Anyhow, there's only one bike there. Be quick, because, all the same, I'd rather you weren't seen."

"I'll bring it back to you at once," said Blomart.

[50]

She let herself drop onto the wooden bench. Would he get there in time? Supposing he were caught . . . better not think of it. Not to think was the only way of getting things done. As one grew up, one began to think too much.

"What are you doing here?" asked Paul. He had suddenly appeared and he was looking wrathfully at Hélène; he was flushed with anger.

"I'm waiting for your friend," said Hélène. "He's nice, he is. He doesn't seem to find me so repulsive."

"Where is he?" asked Paul.

"I sent him on an errand."

"You've certainly got a nerve," said Paul more gently. "Well, you'd better stay since you're here. But you won't enjoy yourself." He sat down.

"I'm enjoying myself very nicely," said Hélène. She stared at the frosted glass panel of the door. Seven minutes had already elapsed; he should have been back.

"What do you want to eat?" asked Paul.

"I don't know," said Hélène. "I'm not hungry."

It would be lousy if anything happened to him because of her. He was good to look at in his big rolled-neck pullover, with his thick black hair, his strong neck, and his slender figure; he did not look working-class, or middle-class, or bohemian. She started: he was framed in the doorway, smiling.

"Your bike's here," he said. "Do you want to use it now or shall I bring it in?"

"Oh, I am grateful to you," said Hélène. She wanted to throw her arms around his neck. My bicycle, it is really mine! By and by I'll go through the streets, I'll go right across Paris; I'm sure it runs perfectly. It seemed to her that her whole life was transfigured. "Please bring it in."

"Your bike?" said Paul. "What's this cock-and-bull

story?" He looked at the magnificent pale-blue bicycle that Blomart was putting against the wall. "Is that yours? Since when?"

Hélène smiled without answering. Paul looked questioningly at Blomart. "Is that bike yours?"

"No, it's her own, which I am bringing back for her," said Blomart. "She asked me to go and get it for her." He too was looking uncertainly at Hélène.

"Well, that's the limit!" said Paul. He seized Hélène by the shoulder. "I say, you might do your own dirty work instead of making other people take risks. Can't you understand? Supposing he'd been caught!"

Blomart began to laugh. "Well, I've been nicely taken in," he said shamefacedly.

His laughter was young and friendly, but in his eyes and at the corners of his mouth were depths of reticence that Hélène could not fathom.

"You know, I apologize," said Hélène, "but I couldn't go myself, all the concierges in the neighborhood would have recognized me."

"Not at all!" said Blomart. He sat down and passed the menu to Hélène. "What would you like? You must be hungry after all this excitement."

"I'll have some *pâté* and beefsteak and fried potatoes," said Hélène.

"The same," said Blomart to the proprietor, who had come up to them, "and a bottle of red wine."

"For me as well, *pâté* and beefsteak," said Paul sulkily. He was deep in a pigheaded meditation. "This business is idiotic," he said abruptly. "I'm going to take that bicycle back."

"My bicycle!" gasped Hélène. "Paul, if you do that I'll never speak to you again."

"I'm going to take it back," said Paul. He stood up.

Tears rose in Hélène's eyes. Paul was stronger than she was and he was obstinate.

"If you go," she said through clenched teeth, "I'll follow you down the street screaming, and you'll see the nice old hullabaloo it'll create. Just you try and go, just try. . . ."

"Listen," said Blomart. He looked at Paul in a conciliatory way. "Now that I've had the trouble of pinching that bike, let her keep it!"

Paul hesitated. "But it's idiotic, she'll be suspected at once."

"I don't care a damn," said Hélène. "There's no proof."

"Where will you hide it?"

"Why not at your place?" said Hélène.

"No," said Paul. "I don't want to be mixed up in this."

"We could put it in my place," said Blomart.

"Oh, that would be wonderful," said Hélène. "Could I repaint it there? Wouldn't it be in your way?"

"Not at all," said Blomart. "What color will you paint it?"

"Dark green," said Hélène. "Don't you think that will be nice?"

"Dark green?" said Blomart. "Not a bad idea!"

"Those kinds of jokes were all right when you were small," said Paul, "but now they're completely lousy. Come now! Put yourself for a moment in that poor creature's shoes when she can't find her bike."

"Exactly!" said Hélène. "The thought delights me. That poor creature — she's an appalling redhead, covered with furs, with layers of carpets all over her flat. And besides, she never uses her bike, it had been standing in the courtyard for a week."

"You'd steal anything — you don't care a damn," said Paul.

"That's not true," replied Hélène. She shrugged her shoulders. "I don't understand why you wear yourself out defending the rights of property when you're a Communist!"

"That's got nothing to do with it," said Paul. "You sound like a bourgeois who always thinks that you become a Communist in order to pick your neighbor's pocket."

"I see no reason why dirty plutocrats should not be robbed," said Hélène. She turned toward Blomart, hoping to find agreement in his eyes.

"Personally, I wouldn't do it either," he said. He still wore the same friendly and slightly ironical expression. "As though I were four years old," thought Hélène, somewhat annoyed.

"But why?" She was disappointed.

"It doesn't get you any farther," answered Blomart.

"How so? I'm much farther forward. Now the bike's mine."

"Yes, of course." Blomart was smiling. His smile was not transparent like Paul's, and Hélène looked at him in perplexity.

"Then why do you blame me?"

"But I'm not blaming you," said Blomart politely.

"You said you wouldn't have acted as I did," she said impatiently.

He made a vague gesture. "Oh, I always feel awkward about furthering my own interests." His tone was serious; from Paul this serious tone would have been irritating, but Blomart's words did not ring hollow. He had deliberately left home at the age of twenty so that he should not own anything. He must have good reasons for what he said.

[54]

"But we always seek to further our own interests," said Hélène. "And I think we're quite right," she added challengingly. "After all, we only have ourselves."

"You certainly only have yourself," said Paul.

"Because I'm lower-middle-class, I know," Hélène cut him short, baring her teeth at him.

"Our interests, yes," said Blomart. "But it all depends what they are."

"What do you mean?" said Hélène.

His manner was reluctant and superficial; it was evident that he took her for a child and did not wish to lower himself by discussing the question with her. "Our petty personal desires don't seem to be very interesting to me," said Blomart. "I can't see what's to be gained by satisfying them."

"My own interest me," said Hélène.

She was put out. In one way she quite liked talking to him. He seemed to have a store of secret resources, and it was pleasant to think that he was choosing his words specially for her, and that she was the focal point of those intelligent eyes. But how sure he seemed of himself! She was immediately seized with a desire to contradict him.

"I think one ought to have more pride about it," said Blomart.

"More pride?" Hélène was surprised.

"Yes."

She did not fully understand what he meant, but in her ears the words had an insulting ring. What it amounted to was that he took an indulgent view of the theft of the bicycle because he considered it to be childish. Hélène to him was a mere child, as he looked down on her from his adult masculine superiority.

"In that case, if you're not even interested in what

you desire," she said aggressively, "I wonder what's left."

"A good many things," said Blomart pleasantly. There was something brotherly in his voice. Were there other people to whom he always used that tone? To a woman, perhaps? It was queer to think that there was a whole life behind and around him.

"What things?"

"It would take a long time to explain," said Blomart gaily. "You'll soon discover them for yourself if you really don't know."

Anger once more colored Hélène's cheeks. He was decidedly not going to bother to talk to her; he insulted her to her face, and then calmly ignored it.

"Oh, I know: I ought to take an interest in the happiness of mankind." She sneered at Paul. "The working class! Now they have a sense of solidarity."

"Exactly," said Paul.

"But it's much simpler if each person fends for himself. I fight for my own rights myself; my neighbor only has to do the same.

"I think you were born fully armed," said Blomart.

Hélène felt a lump rise in her throat; there was no point in her smiling so sweetly at him if he ended by laughing at her.

"Her bark's worse than her bite," said Paul with a laugh. "She can't bear to see anyone hard up without giving them her last penny."

There was no need for him to come to Hélène's rescue, she could stand up for herself. Moreover, she had no objection to shocking Blomart.

"I agree that I don't like to see anyone suffering," said Hélène. She looked provokingly at Blomart. "But then, you see, I may be a monster: I don't care a rap for people I don't know."

"That's not being a monster, it's quite a usual state of affairs," said Blomart.

His tone was impartial. Hélène cupped her glass of wine between her hands; she wanted to throw it in his face. He was having a great time making a fool of her, he who spent his time in discussion groups and meetings. "He'd merely take it as a joke." She emptied her glass and put it down on the table.

"In any case, it's better than strutting about self-importantly as if you held the fate of mankind in your hands," she said uncertainly.

"Of course," said Blomart. He was laughing; he was not even trying to hide his contempt.

"I'm sure that mankind doesn't give a damn for all your talk." She could no longer stop herself; she did not quite know why she had begun to adopt that angry tone, but there was no going back on it, her anger grew with every answer — and Blomart was laughing. She got up and took her coat.

"Have a good time without me," she said.

She seized hold of her bicycle, went out through the restaurant door, and jumped onto the saddle. They were still grinning behind her back; Paul must be rather embarrassed, but Blomart must certainly be finding the incident amusing. Tears of rage rose to Hélène's eyes. Those two old schoolmarms! Now they were talking as man to man, and she was only a wayward, superficial little girl to them. She shuddered; the damp went right through her too thin coat, riding a bicycle in this cold weather was unpleasant. "Did I really make such a fool of myself? I never know how to behave." She braked and stood her bicycle against the curb. Perhaps it wasn't wise to leave it there. Never mind! After all, it was only a bicycle, no more, no less. She pushed open the door of a large, brightly lit café

and put her elbows on the counter. "A rum." The rum
burnt her throat. It was Paul who had exasperated her;
if only he hadn't been there. Was he really interested
in people? Really and truly? Take these people here.
men and women, young and old — they laughed, they
drank noisily. What could anyone see in them? What
is there about them that I haven't got? I know myself
backwards and it's always the same old thing. But
they're no better. "You'll soon discover them for yourself." But no, I can't discover anything. Who is interesting? Who is worth troubling about?

The bicycle, faithful and obedient, was in its place
beside the curb. Hélène grasped the handlebars in a
thoroughly bad temper; must she drag it about with
her all night? She did not want to ride it again, it was
easier to think while walking. "What purpose do I
serve?" It was difficult to think it out from any angle,
her ideas fled in all directions. "What I need is another
rum." She went into a café Biard. "A double rum."
The bartender was wiping the counter with a cloth.
"This dreary light, the dampness in the street. And I.
I'm here. But why should I be here? I, who am I?
Someone who can say 'I.' And some day no one will be
aware of my identity." She rested her hand on the top
of the bar. "It's impossible. I've always been here, I
shall always be here — it is eternity." She stared at her
feet, they were riveted to the ground. How could she
ever move? And where should she go?

Hélène found herself back in the street. She looked
at the bicycle in disgust: just where she had left it, like
a patient and unwelcome dog. She walked away, sick
at heart; it was better to keep her hands free, it was all
she could do to manage her feet; they had to be placed
one in front of the other, it wasn't as easy as one might
think. She took a few steps. "I'm getting nowhere," she

said. She leaned against a tree. The trunk was running with damp, and icy drops fell from the bare branches; Hélène felt the cold penetrate into every fiber of her body. She started to walk again. "I'm getting nowhere," she repeated. No matter what steps she took, she remained in the same place, as in a nightmare. Should she go forward, should she go back — but she had no aim.

"He could tell me a way out." His smooth face, his careless and serious voice. It did not seem absurd to him that he was on this earth; he seemed to have good reasons for it. "If I could talk to him without Paul being there." Suddenly, in the icy wilderness, there was a sparkling flame: she had only got to write to him. An aim — now the aim was there; once more time flowed on, warm and sentient. Hélène tripped against the curb and began to laugh.

3

A KNOCK. The door is opened quietly.
"Do you want anything?"

He shakes his head, "No, thank you."

What do I want? And for what? Out there, no
doubt, these words still have a meaning. There is a
room on the other side of the door, a whole house, a
street, a town, and other people — other people who
sleep or watch.

"Has Laurent gone to get some sleep?"

"Yes. He'll come to see you at six o'clock." Madeleine comes nearer the bed. "Is she still asleep?"

"She has slept the whole time."

"Don't forget, I'm next door, with Denise," said
Madeleine.

She shuts the door again. On the bed there is a slight
movement.

"What's the time?" The words are faintly whispered,
in a childish voice. He bends over and lightly strokes
the hand that lies on the sheets. "Two o'clock, my
dear."

She opens her eyes. "I've been asleep?"

For a moment she is tense, she listens; she is not
listening to what is happening around her, but to something within herself.

"They're still making that noise up there. Do you hear
them?"

He cannot hear; he bends hungrily over this agony,
but he cannot share it.

"I wish they'd be quiet."

"I'll go and tell them. Go to sleep again."

"Yes." The blue eyes waver. "Paul," she asks, "where is Paul?"

"He is safe. Tomorrow night he'll have crossed over to the free zone. He'll come here before he leaves."

She shuts her eyes again; the words have not entered into her dreams, that heavy dream in which pulses the drumming of the blood in her arteries, a dream I cannot dream. "No, don't go to sleep again. Wake up for good, wake up for ever!" She opened her eyes, she opened her lips, and she was once more beside me, but I could not keep her there. I would have to force my way to her heart, to break through the fog and make her listen to me, to beg her: "Don't die, come back to me." Come back — yesterday it was still so easy. With your hands on the steering wheel, you looked at the sky and you said: "What a lovely night!" A far too lovely night, so warm! You smiled. "I'll come back." Never again shall I see her smile. Her upper lip seems to have shortened, it reveals her teeth, and her nostrils are pinched. Already a dead body is taking shape in her living body. I must close my eyes and forget that death-mask; tomorrow I shall be unable to do so; I shall see nothing else. "I'll come back." I should have put my arms round you and never unclasped them again. "Don't go away; I love you, stay with me." And you heard those words in the silence, and you went away — I should have shouted them out aloud. "I love you." Now I speak and you no longer hear. You listened to me so passionately, and I spoke no word. Will things ever be again as they were, in any other life?

She is there, so near and so young, in her light-colored blouse, as young as the hope of that triumphant summer. She was wearing a pleated skirt with red and green checks and a white shirt-blouse and a wide red leather belt round her waist. Her hair fell smoothly on either side of her face, with a fringe over her forehead. When she was suddenly framed in the doorway, all eyes turned toward her; she did not look like a working man's wife, and yet as she passed through the workshop she did not seem out of place; it was probably due to the unstudied grace in her dress, in her movements, in her whole person. She came up to me with a scared and aggressive expression; abruptly she held out a parcel to me.

"I've brought you something to eat."

I took the parcel, an enormous bundle covered with loosely tied brown paper.

"You're too kind." I looked at her uncertainly; she was shifting awkwardly from one foot to the other. I felt awkward because I had not answered her letters, and most of all because I had received them.

"Well," she said impatiently, "aren't you even going to open it?"

She must have thought that we had been fasting during these two days of voluntary captivity, for she had stripped the confectionary shop, choosing the most substantial and masculine-looking goods from the sickly stock — slabs of gingerbread, sticks of unsweetened chocolate, thick biscuits — but she had not been able to resist slipping in a soft caramel here and there, a crystallized banana, or chocolate almonds. She sniffed at the food with a greedy smile.

"Share it with your friends quickly; you must certainly be hungry?"

I looked round the workshop to meet six pairs of twinkling eyes. "Who wants some dessert?" I called out. I sent over a shower of *petits beurres,* boxes of dates, dark and light caramels, and I bit into a piece of gingerbread.

"Aren't you going to have anything?"

"No, it's all for you," she said.

Her eyes were shining; she followed every movement of my jaws and I felt that she tasted in her own mouth the honeyed mess that my tongue pressed against my palate. I became more and more embarrassed; her glance minutely searched my face, it noted the shape of my eyebrows, the exact shade of my hair; no one had ever scrutinized me like this. Madeleine never looked at me, she never looked at anything; she was surrounded by things, confused and vaguely terrifying things, which she tried rather not to see. Marcel sometimes looked at me, but he merely noted my features with melancholy detachment; whereas Hélène's eyes were asking questions, weighing up, demanding an account. Who was this other personality who dared to be there, confronting me? I masticated a large piece of gingerbread in silence; then I said: "They let you get through?"

She shrugged her shoulders. "Well, I'm here!"

"Their instructions are to let in no one but mothers and wives. . . ."

She smiled with slight defiance. "I said I'd come to see my fiancé."

"Perrier is in the next workshop," I said hastily.

"But I gave your name," she said. "I even think that's why they didn't turn me away."

I must have looked annoyed, for she asked: "Do you mind?"

"I do, rather. I gave the orders and I don't want to take advantage of any exceptions that are made."

She sat down on a stool and crossed her legs; they were fine sunburned legs. She was wearing leather sandals and white socks.

"And why not?" she said.

"See here, if you absolutely insist that we have a talk, let's fix a meeting. The strike won't last long, but you mustn't stay here."

"Ah, but I've come a very long way," she said. "No, I'm staying, so that you'll just have to answer me."

I smiled. Her letters had annoyed me; they were the letters of an aimless little girl. But she must be worth more than that. On her forehead, in her eyes and her cheeks, was a wild-animal passion, but her mouth trembled with a thousand tender promises; I liked that face. I glanced at my companions; they were paying no attention to us. Some of them were playing cards on a marble slab; others were stretched out on the floor, smoking; Portal was heating up on a spirit-stove the lunch-pail that his wife had brought him, Laurent was writing a letter. It was like being in a working man's club, except that the background was still that of our daily work; it was surprising to watch the leisurely development of individual lives in these workshops where formerly we all labored together under strict discipline. The lead had hardened in the crucible, the fire was out, the letters on the keyboard were no more than indistinct signs, the lead type had become so formless that we might have been illiterate; we alone existed, heedless of these inanimate objects, entirely absorbed in ourselves. We were free and we were putting our strength to the test. We obeyed no orders and we had not asked anyone to act on our behalf. The strike had blossomed spontaneously, without pressure being applied by any particular party, without a political aim, from the hearts of the workers themselves, their needs and their hopes. I had reached my goal. For years I had patiently struggled to get there, to the confirmation of that serene solidarity where each man found in his comrades the strength to impose his own will, without infringing the liberty of any one person and nevertheless remaining responsible for himself.

Her foot was swinging impatiently; the tip of her sandal brushed against my arm. "You're furious?"

"Me? Why?"

"You haven't uttered a word."

"I was considering the position; these strikes are a great success. Just think! At this moment, throughout the whole of France, the same thing is happening in thousands of factories and workshops."

Under the fringe, which accentuated her obstinate expression, her blue eyes turned black.

"Why do you always laugh at me?"

"Am I laughing at you?"

"I didn't come all this way for you to talk to me about your strike."

Her eyes boldly searched my face, they delved into each line of my face and each wrinkle of my forehead; but she was aware that the tenderness of her mouth was giving her away, and she timidly moistened her lips with her tongue.

"Why didn't you answer my letters?"

"But I did."

"Once, four lines."

"There was nothing more to say."

She looked at me as though she wanted to hit me. "Is it very wrong for me to try to see again someone whom I've met and who might help me?"

"But is it wrong, when someone can't help you, for them to refuse to see you?"

I had definitely made up my mind to put her off, I had no time to waste on her; but she was charming with her serious, angry face; a rush of blood had brought a glow to her cheeks.

"Yes, obviously you don't care if I go on stagnating without knowing what to do."

"I'm bound not to care — I don't know you."

"But now you know me." She gave me an engaging little smile.

"Listen," I said, "I understand you very well. You've got to the aimless stage, any amusement seems good to you. But in my case it's different; I've got only too many things on hand; I've absolutely no time to give you."

"No time . . ." Her foot was still swinging impatiently. "You can always find time if you want."

"Let's say that I don't want," I replied.

She stopped dead, the better to let the meaning of my words sink in. She hung her head. "Don't you like me?"

The tone of the question was so sincere that I was disconcerted; her way of laying herself open to the most cruel replies showed a courage that compelled one's admiration. It was the first thing that struck me about you, your reckless taste for sincerity.

"I like you very much. But, you know, you are full of illusions about what I could do for you. I've nothing to teach you, unless you're interested in trade-unionism."

She shrugged her shoulders. "I'll soon see if you're no use to me."

It was difficult to escape her rapacious little claws.

"No, let's drop it. If I made a point of frequently seeing all the people I like, my life wouldn't be long enough."

"Do you know so many? You're lucky." She sighed. I don't know a soul."

"First, you've got Perrier. . . ."

The black flame gleamed again in her eyes. "Oh, it's

[66]

because of Paul. Don't worry, I've no intention of falling in love with you."

"I've never thought that," I said. I was not so sure; she seemed to me to be agog for a passionate affair, and to her it would clearly have seemed dull to be in love with her fiancé.

"Only," she continued, "Paul and I have been stewing in the same juice for years. I'd have liked to hear a new note."

"You like reading. There's nothing like a good book to take you out of yourself."

She shrugged her shoulders in a fury. "Of course I read, but it's not the same thing." She kicked the stool with her heel. "It's quite clear that you don't know what it's like to be stuck alone in a corner from morning to night."

"Your circumstances will certainly change. I'm not worried about you." I took a step as if about to leave her. "Excuse me, but there's some work waiting for me to do."

"Some work? But you're on strike."

"That's so, I'm writing an article about the strike."

"Show it to me."

"It's not finished. And besides, it doesn't interest you."

"Tell be about it," she said. "You aren't a Communist?"

"No."

"What difference does that make?"

"Communists treat human beings like pawns on a chessboard; the game must be won at all costs; the pawns themselves are unimportant."

She looked arrogantly about her, "And you really think that they're so important? The only thing that could be amusing in politics would be to feel that you held a lot of strings in your hand and to keep on pull-ing them."

"You don't know what you're talking about," I said.

It's an accident — you're not going to leave the party for that. The party comes first, my son. We'll avenge him. A pair of fists and a head don't count. There are so many heads and fists left. I knocked on the door in the night and Marcel opened it — his only brother was dead. For God's sake, kill me and bury me deep in the earth. Dangerous as the tree round the bend of the road, as that loaded revolver, as war, as pestilence. Hide me; blot me out. I am alive. I can at least never de-liberately take any action again, never again.

"But when you organize these strikes, aren't you pull-ing strings?"

"They were organized without my help," I said.

After I left the party, I did nothing for two years, and then, little by little, I began to take an interest in trade-union activities. That work seemed to me to be justifiable, because it was in no way political work; its standards were human. I did not have to make a choice for someone else; I took no decisions; each member of the union expressed his own will in the collective will; I did not try to influence the group to which I be-longed; I was merely the instrument through which it expressed its existence; in my person, its fumbling aspi-rations became coherent thoughts, its scattered aims took on a tangible form, they borrowed my mouth to give it a voice, but that was all. Because of me, nothing unexpected or arbitrary happened in their lives, noth-ing that did not spring from within themselves. But I did not feel like explaining all that to Hélène. I held out my hand to her. "Good-by. Go away, like a good little girl."

"And suppose I don't want to go?"

"I can't force you."

I went and sat down by the marble slab on which I had spread out my papers. She hesitated for a moment and then came toward me.

"Good-by, then," she said sadly.

"Good-by."

I had put up a good defense, I was extremely proud of my incorruptible prudence. Blind, again. I conscientiously drove you away; I pretended to drive you away, but were not my voice, my face, my past — all the things that attracted you — only the sum total of myself? Even my denial gave me a new attraction. "I did nothing to bring it about." Madeleine shrugged her shoulders. She was right, I was responsible. Responsible for the hardness and the gentleness of my eyes, for my past history, for my life, for my being. I was there, standing across your path; and because I was there, you met me, without any reasonable cause, without having wanted to do so: from that moment you could choose to come closer to me or to run away from me, but you could not prevent my existing in your consciousness. An absurd constraint weighed on your existence, and it was myself. I thought that I could make my life what I willed it should be, I felt free and guiltless. And I was continuing forever to be the origin of evil for others. But I did not know. I thought it was enough to say no. No, I would not see you again. No, I would not drag my comrades into a political struggle. No, we would not ask for anyone to intervene.

"And yet their objections to your attitude are sound," said Marcel. "Not to take part in politics means that you are still taking action in some other way."

"You're a fine one to talk," said Denise. "You haven't even voted."

She was serving coffee in the middle of the big, bare

[69]

studio. To prevent the bailiffs distraining the goods, we had secretly taken away, on the previous day, the valuable furniture, the hangings, and the few canvases that Marcel still owned.

"It's as absurd as voting," said Marcel. He smiled. "Only it's not so much trouble."

"As far as I'm concerned, that objection is mere sophistry," I said. "You must prove to me that politics come before anything, that man is a political animal, and that his attitude is political, whatever he may think. I deny that. Politics is the art of acting upon men from without; the day when humanity as a whole can organize itself from within in its entirety, there'll be no further need for politics."

"How well you speak!" said Marcel. "Are you trying out on us the speech that you are presently going to make?"

I amused him, I think, more than anyone else in the world. For me to pretend that I was not involved in the universal absurdity was a degree of absurdity that he had never met in anyone else. The assurance with which Denise walked into every pitfall was less screamingly funny to him than my efforts to avoid them. As for him, he submitted with complete indifference to being trapped in the snares of this world; that was far from being the thing that mattered for him.

I smiled at him without resentment. I had never felt so happy for the last eight years. In the scarlet glory of the 14th of July I was saluting my own personal triumph: the triumph of my life, of my ideas.

"Don't you feel like taking a stroll toward the Bastille?"

"With a sky like that?" He looked significantly at the startlingly blue sky. "No, I'm going to have a nap."

He only really lived by night; he slept for the greater part of the day.

"What about you?" I asked Denise. "Will you come?"

She was staring gloomily at the door through which Marcel had just disappeared.

"I'm not particularly keen." She turned and looked at me, "To think that we could have been so happy."

"You won't change Marcel," I said. "You must take him as he is."

"I do try," she said, "but he's incurable. He does it on purpose. . . ." The tone of her voice was tearful, but she managed to control it. "I'm sure that he is weaving a web round himself from which he'll never get out."

For many years now Marcel had given up painting those pictures of his, whose only justification was that they attracted the attention of someone else. He wanted to create. He had carved wood, modeled clay, chiseled marble; he stroked with satisfaction the hard matter from which his hand had shaped forms with individual life; they stood on their own. You could walk round them, they had nothing that a chair or a table had not got. But soon he began to look gloomily at his work. The marble existed in its own right, in its pristine state of heavy stone. "But the features, where are the features?" Marcel would rave. He would point two fingers at me. "They are in your eyes — nowhere else." One morning he loaded his works on a handcart, harnessed himself to the shafts, and dragged the cart to the wharves at Bercy and there upset the stuff into the Seine. Denise had cried for days.

"As for living, he no sooner gives up one thing than he discovers that he must at once give up something else as well. Where will he stop?"

Under the flaming hair, her face was care-worn; her eyes had learned suspicion. She had on a smart frock, but it was worn at the elbows and held at the waist by a cheap belt.

"You ought to try to live a life of your own," I said, "and not to remain dependent on Marcel's life."

"What do you expect me to do? I've no real gift for anything."

"It's not absolutely necessary to be extraordinarily gifted."

She looked at me doubtfully; she liked gilt-edged securities.

"I loathe mediocrity." She wheeled round and took a step in the direction of the table. "Do you think that's beautiful? Do you?" She pointed to a kind of little mound made from a conglomeration of shells and pebbles. Marcel now spent all his time in making these things; he plaited pieces of string, straw, strips of felt, he made mosiacs from pieces of chromo. These objects satisfied him because they could not be separated, even in thought, from their obscure meaning and their flesh-and-blood existence.

"Marcel doesn't pretend that they are beautiful," I said.

She shrugged her shoulders. "A failure — that's what he's turning himself into."

It was difficult to explain to her that success and reputation did not deserve such burning regrets. "Then what is important?" she would say. I could not answer on her behalf. I knew what was important for me, and Marcel knew what was important for him. But nowhere under heaven had we found these definitive and absolute standards of value which Denise insisted should be revealed to her.

"Trust him," I said.

[72]

"Haven't I been patient?" she asked.

I looked at her with pity. She was a very worthy person. She accepted poverty without complaining, she never upbraided Marcel, she tried her hardest to understand what she called "his complex." Loyal, intelligent, brave — but an inner sense of inferiority canceled all these virtues.

I touched her arm, "You oughtn't to stay here. Do come with me."

"I'm afraid that it will be too tiring." She smiled joylessly at me; she was afraid of intruding. I did not insist. I could not manage to arouse any real feeling of sympathy for her. I blamed myself sometimes for this.

"Don't take it so hard," Madeleine used to say to me. "That's only bourgeois unhappiness, well-to-do unhappiness." Madeleine could never understand that anyone could either complain of their lot or delight in it, or indeed that anyone could fear or hope for anything.

"What on earth goes on in their minds?" she said, pointing to the red-and-black stream of people flowing down the middle of the street.

She limped along beside me. Her shoes always hurt her because she picked them up here and there, either as a bargain, or in exchange for something else, or to help someone out.

"They think tomorrow will be better than today," I said. I thought so too. So many promises were breaking through into fruition from the initial uncertainties of a new experiment.

"Pooh! Whatever they do, human life will never have much value."

I made no answer. I never tried to discuss anything seriously with Madeleine; the more convincing the arguments presented to her, the more she suspected their guile. Besides, it was true that her life had no value, since she herself set so low a price upon it. Her body had no value, she gave it with indifference to anyone who asked for it; her time had no value, she spent it chiefly in sleeping or in smoking while she stared into space; she would not have been lacking in intelligence had she not considered that her thoughts had no value either, and rarely did she deign to consider them. Her pleasures, her interests, her worries, even her feelings were of little importance in her eyes, and no one could make her feel they were of value to her; no one but herself could make it seem important for her to exist. But to the men who marched by, singing, to be a man was an important undertaking. Tomorrow life would have a meaning, and already had acquired one through the power of their hopes.

"Are you coming with me, or will you wait for me in a bistro?"

"Are you going to spout again?" she asked.

"Yes. I've promised to address the comrades."

In the middle of the open space, perched on a platform, Gauthier was making a speech. There must have been a zone of silence around him, but we were too far away and his words were lost in the murmur of the crowd.

"What's he talking about?" asked Madeleine.

"I don't know."

"And you — what are you going to say?"

"Come along, you'll soon find out."

"No," she said, "I'm waiting for you here."

She leaned up against a tree and took off her shoes, exposing her stockings, which were riddled with holes and dotted with red blobs; to stop the runs, she painted them with nail varnish.

"It may take some time," I said.

"I don't care."

A band of children was processing past us, red scarves round their necks, red berets on their heads; there followed women shouting rhythmically: "Hang La Roque." The flags flapped above our heads, the tricolor mingled with the red flag; at all the squares in Paris platforms had been erected and festoons were swaying between the trees: 1936, the 14th of July 1936. How proud was our bearing! It was true that our victory was not complete, there was still much to be done, but for the first time, rising above party factions, we had achieved a coalition of all the forces of hope. Was that only yesterday? He made his way through the crowd. He wanted to shout out loud to relieve the joy that swelled his heart, he wanted to shout aloud — his joy, your joy.

"Comrades." He was speaking. The words that he spoke came from his own brain, and yet they did not listen to them with their ears, but from the depths of their souls. He spoke for himself and they acclaimed him: he was speaking for them. He told them of the great wave of goodwill that had been born in France, which was going to spread throughout the world; he promised them that their methods of establishing peace would be adopted throughout the world. "For above all, trade-union comrades, this day is a day of triumph for us; the results that we have achieved are only a beginning, but what fills our hearts with pride, what allows us every hope, is that we have succeeded in doing this through industrial and not political action." He spoke and his words were neither appeals nor orders, but a song, a song of rejoicing. Through his mouth they all sang together in unison.

As though each of us had not occupied space on earth; as though each of us had not been the other's stumbling-block; each man for himself alone, existing

*side by side with the others, forever separate from them
— another human being.*

They sang of the magic of liberty, the strength of brotherhood, and the supreme glory of humanity. Soon war, violence, dictatorship would be impossible; even politics would cease to be of use, for there would be no separateness among men, only a brotherhood of mankind. That was the supreme hope that they hailed for the coming years: the brotherhood of all men in the free recognition of their liberty.

"Let me have your notes," said Gauthier. "I want to publish your speech in the *Vie syndicale.*"

"You spoke jolly well," said Laurent.

Blomart put his hand on his shoulder. "He's a comrade from the works."

"You also spoke damn well," Laurent said to Gauthier. "Are you the man who writes in the *Vie syndicale*?"

"He's the editor," said Blomart.

He was smiling. He was happy. The flags flapped in the breeze, the crowd was singing, and the fellows from the workshops, the comrades from the union, those who did not speak and those who were loquacious, the leading lights of the movement and the mere nobodies, one and all slapped him on the back and slapped one another on the back, and shook hands with one another. Our celebration. Our victory. He remembered another crowd, in the underground railways of his childhood, and the old odor of guilt. It was over. Freed from guilt, he breathed the smell of ink and dust, the smell of sweat, the smell of work; freed from guilt, he strolled beside blank walls, he looked at gasometers and factory chimneys, for beyond weariness and gray horizons these men knew how to

[76]

assert their will, and their life was not a blind accept-
ance. They chose their own fate; it was with pride that
he identified himself with them, thinking: "I am one
of them."

"I've kept you waiting a long time; I hope you
weren't too bored."

"No," said Madeleine. "I could see you getting all
excited over there."

She had remained standing, leaning against the tree
trunk. I took her arm. At that very moment you appeared before me. You held Paul's arm; a scarlet rosette
stained your white blouse; your cheeks glowed with
animation.

"We've been looking for you everywhere," said
Paul.

You shot a withering glance at him and then you
looked at Madeleine, who was clumsily trying to slip
her foot into her shoe. I made the necessary introductions.

"We listened to your speech," said Paul ironically.

"Oh, were you there?"

"Yes." He shrugged his shoulders, "As if France
could separate her fate from that of the world!"

I wanted to reply, but you stopped me impatiently.
"We're not going to stick around here for another
hour."

"Standing is tiring," said Madeleine.

You looked her up and down arrogantly. "Oh, I'm
not tired."

We followed the black flood that flowed haphazardly
between the beflagged houses; the ground was strewn
with bits of paper, flags, rosettes, and pamphlets; we
went and sat down outside a dance hall at the corner
of a street. The waiter put three half-pints and a grena-

[77]

dine on our table; Hélène adored those deadly colored drinks.

"All those damn fools who are singing," said Paul. "They think they're going to build a comfortable little nest in the middle of Europe. Nice and comfy, all doors locked, with the Pyrenees in the south and the Maginot Line in the north. And meantime, Fascism is taking up its position at our gates. And yet they know very well that we can't remain on a national basis."

"No doubt," I said, "but all the same, we must start by winning on that basis."

Silence fell. With a smile Madeleine was listening to an accordion. Hélène was swinging her legs backwards and forwards like an abandoned schoolgirl. I did not feel like carrying the discussion any farther. I was well aware that France was not the only nation in the world. Neither was I the only person in the world; but I had managed to gather round me a life free from compromises and privileges, which owed nothing to anyone and which could not be a source of unhappiness to anyone. I smiled at Madeleine. Her face wore an expression of beatific peace. It was doubtless true that I did not give her much of myself, but she did not ask for more, she would not have known what to do with it. She could only drift through life, and her happiest moments were those she spent with me. I only felt responsible for myself, and it was a responsibility that I accepted with a quiet mind; I was what I wished to be, my life did not differ from the way I planned it to be. And yet across the little iron table you were looking at the face that I had not chosen for myself.

"Of course, you don't know how to dance?"

"I did know, but I'm afraid I've forgotten."

"You ought to try," said Madeleine.

She examined Hélène without hostility or liking,

once and for all, so that she need not think about it again.

"Let's try," I said.

I put my arm round Hélène; I had entirely forgotten how to dance, but I only had to follow her, she could dance for both of us.

"Who is that person with you?" she asked.

"She's a friend of mine."

"Is she interested in your trade-union affairs?"

"Certainly not; it bores her almost as much as it does you."

"What does she do?"

"Nothing at all."

"Nothing?" She looked at me with that expression of hers which seemed to be asking me to give an account of myself. "Why do you go out with her?"

"Because I'm fond of her."

"And she?"

"She's fond of me, too," I said rather shortly.

There was a silence.

"It was funny seeing you on that platform just now," she said.

I smiled. "I must have bored you very much."

She looked at me seriously. "No, I tried to understand. What you said about liberty interested me."

"Who knows?" I said. "Perhaps it's a beginning. Perhaps you're going to take a great interest in politics."

"I shouldn't think so." She looked around her. "Of course, when you're caught up in a crowd like that, it works you up, singing and marching with the others; but as soon as you stop, I think you feel slightly sick, as if you were a bit sozzled."

"I agree," I said. "But political or trade-union work has nothing to do with these public demonstrations."

She pondered. "What I liked in your speech was that you seemed to think that people exist as individuals, each for himself, and not only in great masses."

"The masses are made up of people who exist as individuals; it isn't a question of numbers."

"Oh, do you really believe that?" she said. Her face lit up. "Paul always seems to think that we're just ants in an antheap. So whatever you do or feel has so little importance! It's really not worth while being alive."

She was dancing, her head slightly bent back, her fair hair floating freely round her slender face; it shone in the sun and her white blouse gleamed; but it was not her hair, her youthful complexion, nor the blue of her eyes that lit up her personality, but that zest for living which drove her on toward the future. Her eyes rested on my forehead, on the sky; they searched the horizon to wrest from it all its promises; her legs, eager to spring forward, trembled with the effort to control them; the world was before you, such a vast, such a beautiful prize.

There is no more future, and the world is drifting away. Your eyes are shut: pictures are whirling round and round in your throbbing head, like the blood that is pulsing from your heart back to your heart. Even when you lift your eyelids, things are there, perceptible and lifeless, as in a dream, and they are no longer distinguishable from yourself. The world dematerializes and is absorbed in you; it shrinks until it becomes only the flickering light that is growing pale and must finally be extinguished; the future is telescoped into the stationary moment; soon the present will be absolute; there will be no time, there will be no world, there will be no one at all.

You were dancing, pressed close to me, and already that bond was being woven between us, the bond that fetters me to your agony; already in spite of myself I had entered into your life, so that one day, in spite of myself, I should remain thus at the portals of your death.

The music stopped. Hélène looked regretfully at the garlanded platform. "What a pity! I'd so have liked to go on talking!"

"We'll have another dance later."

She gave a petulant shrug. "There's no point, if we've got to break off all the time."

Her voice carried an imperious request, to which I turned a deaf ear. We went back to our places. Madeleine was talking to Perrier; she got on well with him and she was smiling at him. I liked the smiles she gave in spite of herself; she would have been attractive if she had only allowed her features to keep their natural expression; in spite of her poker face, there was something attractive in her slow movements, in her soft body and her dreamy look.

Hélène was sucking up through a straw the pink drops that clung to the sides of her glass.

"I'd like another," she said. Once again she was swinging her legs from impertinence and boredom.

"We've decided that we'll all four go and have dinner together," said Madeleine. "Does that suit you?"

"Of course it suits me. Where shall we go?"

It was not a question that could be answered lightly. Madeleine was sensitive to atmosphere; in some places she felt defenseless, like a hunted animal; in other and more friendly places she could forget for a moment the fear the outside world aroused in her. We had started a discussion. Hélène was ostentatiously silent; she had been brought a second grenadine and was blowing bubbles through her straw into the pink liquid. She rose abruptly.

"You promised to dance with me again."

I rose willingly and we danced in silence for a moment. Suddenly she moaned: "Oh, how my head aches!"

I stopped. "Would you like to sit down?"

"If you were kind you'd go and get me a headache tablet."

"I'll go at once."

I left at a run; the first druggist's I came to was shut; I had to go as far as the Hôtel de Ville; I was pleased to be able to do this little thing for Hélène; I would have liked to do something for her if I had not felt that the slightest move on my part might endanger her safety.

I put three tablets on the table; Hélène was sitting alone, with four empty glasses in front of her.

"Where are the others?"

"They've gone on ahead to keep a table. They said that if we didn't hurry we wouldn't get in anywhere."

"Where have they gone?"

"To Demory's, rue Broca."

"That's a long way away," I said. "Well, let's join them. Aren't you taking your tablet?"

She hesitated. "It isn't so painful now. I'd rather wait a little."

We went off gaily through the streets, in which the heat of the day was wearing off and becoming milder. This unexpected tête-à-tête was far from boring me. I did my best to answer her questions; she hurled questions at me, as if I had been God the Father.

"But in the end," she said, "why does one live at all?"

We were going into Demory's; I went right in to the back of the room, but there was no sign of either Madeleine or Paul.

"Are you sure this is where we were to meet?"

"Of course," said Hélène.

"You don't look very certain. . . ."

"I'm quite certain." She went toward a table. "All we've got to do is to sit down and wait."

"Yes, they certainly won't be long."

Hélène leaned her chin on the palm of her hand. "Tell me, why do we live?"

"I'm not one of the Evangelists," I said with slight embarrassment.

"And yet you know why you live." She spread her fingers fanwise and studied them attentively. "I don't know why I do."

"Surely there are things you like, things you want. . . ."

She smiled. "I like chocolate and beautiful bicycles."

"That's better than nothing."

She looked at her fingers once again; of a sudden she seemed sad. "When I was small, I believed in God, and it was wonderful; at every moment of the day something was required of me; then it seemed to me that I *must* exist. It was an absolute necessity."

I smiled sympathetically at her. "I think that where you go wrong is that you imagine that your reasons for living ought to fall on you ready-made from heaven, whereas we have to find them for ourselves."

"But when we know that we've found them ourselves, we can't believe in them. It's only a way of deceiving ourselves."

"Why? You don't find them just like that — out of thin air. We discover them through the strength of a love or a desire, and then what we have found rises before us, solid and real."

While I was talking, I kept watching the door. I was beginning to be anxious. This tale of hers seemed to me to be a little suspect. Why hadn't they waited ten

[83]

minutes? Madeleine was never given to attacks of punctilious uneasiness.

"It's funny that they don't come," I said. "I wonder if you haven't mixed everything up."

"No, no," she said with slight impatience. "They must have gone for a stroll before coming here, that's all." Once more she looked me full in the face. "How can we find within ourselves good reasons for living, since we die?"

"That makes no difference."

"I think it makes all the difference." She stared at me with curiosity. "Don't you mind thinking that some day you'll not be here, and that there'll not even be anyone to think of you?"

"If I've lived my life as I wanted, what does it matter?"

"But for a life to be interesting it must be like going up in an elevator; you come to one floor, then another, then another, and each floor is only there because of the floor above it." She shrugged her shoulders. "So, if once you get to the top, everything falls to pieces — it's just ridiculous from the start, don't you think so?"

"No," I said absentmindedly. I was no longer following the conversation, I was really worried.

"Listen," I said, "I'm going to take a taxi and go round all the restaurants we mentioned. You can stay here. If they come, tell them that I'll be back in a quarter of an hour."

She looked at me slyly. "We're getting on quite well without them."

"I'm sure you made a mistake and they're waiting for us somewhere else."

"Let them wait," she said with annoyance.

I was on the point of getting up. "You don't mean that."

[84]

"I certainly do mean it."

"Well, I don't."

"All right." She looked at me triumphantly. "In any case, it isn't worth while looking for them; you won't find them."

"Why not?"

She ran her tongue over her lips. "I sent them to the other side of Paris." I looked at her without quite understanding her. "I said that you had suddenly remembered an appointment and that they were to go on ahead to keep the places in the restaurant and we would join them there."

"Which restaurant?"

She looked round her with a cunning expression. "Quite a different one."

I was annoyed; too many people treated Madeleine in an offhand manner, so that I was all the more careful never to be discourteous to her. "Why did you do such a silly thing?"

"I wanted to talk to you."

"Well, now that we've had a talk, tell me where they're waiting for us and let's go there quickly."

She shook her head. "I shan't tell you."

"It's ridiculous," I said. "You don't think that you can forcibly compel me to talk to you."

She tightened her lips without answering. I rose.

"If you refuse to tell me, I'm going home."

Her face hardened. "Go home, then."

"You're ruining an evening that might have been enjoyable."

"So you say!" She angrily shrugged her shoulders. "It was boring enough just now."

"And so that you shan't be bored, you don't hesitate to wreck three people's evening? You're a filthy little egoist."

She grew scarlet. "I enjoy being damned annoying. You're so hard with me."

"I'm not hard. I don't want to become involved with you."

I pushed open the door of the *brasserie* and strode off toward the bus stop. She was trotting by my side.

"Is it because of that horrid woman?"

She was so shamelessly choking with jealousy that I shook with silent laughter. Never had I met a woman so ignorant of feminine wiles.

"Madeleine has nothing to do with it."

It was true; we were bound by no understanding; over certain periods of time we met every day, and then Madeleine would disappear for weeks on end; she confided her sentimental escapades to me with candor. If I'd had any amorous adventures, if I had fallen in love with a woman, I would have told her without the slightest embarrassment.

"I can do without your company," I said. I lengthened my stride. It would be best to tell the whole story to Madeleine; it was easy to affront her in small things, but if she was handled carefully, she was capable of accepting anything.

I came out onto the Place des Gobelins; the café terraces were overflowing onto the pavement; the fairy lights were lit, Japanese lanterns were swinging under the trees. I heard a little panting voice behind me. "Wait for me!" I turned round. You came quite close to me and you looked at me; you looked at me with an insistence so mysterious that I felt that I was being born again in your eyes; I was not very clear about what you saw. You got your breath back.

"I'll tell you where they are: I sent them to the Port Salut."

"It's not far," I said. "Come on quick; we shan't be too late."

"I don't want to come."

You held out your hand and you said to me, with your tail between your legs: "Good-by, I beg your pardon." And I felt a great urge in my arms to draw you to me, to hold you to my heart; to my arms the gesture seemed so easy — easy to do, and easy to undo, a transparent gesture and exactly equal to its own weight. But I kept my arms close to my sides. I made a gesture, and Jacques died. A gesture, and something new appears in the world, something that I have created and that grows outside my orbit, without me, dragging unpredictable avalanches with it. "He held me in his arms." Already I felt that my face was no longer my own under your gaze; had I burdened your past with some definite event, what would have become of it in your heart? I shook your hand with indifference; I let you go off alone through the festive streets; you were crying, but I did not know it. I set off on my way, thinking that I too was still alone, and, after my fashion, nursing a vague regret. As if all the kisses that I did not give you had not bound us to each other as surely as the most ardent embraces, as surely as the kisses that I shall give you no more, as the words that I shall no more say to you and that bind me to you forever, you, my only love.

✺ 4 ✺

Hélène stretched herself. She was curled up in a ball in front of the fireplace and the flames were toasting her face. Her eyes on her work, Yvonne was sewing; with mechanical regularity the needle stabbed into the piece of raspberry-colored silk. A dull gray day closed in upon the windows of the room. "That's torn it,"thought Hélène, "it's going to happen. It's happening." Her hand tightened on a shred of golden rind, which spurted between her fingers. "I don't like Sundays," she said.

"I rather do," said Yvonne.

Sunday, Monday . . . it didn't really make much difference. On Sundays she stayed at home, but she carried on with her sewing; she never stopped sewing. There was a little dry pop among the ashes.

"Do you remember," said Yvonne, "the first time we roasted chestnuts, how they popped!"

"Yes," said Hélène. "What fun we had!" she added regretfully. She pushed the tongs into the smoldering ashes. "I think they're cooked."

In the neighboring room a voice called: "Yvonne!"

"Coming," said Yvonne. She put down her work, made a face at Hélène, and left the room. Hélène peeled a chestnut and put it into her mouth whole; her fingers smelt of burnt wood, tangerines, and tobacco — a good smell. The chestnut cracked between her teeth, it was hot. "All that exists," she said. But it was not true; there was only emptiness around her. "It's going to happen, it's here," she said. "How I hate to suffer!" She closed her eyes. In the next apartment a voice on the radio sang: "On all the roads there are stones, on all the roads there is sorrow." Hélène did not try to fight, it was useless.

"Exactly one year has passed and I can count on the fingers of my hand the days on which I've seen him. And now only he exists."

"Do you know what she wanted?" said Yvonne with laughter in her voice. "She wanted me to blow her nose. She has made up her mind that she's in agony if she raises her arm from under the sheet."

Hélène kept her face turned toward the flames so that Yvonne should not see the mist in her eyes. "You ought not to give in to her."

"Bah, that's the only pleasure she gets."

"The pleasure of persecuting you, since she's no more ill than you or I."

"All the same, she can't have much fun."

Yvonne had picked up her work again. Hélène put a handful of chestnuts on her lap.

"They're first-rate," said Yvonne, "all crisp and rather burnt; that's just how I like them." She glanced quickly at Hélène. "You don't take sufficient advantage of the small pleasures in life," she said pontifically.

"Idiot," said Hélène.

Yvonne had certainly guessed, but she would never ask questions; she knew how to see, understand, and be silent; Hélène felt safe near her.

"I'm sure that you're going to sit up all night," she said, almost resentfully.

"What has to be must be, mustn't it?" said Yvonne. She puffed out the shining bodice. "A bridesmaid's dress always exaggerates the figure. That piece goes there, so that it matches. Pity the bride carries her stomach below her navel."

"Below her navel?"

[89]

"She's so thin that everything has dropped to hell. She's rubber-plated all round her stomach and hips."

"The bridegroom will get a shock," said Hélène.

Yvonne began to laugh. "If you only knew the number of women who turn out to be surprise packages. When we deliver an evening dress, we often deliver the bosom with it."

The needle pricked into the hem, in, out; it was hallucinating.

Never, never. He will never love me.

"You know," said Yvonne, "I don't want to turn you out, but if you want to be at Paul's by six o'clock . . ."

"What's the time?" asked Hélène.

"Exactly six o'clock."

Hélène yawned. "I'll go by degrees."

Paul. My life, my real life. I've no life left. Only this absence. I shan't see him again for days and days. And it doesn't occur to him that he'll not see me again; he doesn't even think about not loving me. Everything is complete about him. I don't exist for him. I don't exist at all.

"Poor Paul," said Yvonne. She was intent on threading a needle.

"Why poor Paul?" Hélène rose to her feet. "He's in excellent health." She put on her coat, bent over Yvonne and kissed her black hair. "See you tomorrow. I'll be at the Biard by six o'clock."

"See you tomorrow. Enjoy yourself," said Yvonne.

Enjoy yourself — "I ought to be ashamed of myself." To sit up all the night crouching over a pink garment, with a madwoman whining in the next room. Hélène quickened her pace. It was strange; Yvonne did nothing but sew, peel potatoes, and look after a neurotic invalid, and yet her life did not seem to be absurd; it was even satisfying to think that Yvonne existed, just as she was, crouching over her work in her lonely room. "Is it my fault that my life is absurd?" My life! Perhaps it would have been enough to say with conviction: "It is my life." But Hélène could say it no longer, she would not do so. "And yet I shall never have any other life. Never. Never."

"I'm rather late," said Hélène.

"That doesn't matter," said Paul. "The coffee's still warm." He cleared the armchair and brought it up to the stove. "Sit there." He filled a cup and held it out to Hélène.

"Your coffee's excellent," she said. "You're a wonderful man about the house."

"Well, the girl who marries me won't do too badly," said Paul.

He sat down on the arm of the chair and she leaned her head against his hip. Handkerchiefs were drying on the iron piping; a kettle of water was bubbling.

"Poor Paul," thought Hélène with sudden gentleness. "I ought to be kinder to him. Poor dear Paul."

"You'll see how I'll fix up a nice little home for us," said Paul. "I'll make you a big work-table, strong, in nice-quality wood, and a bookcase for your books. We'll hang your watercolors on the walls; it'll be damn fine."

"You are sweet!" said Hélène. She quite liked the feeling of his hand as it lightly stroked her hair in a slow, monotonous caress.

"I'll buy a tent, and in the summer we'll go camping on Sundays."

"You're so sweet," repeated Hélène.

Peacefully she allowed these pictures of homely happiness to pass before her mind's eye: the neat little room, the beef simmering among baby onions, the movies with ice cream in the intermissions and those bunches of mauve and yellow flowers, brought back on Sunday evenings on the bicycle carrier. It was Sunday today and they were making Sunday plans.

"Are you comfortable?" asked Paul. He drew Hélène to him.

"I'm comfortable," she said.

In a flash she beheld a dark head rising out of the rolled collar of a pullover. "He's somewhere; at this very moment he exists in flesh and blood." And then the picture faded. A dream without any foundation. There was only the flesh-and-blood hand stroking the nape of Hélène's neck; lips that were touching her cheeks, her temples, the corners of her mouth, until she felt enveloped in some pale, sickly vapor; she closed her eyes. She abandoned herself unresistingly to the charm that was slowly metamorphosing her into a plant; now she was a tree, a great silver poplar whose downy leaves were shaken by the summer breeze. A warm mouth clung to her mouth; under her blouse a hand caressed her shoulders, her breasts; warm vapors increased about her; she felt her bones and muscles melt, her flesh became a humid and spongy moss, teeming with unknown life; a thousand buzzing insects stabbed her with their honeyed stings. Paul picked her up in his arms, laid her on the bed and stretched himself beside her. His fingers wove a burning tunic about her belly; her breath came in quick gasps; she could hardly draw breath, she was sinking into the heart of the night, she was out of her depth; her eyes closed, paralyzed by that net of burning silk, it seemed to her that she would never rise again to the surface of the world, that she would remain forever enclosed in that viscid darkness, forever an obscure and flabby jellyfish lying on a bed of magic sea-anemones. She pushed Paul away with both hands and sat up.

"Leave me alone!"

Without looking at him, she jumped off the bed; her cheeks were burning. She went up to the looking-glass; her face was flushed, her hair disheveled, her blouse crumpled; the sight of herself filled her with loathing. She pulled from her bag a comb and her powder compact; her heart continued to beat too rapidly and the squirming in her body, as of a thousand earwigs, had not ceased. She started; Paul had come up to her and put his arms round her shoulders.

"Why won't you?" he said. He had asked the question in a colorless voice, his limpid eyes looked straight at her. She turned her head away.

"I don't know."

Paul's smile was kindly. "And yet you're no longer a little girl. What are you frightened of?"

"I'm not frightened," said Hélène.

She disengaged herself and began to run the comb through her hair.

"But you are frightened," said Paul. He took her gently by the shoulders. "It's only natural; women are very often frightened, the first time. What astonishes me is that, brave as you are, you should let yourself be frightened like other women."

He looked perplexedly at Hélène; she went on combing her hair in silence. How could he discuss the matter so calmly? She was as embarrassed by his questions as if he had asked her to stand naked before him.

"And yet we trust each other enough and are good friends enough for you to have got beyond that," said Paul.

"Yes," she said. She did not know what to say to him — what had trust and friendship to do with that cocoon-like solitude of which her body held an anguished memory?

"Well?" said Paul. Already his grip was tightening; of course, so long as she was silent, he thought he was in the right. She stiffened.

"Well, I don't want to," she said violently.

Paul did not let go; a slight flush had risen to his cheeks. "That's not quite true."

Hélène gave a short laugh. "Do you suppose I don't know?"

"I certainly do," said Paul.

Hélène's cheeks flamed; he had ears that understood the beating of her heart, he had eyes and hands. . . .

"The trouble is that you're immediately standoffish," he continued. "But if you'd let yourself go . . ."

"Of course, if a man paws me, it has an effect on me," said Hélène. She was stuttering with anger. "I'm not made of ice, but then you might as well say that I want to go to bed with all the riffraff who paw me at the movies."

"Why do you take things that way?" asked Paul. "I think we ought to have it out once and for all."

"But there's nothing to say," said Hélène, controlling her voice. "Let's agree that I'm afraid; it's idiotic, I know, but be patient and I'll get over it."

"Obstinate little thing!" said Paul.

He kissed the corners of her eyes; she pursed her lips. She wished neither to hit him nor to cling to his mouth, nor to cry, but she had to tense every muscle in her body in order to avert the storm raging within her.

"Let's get out of here," she said.

"As you like," said Paul.

He followed her obediently down the stairs. Once more he gave up attempting to understand her; he gave up quickly. She looked at him with a resentment that almost immediately changed to distress. She did not understand herself. In the streets the weather was neither hot nor cold, people were walking languidly up and down the boulevard; she felt that under their skin they were just like the weather, neither hot nor cold. Inwardly Hélène felt both intoxicated and fragile. In Paul's arms she would have been protected against the insipid humidity of this particular Sunday. Why had she denied him? The wave of sadness in the hollow of her throat, the iron bar across her stomach, the dry taste in her mouth, these were nothing else but desire.

"Listen," said Paul. "I'm going to suggest something: why shouldn't we get married at once?"

"Get married?"

"Why, yes!" said Paul.

For a moment Hélène was dumbfounded; this marriage was like the idea of the great social upheaval to come, it was mythical; it was discussed with perfect seriousness, but no one really believed in it.

"But where shall we live?"

"At my place; I can manage. There's no reason why you should stay with your family until spring." He pressed Hélène's arm. "Poor little rabbit, I can quite understand that you're highly strung; it's no life for you."

She looked at him resentfully. She wanted to shout at him: "Don't be so nice!" She wanted to claw his pink cheeks to stop him at long last being so obstinately nice. It was so utterly absurd: he loved her and she did not love him; and the man she loved did not love her.

"It won't make much difference," said Hélène, "considering that I couldn't work in that rabbit-hutch. So long as we haven't an apartment, I'll still have to spend the day in the rue Saint-Jacques."

"It'll make a great deal of difference," said Paul.

"I shan't see much more of you than I do now."

"But our relationship will be quite different."

A flush of humiliation and anger colored Hélène's cheeks. "He thinks that I need a man, that a few good nights of love would put me straight."

"I told you that I'd no wish for such relationships," she said definitely.

"Well," said Paul, "you don't intend to remain a virgin all your life?"

"Do you think you're the only man in the world I could go to bed with?"

Paul looked at her reproachfully. "Listen, Hélène, if I was clumsy just now, forgive me, but don't be unkind; you know that all I want is for you to be happy. Let's have a talk in all good friendship."

She was unfair, she was wicked, and she knew it; but she wanted to stir up those limpid waters; he was too certain that she loved him. Was that his fault? It mattered little; he must surely be in the wrong since she had longed so fiercely to hurt him.

"And in the name of good friendship," she said, "why did you decree that I must sleep with you?"

"Oh, that's all right," said Paul impatiently.

Her smile was self-satisfied; it was difficult to anger him, but sometimes she managed to do so.

"I'm not fooling," she said. "If you want to talk, let's talk seriously. Why?"

"I thought that you loved me," said Paul ironically.

"And what about you?"

"How — me?"

"Do you love me?"

He shrugged his shoulders. "What do you expect me to do? What do all these idiotic questions amount to?"

"Oh, I know," she said. "It's understood that we love each other, it's been understood for so long. It's indecent to try to find out what it really means."

"That's obvious to me."

"Not to me." She looked at him provokingly. "Would you kill yourself if I died?"

"Don't be childish."

"You wouldn't kill yourself. And if you had to choose between me and your political work, which would you choose?"

"Hélène, I've told you fifty times that I am my work. I can't choose not to be what I am. But such as I am, I love you. I've only one wish, and that's to share everything with you."

"I'm useful to your happiness," said Hélène, "but I'm of no use to your life."

"Who is necessary to whom?" said Paul. "You go on living."

"You live," said Hélène.

For Paul the bond was strong enough — their common interests as children, their mutual stand against mediocrity, the friendship of their bodies ready to be united — but love was something quite different. It was a curse.

"Yet you're not a romantic young thing," said Paul. "What? Would you really like our hearts to beat violently when we meet, and to exchange locks of hair?"

"It's easy to laugh," said Hélène. "You think that so long as we get on all right together and are not physically repulsive to each other, it amounts to love."

"Don't beat about the bush," said Paul. "You think you don't love me any longer?"

There was anger in his voice. Hélène was silent; her courage suddenly failed her.

"I don't know," she murmured. She looked anxiously at Paul. Supposing she were to lose him — he was all she had in the world. What would happen to her without him?

"What?" he asked. "Are you bored with me?"

"No," said Hélène.

"Don't you like me to kiss you?"

"No," she said again.

"Then what is it?"

They were walking through the Observatoire gardens; a thin layer of mud covered the cold earth, a few leaves hung from the trees.

"What is it?" repeated Paul.

"I'm fond of you," she said tonelessly.

"But you think it would be rather dull to spend your life with me?" Paul was grinning; he was uneasy, but in spite of everything he was thinking that he only had to deal with the mood of a hysterical little girl. She had so often treated him badly for no good reason.

"I don't think that marriage would suit me," she said.

"An hour ago you were making plans with me."

"Oh, it's difficult to contradict you," said Hélène in a voice more aggressive than she wanted it to be. "You seemed so sure of yourself; you haven't often asked my advice."

"Usually you're not backward in giving it without being asked for it," said Paul. He stared at Hélène uncertainly. "You're annoyed with me," he said, to conciliate her, "and you say anything to be nasty to me."

"But I'm speaking the truth," said Hélène. "Does it seem so extraordinary to you that I'm not dying to be married to you?"

Paul stopped and put his hand on the balustrade that enclosed the gardens.

"It's true, isn't it? You don't love me?"

She did not answer.

"Then you've lied to me all this time."

His voice had taken on the self-assured cutting tone that he only used in political discussions; his face had become stern. Hélène suddenly felt intimidated; he no longer belonged to her; he stood there before her, he was judging her.

"I didn't lie," she said. "I'm very fond of you." She looked at him imploringly; she had behaved so badly to him! He must not become aware of it or she would die of shame.

"Don't quibble," said Paul. "You should have warned me that there was a misunderstanding between us."

"But I tried," said Hélène.

"You've had fifty absurd shopgirl quarrels with me, but you've never had it out with me straight."

Tears rose to Hélène's eyes; he really seemed to despise her; were there times when he had despised her and she had not guessed it? She suddenly had the feeling that it was only out of the kindness of his heart that he had let himself be so easily led.

"I was afraid of upsetting you," she said piteously.

"Hélène! Do you understand what you're saying?" He really despised her; his eyes had grown dark; it was no longer possible to see what he was thinking; it was terrifying—all those thoughts in his mind which she no longer knew how to control. Hélène began to cry.

"Oh, don't howl," said Paul.

She bit her lips; she had behaved like a spoilt child throughout this scene; was she not capable of answering him on the same plane?

"What has happened," she said, "is that I had never thought about it; I was accustomed to the idea that I loved you."

"How did you discover that it wasn't true?"

She had not the strength to meet his gaze. "Little by little," she said vaguely.

He seized her arm. "Then you love someone else?"

Now it was he who was reading her; he went too quickly, she did not know what to invent, she was going to lose him, and she did not want to lose him. . . .

"Who is he?"

"You're wrong," said Hélène.

He shrugged his shoulders. "You won't tell me?"

What must she say to him? She had never dreamed that Paul meant so much to her! Never had he seemed so solid, so real to her.

"All right," said Paul. "Good night."

He turned his back on her; before she could make any move, he had gone. She began to run. "Paul!"

He turned round. "What do you want?"

She stood before him tongue-tied; she wanted to keep him; she wanted him to go on loving her without any hope of return; there were no words with which to say that.

"Good! Well, when you make up your mind to speak, you can let me know."

She watched his retreating figure. "He thinks I'm foul," she thought despairingly, "I was foul to him." She let herself drop on a damp bench. "And now I've no one left. It's my fault." Tears choked her. He wasn't crying, he wasn't; he knew how to behave; but he was unhappy because of her. "I've never bothered about him; I only wanted to have him beside me, nice and snug and faithful. Cowardly, unfair, flighty, and treacherous — disgusting, I was disgusting," she repeated despairingly. This devastating remorse was intolerable; it was a useless remorse, it made no amends for any fault. "Forgive . . ." But there was no heaven toward which the soul could leap, freed from its heavy past; it remained snared in its own net, as solitary and unavailing as a dead body buried in the earth.

"I want to see him." Hélène rose to her feet and began to run. "He'll tell me to go and have it out with Paul. But it's him that I really want to see." She jumped onto a bus. Never mind his poker face; never mind his icy words. He must be made aware of it. Everything would be less horrible if she could only think that he would know that it had happened. This sultry afternoon, remorse, anguish, all that would begin to exist for him, and then there would be nothing to regret, nothing to desire.

Hélène jumped off the bus. Rue Sauffroy — his street — his house. A shiver ran down her spine. The world around him was so charged that she could scarcely breathe in its atmosphere; when she stood before him, it seemed as if there were no air and she felt stifled. Third floor on the left. Which was his window? There were lots of windows, some of them dark, some lit up. "Shall I ever dare?" From time to time he gave her an hour of his company to keep her quiet, but if he thought she was being indiscreet, he lost his temper; perhaps he might take advantage of it not to see her any more. She climbed the stairs. There was a light under his door. She thought, with beating heart: "He's there, in flesh and blood." She held her breath: she had caught the murmur of voices.

She ran down the stairs again, her cheeks burning. "What am I going to do?" She looked at the house. There was no question of going away; life was here. She leaned back against the wall and counted the windows. The whole of life lay behind that little shining square of light.

The light went out. Hélène moved away and slipped behind the cover of the main entrance. She must have been standing stock-still for a long time; she was chilled to the bone. She waited for a few more minutes and Madeleine came out from the building. Blomart was following her. He took her arm. Why should it be she? Why did he love her? "I ought to have looked at her more carefully," thought Hélène. She had thought her ugly, old, and stupid, but she must have something more precious than beauty and intelligence, since he loved her. Hélène moved forward with careful steps, keeping close to the wall. Madeleine was wearing a thin blue coat with a red scarf and a felt hat that hid half her face.

They went into a restaurant. It was a little yellow-painted restaurant, with a kind of palisaded enclosure all round the entrance, which must be used as a terrace in the summer. Hélène went up to the window. They were sitting at a table facing each other; Blomart held the menu in his hands, she could see his profile; he probably came there often. Hélène looked at the waitress, at the zinc counter, at the dumb-waiter, with baskets of bread, fruit, and a large sausage on it. In one way it was deceptive; it was impossible to guess why he had chosen this restaurant rather than another; the oil and vinegar bottles and the paper napkins gave away no information about anything else but themselves; after twenty attempts she was no farther forward in her knowledge of Blomart's inner self. And yet Hélène found that she could not ask for more. She would have never been able to imagine on her own, and with certainty, this setting which was now presented to her, all of a sudden, through no effort on her part.

"What are they eating?" Hélène stood on tiptoe, but she could barely see their table. It was funny to think that he ate like anyone else. He looked at the food on his plate, he tasted it in his mouth, he chewed it carefully. Hélène had the impression that he ate out of pure condescension, so that he should not be different from other people; he seemed to have no desires, no needs; he was not dependent on anyone or anything, not even on his own body.

Hélène turned away from the window. "I ought to go away." No doubt they would go back together and she would not be able to speak to Blomart. "I'm going away." To be sucked under the surface once more and to be sucked under together with her hopes, her deception, and her fatigue — her courage failed her. At least she had this period of waiting; if she gave up that, then there would indeed be nothing left, neither absence nor presence, absolutely nothing. Eight o'clock — then she ought to telephone. But the dining-room at home had become so remote, with its china plates and its smell of stale cocoa; she could not imagine that it was possible for it to become a reality at the other end of a line. There was an abyss between that dully vegetative world and these streets lit up by Blomart's presence.

She shivered. "Where are they going?" They were leaving the restaurant. Once more she began to trail them. To see him, to follow him, was to establish a bond between him and her. "I will follow them all night." There was a lump in her throat. They were near the entrance to the subway station, they were shaking hands. Madeleine went down the stairway and Blomart turned on his heel.

Hélène hid behind a lamppost to let him pass; she did not want to intrude on his solitude at once. Alone — he only existed for himself. "What's going on in his mind?" He walked more quickly than with Madeleine on his arm, with a rather heavy step. At that instant he was really himself; it was fascinating to feel him existing before her in his absolute truth.

[103]

"Good evening," said Hélène. She lightly touched his arm.

He turned round. "What are you doing here?"

"I was following you."

"For how long?"

"I've been following you the whole evening."

She was smiling; it was hard to speak and to smile when she received the full impact of his face on her heart. She could never exactly recall that expression which was both distant and welcoming.

He stared at her, hesitating. "Did you want to see me?"

"Yes," she said, "I must speak to you. Let's go to your place."

"If you want to."

She began to walk silently beside him. Not behind him, beside him. Not long since, she had prowled in his wake, as insubstantial as a dream; now she was actually there; these streets had now come into her own life. He himself was inviting her to climb the stairs up which she had crept as an intruder.

"So that's where you live," she said.

"Yes. It seems to surprise you." He was smiling. When she thought of him he seemed to be ageless, his face was severe and definite; she forgot the ironical fire of his eyes, his sensitive nostrils, and the repressed ardor that sometimes gave him an extremely youthful appearance. He went up to the fireplace and poked the glowing coals that filled the grate.

"Warm yourself. You seem to be chilled through and through."

"I'm quite all right," she said.

His room. She looked at the carpet, at the divan bed covered with a pretty printed linen, the shelves laden with books, and the strange pictures hanging on the walls. He appeared to be so entirely responsible for himself that it did not seem that anything could happen to him accidentally; and yet she could not imagine him choosing his furniture with care. It was rather as if his clothes, the setting in which he lived, the food he ate, had belonged to him for all eternity.

"Well?" He looked at her curiously. "What's the matter?"

"Well, it's this." She hesitated a second. "I've broken off with Paul."

"Broken off?" said Blomart. "You mean to say you've quarreled."

"No, it's really over."

"Why?" asked Blomart.

He was there, sitting in front of her. She no longer had the slightest wish to tell him her troubles. He was there, nothing else was important.

"I don't love him," she said.

"Are you sure?"

"Quite."

He bent his head over the fire with a rather worried expression. He was thinking about her, about himself. There was no need for her to do any thinking; without remorse, without anxiety, she peacefully gave herself into his keeping.

"What does he say?"

"He isn't pleased," said Hélène.

"He loves you." Blomart looked at Hélène. "Even if you've no passionate love for him, is that a reason for breaking off?"

"Oh, I'm quite willing to see him again," said Hélène. "Only there must be no more talk of marriage, nor of — of emotion," she ended.

[105]

There was a silence.

"Would you like me to speak to him?"

"Oh, no," said Hélène, "there's nothing to say."

"Then what can I do?" asked Blomart.

"Nothing," said Hélène. "There's nothing to do."

"If so, why did you come here?"

"I wanted you to know."

Blomart's face became serious.

"Are you annoyed at my coming?" she asked.

"It seems to me to serve no good purpose."

"Of course. It never seems to you that it's a good thing to see me."

Blomart dug the poker into the red coals without answering. He's talking to himself. He's saying things in his head. So many things that I cannot know, under that black hair which would be so pleasant to touch.

"You know, I did some reckoning up; you see me for about three hours a month. That's the two hundred and fortieth part of your existence."

"I've explained to you twenty times. . . ."

"Your reasons don't hold water," said Hélène. She turned her head aside. "If you're afraid that I might grow fond of you — well, I've already done so."

He was again silent; he was looking at the fire with an inscrutable expression.

"What are you thinking?" she asked.

"I'm thinking that now we must not see each other at all."

Hélène clutched the arms of the chair. "Ah, I won't let you do that to me." The terror that had seized her was so violent that it seemed to her as if her bowels were being torn from her. "Every day I'll go and look for you when you leave the workshop, I'll follow you in the streets, I'll — "

"No, you'll do nothing of the kind. You know perfectly well that you'll never get anything out of me by those methods."

Tears of fury rose to Hélène's eyes. "But why? Why?"

"I don't love you," he said brutally.

"I know you don't love me, but I don't care a damn," she said violently. "I don't ask you to love me."

"Paul loves you, and Paul is my friend. And then there's Madeleine — she would be unhappy, and she needs me."

"I need you too," sobbed Hélène.

"No. You need something to amuse you. You'll forget me much quicker than you think." He looked inexorable; two little vertical lines gave a hard expression to his forehead, and his voice was quiet. He was a rock.

"It's not true," she said. "I shall never forget you; only so long as you don't know what's happening to me, you don't care — I can be as miserable as hell, but your conscience will be clear." She choked, "You dirty hypocrite."

"You must go now," said Blomart.

She looked at him provokingly and her hands gripped the arms of the chair more tightly. "I won't go."

He rose. "Then I shall have to go."

"If you do that — " she was gasping — "I'll break everything, I'll tear up all your papers."

"There's nothing valuable here," he said. "Enjoy yourself."

He took his coat and opened the front door. She rushed toward him. "No, no, come back!"

She followed him down the stairs, but his legs were long and he ran swiftly. She was out of breath and he was already disappearing into the crowd of passers-by; he turned the corner of a street.

"He'll see," she said. "He'll see." She bit her hand-kerchief. He would see nothing; she could not hurt him in any way, he was invulnerable. She leaned against a lamppost. She felt as if she were going to fall on the pavement, fainting with rage.

"I hate him." She jumped onto a bus. "Never, never. He'll never love me." The pain was there, sickly, nauseating. She did not wish to sink into that tepid morass. "Paul loves you." "Does he think that I am condemned to sleep with Paul? I'll show them." There was one thing she could do — hurt herself. "I'd like to wallow in the gutter and then, in a year's time, he'd run into me at a street corner and I'd say to him: 'Are you coming my way, deary?' and he'd exclaim: 'What — you!' " She looked provocatively at a middle-aged man sitting not far away. The man stared at her and she averted her eyes. "I'm a coward. But I'll be brave. 'You need something to amuse you.' He'll see how I can amuse myself! I'm going to get blind drunk and I'll throw myself under a bus, and Paul will say to him: 'Hélène threw herself under a bus last night.' Then he'll look funny."

Hélène alighted, went into a tobacconist's, and marched up to the telephone booth. "Hello, I'd like to speak to Pétrus." There was a confused sound at the other end of the line, a sound of footsteps. If he's not there, I'll telephone Francis, Tourniel, any fool. I don't care which.

"Hello."

"Hello, it's Hélène."

"Well, well! I thought you were dead. It's not nice to drop one's pals. What's happening to you?"

"Will you come out with me this evening?"

"Do you want to come out with me?"

"I'm damn well fed up. I want to get drunk."

There was a silence. "Why not come and get drunk here?" said Pétrus, "I've got some good port and some gramophone records."

"Suits me," said Hélène. "I'm coming."

☙ 5 ☙

M y only love. Is it really you? Can I still say: "You are there"? Yet someone is there who is no other person but you. During the past hour she has changed, she seems to be suffering. Her breathing is shorter and the network of veins is apparent under the parchment-colored skin. You had not chosen this: the labored breath, the sweat on your forehead, the purple flush that surges to your face, the odor of death that already emanates from your body. "It is for me to choose." Who was it who chose? Seated before me, pale and with disordered hair, you naïvely believed that you were there in your entirety; but I knew that you were also elsewhere, in the far reaches of the future. To which should I give the preference? Whatever my decision might be, it was always you whom I was betraying.

And yet I thought that I had finished with Hélène. I had not seen her for three months; she had already broken off with Paul and he too did not know what had become of her. I thought that she had cut her losses and had forgotten me, and I was relieved; she rather frightened me. One Saturday morning, while I was shaving, the doorbell rang. I opened the door and saw a dark face that I did not know.

"Are you really Jean Blomart?" she asked. She was looking at me severely. She was a thin little Jewess with glowing eyes.

"Yes, I am."

"I am a friend of Hélène Bertrand. Her friend Yvonne. I must speak to you."

I watched her mistrustfully. Hélène had often spoken to me about her; she was her accomplice, her familiar. What fiendish plot had they been hatching?

"Well, what is it? Sit down."

She sat down near the fireplace. The fire was not lit. "Hélène is going to have a child."

"Hélène? What kind of yarn is this?"

"It's not a yarn. That is, Hélène will not have that child. I've found someone who will look after her." She did not look at me; she looked at the grate filled with cold, black coals. I did not know what to think.

"Listen," I said. "Why do you come here to tell me this? It's no concern of mine."

Yvonne's eyes had an angry gleam. "Oh, of course not."

"Hélène's only got to speak to Paul about it; she can trust him."

"Oh, so you think that it's Paul's child!" said Yvonne.

I felt a queer pang in my heart. "Isn't it his?"

"Of course not!" Yvonne shrugged her shoulders. "There's no question of Hélène being able to have that child, do you understand?"

"Agreed. How can I help you? Do you want money?"

"No, we don't want your money."

"Well, then?"

Yvonne looked me up and down in a hostile manner. "Well, then, someone must spend the night with her: I can't, my mother is insane and I can't leave her. And someone must lend her a room."

It was my turn to look at her suspiciously. Hélène had so often outmaneuvered me. Was this not a plot to enable her to spend a night with me? It was impossible to read anything in those black eyes that avoided mine.

"I would do so willingly," I said, "if I thought that the story were true."

"But it is true!" Yvonne was indignant. "Do you think that such things are made up for the fun of it?"

"With Hélène, you can never be sure."

"Oh, it's disgraceful!" said Yvonne. "I understand now why she didn't want to ask you."

"She didn't want to ask me?"

"No, and she was quite right. But we didn't know anyone else."

I hesitated. "Yet, there was only Paul in Hélène's life. How did it happen?"

Yvonne's eyes flashed. "One evening you drove her away. She came to ask your help, and you drove her away. She went and got drunk with friends and — it happened."

"Does the friend know?"

"He's a dirty beast. She hasn't seen him for a long time."

There was a silence. Yes, Hélène was capable of that — because I had driven her away. Once more I felt that pang in my heart.

"Is the person who is to look after Hélène reliable?"

"Yes, so I understand. But I had difficulty in finding her. We lost a lot of time. It would have been quite simple a month earlier." She added: "We should not have needed you."

"What shall I have to do?"

"Just stay beside her. If she is in too great pain, give her some ether to breathe. If things don't go as they should and it isn't all over by tomorrow morning, telephone Littré 32-01 and ask for Madame Lucie;

[112]

say that you're speaking for Yvonne; say that the patient isn't well, and she will come at once."

"You can trust me. Tell Hélène that I expect her."

"She will probably arrive at about six o'clock." Yvonne hesitated a second. "Hélène wants me to warn you that it may be awkward for you if things turn out badly."

"Tell her not to worry about me."

She rose. "Then good-by."

She shook my hand without smiling; she had a grudge against me. She was going downstairs, going round the corner of the street, and with her she bore my image, which she contemplated with fierce resentment.

I picked up my shaving brush again and lathered my cheeks. It was easy to saddle me with the blame. Would she have wished me to betray Paul or to abandon Madeleine? I had no duty toward Hélène. The razor grazed my skin. What an expression in her eyes when she looked at me! As if I were a malefactor! I said angrily: "And yet I didn't give Hélène that child." I repeated these words aloud. But within me a doubt kept on insinuating: "Isn't it me?"

"I hope that I'm not going to be too much of a nuisance," said Hélène.

"Of course not."

She stood outside my room with a timid expression that I had not seen before; she carried a big parcel under her arm. My last hope faded: Yvonne had not lied, it was no jest. Under Hélène's blue dress, beneath her childish skin, was that thing which she fed with her blood.

"Come quick and get warm," I said. "I've made up a good fire."

I had put some flowers on the table and clean sheets

on my bed. She looked round the room undecidedly. "Would you mind going out for a moment, just long enough for me to settle down?"

I took my overcoat. "Would you like me to bring anything back for you?"

"No, thank you." She added, "You can come back in half an hour."

It was already dark outside; women passed on their lovers' arms, women with the red laughter of women. Hélène had had a lover, a dirty beast; a dirty beast who had slipped his hand under her dress. He hurt her; she is going to suffer, and she is a child. In the brightly lit shops the housewives were buying bread and ham for the evening meal; they were going to eat and sleep, this night would only be a hyphen between the day that was ending and the day that was to dawn. But in a room there was Hélène with that thing in her womb, and the night was a great dangerous black desert, that we had to cross without any help. When I went back, she was lying in bed; she had put on a white nightdress, scalloped in red, a schoolgirl's nightdress. The big parcel that she had carried under her arm had disappeared.

"How are you?" I asked.

"I feel queer." Her hands were shaking; I noticed that her whole body was shaking, and her teeth were chattering.

"Are you cold?" I sat down beside the bed and I took her hand.

"No, it's nerves," she murmured. Her teeth were chattering violently and her hands were clutching the sheet. "Do I disgust you?"

"My poor child, what do you take me for?"

"But it's disgusting," she said brokenly. A tear rolled down her cheek.

"Stay still. Take it easy."

Little by little the trembling stopped; she relaxed and looked at me more cheerfully. "You must be furious."

"Who, me? Why should I be?"

"You never wanted to see me again."

I shrugged my shoulders. "It was best for you."

"You see — your reckoning was out."

I looked at her helplessly. Then it was really true! Then it really was my fault! I had treated her like a capricious child; she was such a little girl, and already her body knew that sharp woman's pain. Her mouth contorted and she turned dead white.

"Are you in pain?"

She was motionless, her eyes shut. "It's gone now."

"Hélène, why did you do it?"

"I wanted to revenge myself."

"But what a queer kind of revenge!"

"I thought that if you knew, you'd feel guilty." This time her whole face was convulsed and she dug her nails into the palms of my hands. "Oh, it hurts!"

She had not failed; she had even succeeded beyond her hope. At each spasm of pain, despair and evil tore savagely at my heart. For an instant the pain would ease and then it would start again immediately, each time more violently. He who had laid her on that bed was myself. I had not wanted to enter into her life; I had fled, and my flight had wrecked her life. I had refused to influence her fate, and I had used her as brutally as if I had violated her. You were suffering because of me, because I existed. Who had condemned me?

There were strange rumblings under the sheets.

"Oh!" she said. "Oh, it hurts too much."

She was clinging to my hand as if it were a lifeline

[115]

and she was looking at me; my hand clasped hers, and I could see nothing but her haggard eyes and the little turned-up nose in the middle of a sheet-white face. "Be brave. It will stop. It will all be over." I repeated those words endlessly. Without ceasing the pain tore her belly; it stopped for an instant and then pierced her again relentlessly. "It will all be over." And time passed and it did not end. The whites of Hélène's eyes were showing. Sometimes I felt that a sharp scream was going to break from her lips and I put the palm of my hand over her mouth.

"Oh!" she said. "I can't stand it. Quick, quick. Oh, for some relief!" With a maniac look on her face she registered the ebb and flow of the pain. "Quick, relief. Quick, quick."

A wave stronger than the others lifted her up, submerged her. Her glance failed. "Oh!" she said. "Oh my dear love!"

Tears rose to my eyes. It was too unfair. I did not deserve a love like this; I did not deserve her suffering. I had wanted only not to hurt her. Forgive me, my poor little girl! Forgive me, Hélène! But it was too late.

Ah! It would be too simple. Don't go there. And the whites of his eyes showed in his face, swollen with blows: torturer. A child dies, his chest crushed by blows from rifle-butts, because his elders have not dared to will otherwise. "Forgive me." It will be too late.

Torturer. How slowly came the dawn, that dawn which I would like to thrust back forever; how long was that night, as long as this one is short, this night devoid of hope!

"I'm done for," she said. A sob broke from her. "It will never end. I'm done for."

I took a pad of cotton wool and I poured a few drops of ether on it and held it to her nostrils.

"Who's there?" she asked.

"It's me, it's Blomart."

Her eyes no longer recognized me.

"Wait for me. I'll be back at once," I said.

She did not hear. I went downstairs. The cold air made me shiver. There were a few passers-by in the avenue de Clichy; they had slept, they had just woke up and they walked hastily in that uncertain and dreary morning light, sad as the face of a new-born child. A new morning, but for me the day had not yet begun; there was only that night which would not end — the color of the sky made no difference. I went into a little Biard that had just opened. A waiter in a blue apron was wiping the zinc counter with a cloth.

"I should like to telephone."

"There you are."

I took the charge slip and I called Littré 32–01.

"What's up now?" asked a voice.

"I don't know. Something is wrong. You must come."

"At this hour of the morning! I shan't find a taxi."

"I assure you that something is wrong."

I sensed that the woman was hesitating at the other end of the line.

"Are you sure you're not disturbing me for nothing?"

"No, she's been in pain for twelve hours. She's worn out."

"Only I'm an old woman," said the voice. "It isn't easy for me to get about. Well, all right, I'll come."

I went back home and took my place again beside Hélène.

Her eyes were still shut. Was it the effect of ether or

of exhaustion? She moaned no longer. It was as though not a drop of blood were left in her veins. I listened anxiously to the noises in the street. I was frightened. Twelve hours earlier a stranger had lain down in that bed; but this fight had united us more strongly than an act of love; she was my flesh and my blood. I would have given my life to save her. My child, my poor little child. How young she was! She liked chocolate and bicycles and she went forward into life with the boldness of a child. And now she lay there, in the midst of her red woman's blood, and her youth and her gaeity ebbed from her body with an obscene gurgling.

"Now, little one, what's wrong?" said the old woman.

I looked at her anxiously. An abortionist. She was so exactly like the thing she actually was that she did not look real. She was dressed in black, and had fair hair, flabby pink-and-white cheeks, and an orange mouth; her eyes were the eyes of a very old woman, blinking and rather bleary. Could she see properly? Under the paint I was aware of the badly washed flesh. I looked at her hands with their painted nails. A reliable person. She lifted the sheet and I turned away. A vague odor filled the room.

"It's not happened yet," she said. "You were right to call me. I will help you. It will all be over at once."

"Will it stop?" asked Hélène.

"In a second."

"Is everything all right?" I asked.

"Of course." She began to laugh. "You looked so upset that I expected the worst. Good heavens! Haven't you ever seen anything?" I heard her moving about behind me. "Where's my bag? It's dreadful to grow old; I can't see an inch in front of my nose."

"There it is," I said.

She took the black bag and opened it; at a glance I saw a handkerchief, a powder-box, and a purse. She thrust her hand with its painted nails into the bottom of the black reticule and brought out a small pair of gilt scissors. I went up to the window and stared at the gray houses on the other side of the street. I was cold. I dared not tell her to pass the scissors through a flame.

"Don't be afraid, little one."

I heard Hélène's uneven breathing.

"Push," said the old woman. "Push hard. There, there. . . ."

Hélène moaned; a raucous cry came from her lips.

"There," said the old woman; "it's all over." She called me: "Sir!"

I turned round. She was holding a basin in her hands. Her fingers, her wrist, and the whole of her forearm were as scarlet as her nails. "Go and empty that basin."

Hélène was lying flat on her back, with her eyes closed. Her childish nightdress revealed her knees; under her legs was an oilcloth covered with bloody rags. I took the basin, I went across the landing and opened the lavatory door. I emptied the basin and pulled the plug. The basin was full of blood. When I went back into the room, the old woman was washing the red rags in the sink.

"Give me a big piece of paper," she said. "I'll make a bundle of all these rags and you'll throw them down a drain."

"Is everything all right?" I asked.

"Of course. It isn't very serious." She laughed. "You're probably not accustomed to it."

She washed her hands and adjusted her hat in front

[119]

of the looking-glass. I made up the fire, and when the old woman had left I went and sat down again beside Hélène. She smiled at me.

"It's all over," she said. "I can't believe it. I feel so well!"

"You know," I said, "you can stay here as long as you like."

"No, the woman said I could go home. I'd rather go home." She lifted herself up from her pillows. "Would you mind seeing me again from time to time?"

"If you want to."

"You know perfectly well that I want to."

"I was hoping that you would forget me."

"Yes. You treated me like a troublesome little dog that you chase away with stones. But it was no good."

"I see that clear enough."

"I'm not a little dog." She looked at me reproachfully. "You are funny. You have said to me so often that you respect other people's liberty. And you make decisions for me and treat me like a thing."

"I didn't want you to be unhappy."

"And if I prefer to be unhappy? It's for me to choose."

"Yes," I said, "it's for you to choose."

She leaned her cheek against my hand. "I have chosen."

I took her in my arms and I touched her cheek with my lips.

"It's for me to choose." Did you say these words? If you did, I have not killed you, my dear love. But who may say to me "it is I who chose," except herself? And your eyelids hide your eyes, your lips reveal your teeth, your hard teeth, which grin eternally in your crumbling flesh. You will not speak to me again.

He had not chosen. We were hurrying merrily in the snow and he had passed us; it was dark and I was not sure that he had seen us, but I felt myself blush. We were arm in arm, hugging bags of hot chestnuts: he might have seen us. There was me, there was Hélène — that was complicated enough, but that was not all. There was Paul, there was Madeleine, and the remainder of the world on the horizon — and they had not chosen.

Next morning, when I got to the workshop, I went to say good morning to Paul. The female correctors were already in their places, perched on their high stools, their little tweezers in their hands; the women were always the first to start work. Paul was beginning to make up a page; he was arranging his bundles on the marble with an absorbed expression.

"I passed you last night and you didn't see me," I said to him. "I was with Hélène."

"Yes, I saw you."

He had an open face, with a rather obstinate forehead and something childish about his mouth. I buttoned up my gray overalls. Underneath us, in the printing room, the machines began to purr.

"I have never understood what there was between you," he said.

"I haven't seen her again since you two broke it off. Then she came to see me." I hesitated. "You know what she's like; she likes a change and she's bored."

"Oh, so that's it!" said Paul.

"I did everything to put her off."

"I might have guessed it," said Paul. "And she wasn't put off?"

"I like her very much as a friend. But I don't love her. I've told her that, but she says that it doesn't matter."

Paul shrugged his shoulders. "Well, that's her look-out. It's no concern of mine."

I went and sat at my keyboard; it was useless to explain. Whatever I might say, he would never retrace with me the road lined with hesitation that led to our first kiss; he would have had to be me; since the place of a stranger was allotted to him on earth, he could only apprehend my external actions. I ran with Hélène in the snow and he thought: "He has taken Hélène from me. He doesn't love Hélène and he accepts her love." I had left the party after a long inward struggle and he thought: "He is the son of a bourgeois." What I suddenly understood with despair was that these outward actions were not misleading; they belonged to me as surely as my body, and the embarrassment that brought a lump to my throat confirmed their truth: "It's unfair." But the unfairness did not lie in Paul's resentment; it lay in the center of my being, in that curse so often prophetically sensed, so fiercely refused: the curse of being a separate being.

"It's not true, it's not me." I wanted to shout those words when Hélène looked at me with eyes full of admiration and love. And yet it was true: it was I. I who had emptied my wallet on my father's desk, I who had exchanged my bourgeois suits for gray overalls; that room was mine; that was undeniably my face. It was with my own face that she built up that hero whose memories, thoughts, and smiles were my own, but in whom I did not recognize myself.

"I feel guilty of betraying a confidence," I said to her.

"How do you mean?" she asked. She was sitting beside me on the divan bed, leaning her head against my shoulder like a little trusting animal.

"I feel as though I've slipped into someone else's skin."

"You mean that I don't see you as you really are?"

"Yes, that's it!"

She smiled at me. "What is the real you like?"

"Not particularly attractive," I said. "Look — when you ask me why I don't love you, I tell you that you're too young, that we haven't the same interests. Yes. But it's also because I'm thin-blooded. I've never been capable of passion. I dither about between my guilty conscience and my scruples; my one and only aim is not to dirty my hands. I call that a mean nature, of the constipated variety. I envy Paul. I envy you. . . ."

Hélène interrupted me by placing her soft, fair lips on mine.

"That's what's so wonderful about you, you're so self-sufficient that I feel that you've created your own self."

"It's no effort for me to be self-sufficient; I want so little."

"And what could you want?" she asked. Her eyes shone. It was useless going farther; the truth that dwelt within me — I could only tear it out of myself in words, and those words fell on Hélène's ear with an unexpected meaning; once I had uttered them — from the moment she heard them — they no longer belonged to me; what she discerned in them, despite me, was an effort to be sincere and a moving modesty that delighted her heart.

"You're an obstinate creature," I would say.

"Oh, it would be difficult to be fed up with you."

She looked at me so ardently that I wanted to hide my face. What did she see? "It's not me." It was indeed I, such as I was from the outside, under the eye of a stranger. I was both the faithless friend and the reliable, thoughtful hero, despite myself.

Hélène rubbed her cheek against mine. "Would you like me to be fed up with you?"

[123]

"I wouldn't like you to spoil your life because of me."

"There's no danger of that." She was rolling a lock of my hair round her finger. "It isn't such fun to be loved; it's much more interesting to find someone whom one can love."

"In the end, a love that is not shared becomes dreary." I put my arm round her shoulders. "I want to be sure of one thing, and that is that, because of me, you'll not miss any of the opportunities which might come your way?" She looked at me submissively. "You must go on wanting to know people and get about more. For instance, if your firm suggests that you should go to America, as it was once suggested, you must go off cheerfully."

"Of course," she said. "I hope that there'll be something else in my life besides you." She nestled against me. "But later on — not now."

"No," I said, "not now." I gently kissed her face. There were moments when I found her so charming that I would have liked to say to her without lying: "I love you." But how then? Her presence affected me, but when I was away from her, I never thought of her; I would have left her any day without regret. My tenderness, my esteem were far from being love. She closed her eyes under my kisses with a docile and rapt expression. Then she looked at me again and moistened her lips with her tongue.

"Listen," she said.

"What is it?"

She hesitated. "Later on I'll try to detach myself from you, I promise. But that shouldn't stop us trying to have as deep feelings for each other as possible."

I held her closely to me; her courage touched me

deeply. "Is it really worth while getting fonder of each other, if it's only to be provisional?"

"No matter," she said, "we're not going to spoil the present through fear of the future." She threw herself back, and her hair fanned out on the pillow. "I'd like to be all yours," she murmured.

There was at least that minute in my life when I did not hesitate or argue with my conscience. And you knew how to save me from the sense of guilt. With Madeleine, we made love in silence and nearly always in the dark; she passively accepted both emotion and pleasure with a kind of horror, as she acccepted voices and glances and even the motionless presence of objects; when I caressed her, I always felt like a criminal. In my arms you were not a submissive body, but a living woman. You smiled straight at me, so that I might know that you were there, freely, that you were not lost in the tumultuous coursing of your blood. You did not feel that you were the prey of a shameful fate; in the midst of your most passionate impulses, something in your voice, in your smile, said: "It's because I consent to it." Through your constancy in affirming your freedom, you gave me inward peace. Before you I stood guiltless. Before you — but we were not alone in the world.

"There's something new in my relations with Hélène," I said.

"Yes," said Madeleine indifferently.

I had tried to keep her informed of this affair, but each time I spoke to her about it, she changed the conversation.

"Yes, we ended up by sleeping together."

"I never thought you'd be faithful to me all my life," said Madeleine.

[125]

She had never put herself out for me; I had broken no undertaking in regard to her, and yet I was ill at ease. I was sure that the news was displeasing to her. "She has nothing to say," I thought irritably. Probably she was aware of it herself: she said nothing. She even seemed, by what followed, to have completely forgotten when I had told her. For Madeleine, nothing was ever quite true or quite untrue, she took advantage of this ambiguity and floated along apathetically in uncertain waters. She only asked me not to force her to face up to Hélène's existence. On her side, Hélène never spoke to me about Madeleine. They ignored each other so definitely that it often seemed strange to me to be able to think of both of them at the same time. Hélène walked at my side, with firm steps, rich in her own memories, straining toward a single goal; in her personal world there was no place designed for Madeleine. And Madeleine, in her hotel room, which smelt of insecticide, had also her own world, from which Hélène was entirely excluded. Each of them self-absorbed, they were farther apart than two nebuli at the far ends of the ether, than two shellfish clinging to the opposite sides of a rock. And yet I was there, present to both of them, making them exist together.

"How can you not find that situation painful?" I asked Marcel. "To think that it's you who are shaping another person's life, whether he likes it or not."

We were sitting in a little restaurant in the avenue de Clichy, eating black pudding with noodles. Marcel was wearing a threadbare suit and, round his neck to hide his shirt, a Norwegian scarf, its bright colors dimmed by dust. He shook his massive head.

"But I make no demands on Denise. She can make what she likes of her life."

"You know that isn't true. She can't make the two of you rich, or you famous; she can't make you love her."

They had finally abandoned the big bare studio and had rented a modern seventh-floor studio, strangely shaped, where the ceiling was a large pane of glass and the walls were almost entirely taken up by the windows. The draft came in everywhere, the walls oozed damp. "I waste an hour every morning lighting the stove," Denise would say angrily to me, "and that doesn't prevent us from shivering all day."

"There's always some way of managing things," said Marcel.

"It's too easy to say to others: 'Arrange things for yourself.'"

"Why? My arrangements are all right," said Marcel.

"That's your business. You are you; you are not Denise; the way she sorts herself out in this world is only her business. The thing for which you're responsible is the world in which she is immersed."

Marcel was looking with interest at a large fair-haired whore who was hastily eating a garlic sausage before going on up to the wealthy precincts of Montmarte. He did not appear to be listening, but I knew he was listening.

"People are free," I said, "but only so far as they themselves are concerned; we can neither touch, foresee, nor insist on them using their liberty. That is what I find so painful; the intrinsic worth of an individual exists only for him, not for me; I can only get as far as his outward actions, and to him I am nothing more than an outer appearance, an absurd set of premises; premises that I do not even choose to be. . . ."

"Then don't get excited," said Marcel; "if you don't even make the choice, why punish yourself?"

"I don't choose to exist, but I am. An absurdity that is responsible for itself, that's exactly what I am."

"Well, there must be something."

"But there might be something else. Without you, Denise would have had a different life."

"What kind of life?" asked Marcel. "All lives are wasted."

"If you had gone on painting — "

He interrupted me, "But if I'd been of the stuff of which good little drawing-room painters are made, would she have loved me? If — we are apt to say — if I had done this, if I hadn't done that. But things are as they are." He looked at me with a derisive laugh. "I think you are very presumptuous to be so filled with remorse."

I sometimes thought that I took things too much to heart; other people seemed to live so naturally. Nothing seemed natural to me. I wanted all human life to be a pure, transparent freedom; and I found myself existing in other people's lives as a solid obstacle. I could not resign myself to this. I avoided Paul; I looked at Madeleine with embarrassment. Even with Hélène I was worried. Our kisses, our caresses had soon lost the happy limpidity of the first days. Shadows often passed over her face, and, while I embraced her she closed her eyes with an expression of suffering; sometimes when we clung together, she abruptly broke away. I put my arm round her shoulder. "What is it, little wild thing?"

Sitting on the edge of the bed, she swung her foot, staring into space with a hard look on her face; she had not finished dressing; her hair fell in disorder on her shoulders. She started, "Nothing."

"Nothing what? Why do you look so strange?"

"Oh, I was only thinking that it's a pity to have

wasted all this time; now I shall have to go, and we shan't have been able to talk."

She was prevaricating — that was apparent at once from her limp tones. Certainly I liked her body, but if most of our meetings were spent in making love, it was her fault and not mine, as well she knew.

"I had suggested going for a walk."

"Of course! It's all the same to you."

"What's all the same to me? Not to love you? But it's you who are saying that it's a waste of time."

"It is a waste of time since you didn't want it."

"You're stupid. Don't I seem to like your body?"

"Yes, as you like one body among many."

I was silent for a moment; it was clear that some day we must reach that point. "Why do you say that?"

"I say it because it's true."

"Do you dislike thinking that I have similar relations with Madeleine?"

"Would you rather it pleased me?"

"I thought you didn't mind."

She shrugged her shoulders and two tears fell from her eyes.

"You always knew that there was Madeleine in my life," I said. "Why suddenly today . . . ?"

"It isn't only today."

"Then you should have spoken to me about it earlier."

"What difference would it have made?"

I hung my head. I hated to see her cry, but I knew that Madeleine would be cut to the quick if I proposed altering my relations with her. "Listen, you know perfectly well that I am not in the least in love with Madeleine; personally I'd give up all physical relations with her without the slightest regret."

"When I think of it!" said Hélène. "You look at her

just as you look at me. You make love to her . . . but it's unbearable," she ended in an explosion of despair.

I held her close to me without speaking; I felt her body shaking.

"You used not to be concerned about Madeleine."

"Things can't be now as they used to be."

"Why?"

"Because I've begun to think about it." She gave a kind of laugh. "By the way, you ought to have been more careful; one day you came back from a meeting, and there was lipstick on your neck. The day we went to the dogs' cemetery."

"Oh, the day when you had such a bad headache."

"I hadn't got a headache."

I felt myself blush. It was always the same old story. That red mark on my flesh did not exist for me, and your eyes saw it — a stain I did not feel was the cause of grief in your heart.

"Hélène, I'm very sorry."

"Oh, it's just as well that I should see." She gave a short sob. "But I can't kiss you without thinking that she kisses you too."

I looked at her, I was crushed. She was entirely mine. For that exclusive gift not to be absurd, I should have had to have within me a yawning gap that she alone could fill. I was well aware of the solemnity that my caresses had for her; it depended on me whether the value she gave them was illusion or truth. When I held another woman in my arms, I not only was inflicting on her a passing distress, but was holding in check the most passionate affirmations of her flesh and of her heart.

"Listen," I said. "I'll try to speak to Madeleine."

She dried her eyes with a semblance of goodwill, but her face still bore a pained expression.

"It may be easier to manage than I think," I said.

For some time Madeleine had been lengthening the intervals between our meetings; she was distant with me, more absentminded than usual.

"You are very sweet," said Hélène.

I touched her hair. "You don't look very pleased."

"Oh, all that's so silly. What's the good of not going to bed with Madeleine if you want to."

"I told you that I didn't want to."

"Yes, but still, it would suit you better." She sniffed back a tear. "It's so silly, you might as well go on."

"I'll see what I can do."

"No, I beg you, don't change anything," she said with sudden violence. "I don't care, it can't be otherwise." She hid her face in her hands. "Oh, I am ashamed!"

I took her in my arms, but I could say nothing to her. What ought to have been possible was that I should not have been able even to desire anyone else but her, and that what she had to give me should have been something that I could only get from her. All my tenderness failed to vouchsafe that word; I could only control my actions; I was what I was, in spite of her, in spite of myself, and there was nothing to be done about it.

At least I should have liked to risk a gesture, a word for her. "I'll try to speak to Madeleine," but in front of Madeleine I was tongue-tied. She was there, she was absentmindedly stirring a cup of coffee with cream, absorbed in thinking of nothing and believing in nothing. In her inner depths unhappiness, humiliation, and regret had been deposited day after day; a word would have been enough to stir up that mud, but I had not the courage to speak it. When I went back to Hélène, her eyes asked me: "Haven't you said anything yet?" Her sadness was justified, Madeleine's resentment would also have been justified. Which was I to choose? Madeleine's tears or Hélène's tears? They were not my tears. How could I compare their individual alien bitterness? Neither was I God.

"Then, Wednesday, if you like," I said, holding out my hand to Madeleine.

"No, not Wednesday." She was putting on her gloves with a concentrated expression. "On Wednesday I'm going out with Charles Arnaud."

"Arnaud?" I was surprised. "Have you been seeing him again?"

"Why, yes, for over a month now," said Madeleine; she smiled vaguely. "He's just out of a nursing home; they've cured him of drink, only, in order to stand up to the cure, he swills pernods in secret. The result is that he's completely soaked."

It was the only influence I had ever had over Madeleine; I had stopped her associating with that drug-fiend and taking drugs in his company. So far as drink was concerned, since she had known me, she had indulged in it only in moderation.

"You're not going to start all over again."

"Start what again?"

"Drinking and all those idiotic things."

She looked at me sleepily. "What can it matter to you?"

I hesitated. I could take her by the arm, drag her far away from the entrance to the subway station and talk to her. "Don't sulk. The affair with Hélène makes no difference to us. Let's start seeing each other again as we used to do. Drop that fellow." I could exhort her, beg her. She would have listened indolently to me, but she would have been touched by the warmth of my tones. I was sure that she would have obeyed me.

[132]

But I saw again Hélène's convulsed face. "When I think she kisses you!" To involve myself again with Madeleine would have been a betrayal.

"Oh, nothing," I said. There was a brief silence. "Then would you like Thursday?"

"Let's say Thursday."

I went off. I was not pleased with myself. "I could not have done otherwise." But the old excuse was threadbare. I could not have done otherwise — and my mother had remained alone in the icy rooms of the big apartment, and Madeleine was taking to drugs again. It wasn't a question of what I did — the fault lay in no act of mine. I was beginning to understand; it lay in the essence of my being; it was my own self. For the first time I thought: "Perhaps there is no solution."

Guilty if I spoke, guilty if I remained silent. Whatever I did, I was in the wrong. I fingered the express message. I was certain it was beginning again — the same story, my own personal story. "What does she want of me?" During the whole of this last month I had hardly seen her; twice she had passed me in the restaurant where I was dining with Hélène and she had asked me with a provoking smile to lend her a little money, "to go and have a drink." She was drinking and she was sleeping with Arnaud; she was taking drugs. I was extremely worried when I went into the Café de la Fourche. Did other men weigh less heavily on the earth than I? Or were they less concerned with the traces they left behind them? Everywhere I beheld the uneasy signs of my presence. Or perhaps it was a curse that had been put upon me; each of my actions, like each of my refusals, carried with it a mortal danger. I thought I was only kissing Hélène, and I was betraying Paul and hurting Madeleine.

"What foolishness has she been up to?" I thought as I opened the door of the café.

Madeleine was nonchalantly drinking a cup of chocolate, she was reading an evening paper. Without even offering me her hand, and as if I had returned to my place beside her after a ten-minutes' absence, she pointed to an article on the Spanish War.

"The swine!" she said. "They'll let them rot without sending them any help."

"You know, intervention might entail heavy consequences."

"Why don't you try striking? Perhaps Blum would give in."

"I don't want a strike for political reasons."

I, too, ardently hoped for the defeat of Franco's Moors, but from that lonely wish, that intimate quivering of my flesh, I did not deduce the right to create a will which I would impose on my comrades.

To will to drag someone else into the struggle, into my struggle. A shot, then a second one: Jacques was dead. I had put a revolver into his hands and he was dead. Disaster had overtaken Jacques. And Marcel's stupefied face, the smell of flowers and the candles round the waxen dummy.

Because I had taken action in regard to him. I knew forever that one cannot control the limits of an action, that one cannot foresee what one is actually doing. Never again would I run that insane risk. Never would I raise a finger to bring about an unknown event.

"In any case," she said, "it wouldn't be difficult to get arms through clandestinely and to authorize the signing up of volunteers."

From time to time she was seized with enthusiasm

for a cause. Two years previously this Breton girl had been a passionate Zionist, she had submitted to working eight hours a day as an employee in a Jewish bookshop in order to help the movement financially. I was not untowardly astonished at her new interests, only I was somewhat impatient to know why she had sent for me so urgently. I listened to her for about half an hour, pouring out her indignation against Blum, then I took advantage of a pause.

"I say, tell me, what did you want to talk to me about?"

She looked at me in her placid way. "But about all that."

I began to laugh. "Does it really mean so much to you?"

"Oh, you don't understand. I want your help; you know a lot of fellows in the party; I don't mind how they'll get me across the frontier, but I would never be able to manage it by myself."

"Do you want to go to Spain?"

"I want to join the militia. Why not? What am I doing with myself here?"

She was actually capable of going, and it hurt me to think of it. "But it's absurd, you've no reason for doing so."

"There's no need for so many reasons; life is not so precious."

"It's a mere brain-storm of yours."

She looked wearily at me. "I did not come to ask for your advice, but for your help. Will you give it to me, yes or no?"

I hesitated. "It's a queer kind of help. If once you get there and anything happens to you, I shan't feel very cheerful."

"I absolve you from any guilty feelings." She smiled. "Besides, something might just as easily happen to me here."

"Are you in trouble?"

"I'm not in trouble. I want to go."

There was no hope of getting anything more out of her.

"I'll see what I can do," I said.

It was easy. I had only to speak to Paul or Bourgade. *I had only not to speak to them. They had put him in his bedroom, laid out on the bed, with candles and flowers all round him; he looked like a waxen figure, a strange figure made for some surrealist exhibition. And Marcel was looking at it.* The same story — because I exist. Can I not pretend that I do not exist? I blot myself out of the world, I blot out my face and my voice. I remove the traces I have left — nothing has changed, there is only a harmless little erasure in my place. Hélène is no longer imprisoned in an unhappy love, Madeleine does not get herself killed in Spain, the earth is lightened of that weight which strains its secret fibers, which makes them vibrate and crack in unforeseeable far reaches of the future. To blot myself out, to exist no longer. "I will not speak to Paul." *And in the same room that smells of insecticide, an opulent corpse, stuffed with cocaine, will be found in the morning.*

Light broke upon me. You will not blot yourself out. No one will decide for you, not even fate. You are the fate of others. Decide. You have that power: something that was not before bursts out suddenly in the void, depending only on you yourself, and yet separated from you by an abyss, and thrown across the abyss for no other reason than itself, for which you provide the only reason.

I won't. I won't do it any more. *They make them work in the snow in canvas jackets and trousers, with canvas sandals on their feet. And we say: "All right. We can't help it."* But if a row of apartment houses is blown up — a whole heap of new corpses! *There is a woman asleep somewhere, she has at last managed to go to sleep thinking: "He did nothing, it will not be he." And tomorrow night it will be he. Because of me.* Supposing I blot myself out! Supposing I cease to exist! Even if I kill myself, I shall continue to exist. I shall be dead, but they will remain chained to my death, and that sudden void upon the earth will make a thousand unforeseeable fibers vibrate and crack. Berthier, or Lenfant, will take my place. I shall still be responsible for all those acts which my absence will have made possible. Someone will say to Laurent: "Go," or "Don't go." *It will be my voice.* I cannot blot myself out. I cannot withdraw into myself. I exist, outside myself and everywhere in the world. There is not an inch of my path that does not trespass on the path of someone else; there is no way of living that can prevent me overflowing from myself at every moment. This life which I spin from my own substance presents a thousand unknown faces to other men, it flows impetuously through their fate. *He has waked up and he hopes: "They will forget me." His life lies so wide open before him. And I am there, beside you whom I have killed, and I load the rifles that will murder him tomorrow.* No, I won't. Let us give up. *We give up, we bow our heads; and there, in the far reaches of the future, for every drop of blood that we have spared, all this blood.* Let us go on. . . .

Give up, go on. Decide. Decide, since you are there. You are there, and there is no way of escape. Even my death does not belong to me.

[137]

"I have spoken to Bourgade."

That night had again been merciful — that night I had been able to decide; I was not alone; I was confronted by an individual freedom. If I could not allow myself any rights over it, any preponderating influence, I must consent to be only its instrument.

"Drop in and see him tomorrow. He'll give you introductions for the lads at Perpignan who will get you over the frontier, and also for the comrades at Barcelona. Apparently they are not anxious to put a rifle into a woman's hand."

"Thank you," said Madeleine. "You don't know what you're doing for me."

We were in her room; it was a kind of narrow corridor, cluttered up with empty suitcases and bundles of linen; it smelt of disinfectant and shampoo powders. A saucepan filled with water in which two white tablets were melting was purring on a tiny stove. If I had loved her . . . if I had thought of her more . . . the iron enters my heart. Now everything was clear to me; I was forever at fault, since my birth and beyond my death.

And yet it wouldn't happen this time. This blood and this death-rattle were not for her — as though the infernal machine had amused itself by revolving impotently, as though fate had taken pleasure in that parody. They did not send her to the front. Ten days after she left, a letter reached me from a hospital in Barcelona; they had modestly put her into the kitchens; for two days she had conscientiously washed up and then she had upset a large basin of boiling oil over both her feet. She was in bed for six months and then came back to Paris.

"You know, they say the French are dirty swine," she said to me on her return.

It was spring. In the evening, after I left the work-shop, I wandered with Hélène on the quays at Asni-ères; she bought bunches of violets at the street corner; caramel-colored glasses of beer beside us, we listened to the intermission bells in the cinemas as they rang out intermittently under a purple sky; couples like ourselves went nonchalantly up and down the avenue de Clichy; I watched them anxiously, these men who enjoyed with a quiet heart the sweetness of the evening. They did not look like criminals; the taste of beer and tobacco, the brilliance of the neon signs, the smell of young leaves — none of these things aroused a sense of guilt in them. We were there, bathed in the soft dusk of Paris, and we were doing nobody harm. And yet we were also over there in Barcelona and in Madrid; no longer harmless strollers, but dirty swine. As surely as we existed in these joyous streets, we existed under the dark skies filled with the roar of the Stukas; we existed in Berlin and in Vienna, in the concentration camps where Jews slept in their shirts on the sodden ground, in the prisons where militant Socialists were rotting; a persistent and crushing existence, which be-came part of that existence of barbed wire, unbreak-able stones, machine-guns, and graves. These carefree faces, on which we allowed our smiles to spread, were for others the mask of tragedy.

"Do you realize it! The workers, the clerks — that's how they feed in France!" said Lina Blumenfeld. She was so shocked at the sight of fat garlic sausages lan-guidly resting on a mound of potatoes that the mouth-ful I was swallowing stuck in my throat. I had also been at a meal the first time it had happened, and I had left the table. "I will earn my bread through my own efforts." He had walked on the warm boulevard, kicking a chestnut along and taking deep breaths of air that he thought he was stealing from nobody. "My own efforts." But in exchange for my daily work what right had I to be given underdone beef, and not boiled potatoes with a little margarine? I did not want to benefit by, and I had nobly renounced, my paternal inheritance, and yet, unhesitating, I benefited from a prosperity that in the eyes of starving nations became avarice and oppression. "Do you think that there are any justifiable situations?" Marcel had seen clearly. I had fled from my home, and now whither could I flee? Everywhere, at all the street corners, prowled the sense of guilt, and I carried it with me, stuck to my skin, intimate and tenacious. I felt like my mother as I kept close to the walls, avoiding the glances that would have mirrored back to me my own image: a swine of a Frenchman, selfish and well fed.

"You'll regret it," said Blumenfeld. "Do you think Hitler will stop at Austria? You'll see. France's turn will come."

He looked at us with despair and hatred. He had come on purpose from Vienna to arouse our indignation and our pity. He was one of the most important members of the illegal front who were conducting a clandestine struggle in Austria against Nazism. Denise had introduced us; for some time she had been trying to live on her own account and she gave herself up enthusiastically to anti-Fascist activities. I had taken Blumenfeld to the headquarters of the union, so that he could get in contact with some of my comrades. Denise and Marcel had come along too. Blumenfeld had spoken for a long time; he had described to us the arrogant parades of the white-stockinged militia, the banquets where the amnestied Nazis toasted their future victories, the provocations, the outrages that

[140]

took place under the unmoved gaze of police. Now he was looking at us, and he was silent.

"But why aren't you able to stop their movement?" asked Gauthier. "There are still more than forty-two per cent of Socialists among you."

"We're hunted down," said Blumenfeld. "It's not possible for us to take any effective action. All we can do is to keep unrest alive by clandestine meetings, pamphlets, and lightning speeches."

"But Schuschnigg ought to understand that it's vital that he should join in with you," said Lenfant.

"There's nothing doing there," said Blumenfeld. "He's always refused every attempt at conciliation." His eyes grew hard. "And what's more, do you think the masses feel like letting themselves be killed for Schuschnigg? They have too many memories." He looked at me again. "Only a resolute attitude on the part of France and England can save us."

There was a silence. He had come up against that silence everywhere, except with the Communists.

"What do you actually expect us to do?" said Lenfant.

"If you organize meetings, a press campaign to inform your comrades of what's happening to us, you ought to be able to rouse public opinion."

"But," I said, "it's no small matter to drive a country into war."

"No," said Gauthier. "And moreover all hope of a peaceful solution is not yet lost."

"Oh, the annexation of Austria will be peaceful enough; the Nazis will have no difficulty in usurping the government — they're everywhere." Blumenfeld's voice was shaking. "Schuschnigg is betraying the country to them piecemeal; I've reliable information that he's about to sign a new pact with them. Hitler has only to say the word." He looked at us again in distress and anger. "Only France can restrain him."

"France cannot afford the luxury of a war," said Gauthier.

"You'll regret it," said Blumenfeld. "So you think that Hitler will stop at Austria? You'll see. France's turn will come."

Gauthier looked coldly at Blumenfeld. "Is it possible to stop a country from committing suicide? Everything that you've told us amounts to a suicide story."

He was so sure of his pacifism, so sure of himself. "I am a pacifist." He had given a definition of himself once and for all, he had only to act in accordance with his own idea of himself, neither looking to left or right, as if the road had been already marked out, as if the future had not, at every instant, been that gaping void.

"A suicide is always more or less a murder," I said.

"Ah," said Blumenfeld. "Do you think so?"

For the first time during the whole session Marcel spoke. He smiled. "He's always been convinced that each of his actions was a murder."

It was murder. At that moment and during the whole of the following year I spent many sleepless nights. A press campaign, meetings, strikes. From his side Paul drummed into me: "War would bring about the fall of Fascism." Could we stand with our arms folded, beside blood-bespattered Spain, beside the po-groms that defiled Germany, and that brown tide which was rolling toward Austria? Beneath Blumen-feld's cold and desperate glance I was ashamed, but shame was no argument; the moans of the wounded on the shell-torn and bloody battlefields filled me with pitiless horror. Beyond the Pyrenees the workers of Spain fell beneath the Fascist bullets, but could I redeem their blood at the price of French lives, at the price of a single life that was not my own life? Jews died like flies in concentration camps, but had I the right to exchange their dead bodies for the innocent bodies of French peasants? I could pay with my body, with my blood, but the remainder of mankind was no coin for my use; what superman's mind would allow itself to compare them, to count them, to claim that it knew their just measure? Even a god would have failed in this presumptuous intention; mankind was no set of pawns to be moved, no stake to be risked, no force to be harnessed; each man carried his truth in the most secret depths of his being, out of all reach; what happened to him belonged only to him; it would never be possible to provide any compensation. Hélène's joyous smiles had not neutralized Madeleine's resentment, they had not lessened the scald of the boiling oil. Nothing had erased Jacque's death, no new birth would ever replace that life which had been taken from him, his one and only life. There was no place in the world where the absolute separation of those fates could again be fused.

"I'll take no action, I've never allowed myself to take any political action." I refused to throw into the world, like a capricious god, the weight of my obscure will. To take part in politics was to reduce mankind to their vulnerable condition, to treat them like blind masses, so that I might reserve to myself alone the privilege of existing as a living thought; but even that thought must become a mechanical opaque force, in which I would cease to recognize myself, for it to take effect on inert bodies, or to move them. In the room filled with noise and smoke, I would speak words which would entice men whom I had never seen to uncharted seas; I would use my liberty to become the accomplice of the hideous primeval joke: the absurdity of the man who is as he is without having willed to be so. "No, I cannot drive my country into war."

"I hope that you may never regret it," said Blumenfeld.

And shame was there. I had willy-nilly to get accustomed to living with it — it was guilt in a new guise. It could be hunted from one corner of my life, polished, neatly and beautifully smoothed away — but it was immediately to be found lurking in another corner. It was always somewhere. Without shame, I held Hélène in my arms, but I hung my head before Madeleine's bitter smiles; without shame I looked at my trade-union comrades but my mouth became dry when I thought of our brothers in Spain and Austria.

"You take pleasure in tormenting yourself," Hélène said to me.

The morning papers had informed us of the annexation of Austria; when Hélène had come to get me at closing time, I was incapable of speaking about anything else. Yet I did not like to touch on these questions with her; at such moments she seemed to be a stranger to me. She added with slight annoyance: "After all, it's not your business."

"Not my business? I wish someone would tell me what is my business."

"There's your own life," said Hélène. "Don't you think that's enough?"

"But my life is made up of my relations with the remainder of mankind; Austria is part of my life, the whole world is part of my life."

"Quite, and these people whom we're passing now are part of your life because you see them." Hélène's color had heightened and her voice had taken on a rather sharp tone, as it did whenever she was put out by an argument, "It doesn't mean that you're responsible for what happens to them."

"That remains to be seen," I said in my teeth. It was seven o'clock in the evening; the avenue de Saint-Ouen was teeming with people; at the street corners they tore the last edition of *Paris-Soir* from each other's hands; the brightly lit bakeries were crammed with crusty croissants, brioches, and long golden loaves; in the butchers' shops, with their sawdust-sprinkled tiles, carcasses of beef and mutton, cleaned, washed, and decorated with rosettes, hung in lines from the ceiling, as if on parade, and on the counter reclined enormous bouquets of red meat surrounded with frilled paper. Abundance, leisure, peace. Their elbows on the zinc counters of the bistros, men argued at the top of their voices, without fear. *The iron shutters were closed, the cafés were empty, only the tramp of Nazi boots was to be heard in the desolate streets; silent, their eyes filled with horror, people watched from behind the Venetian blinds. France's turn will come."*

"It's as though you imagined that you'd created the world," said Hélène.

"One day I read: 'Each of us is responsible for everything and to every human being.' It seemed so true to me."

Hélène looked at me sulkily. "I don't understand."

"Of course, if you look upon yourself as an ant in an antheap you can't do anything about anything. I don't say that I could have stopped the Nazis' invasion by stretching out my arms." Once more I saw my mother in the streets of Seville, her little arms outstretched. "Yet if we had stretched out our arms . . ."

[145]

"Maybe, but no one did. The others are just as responsible as you."

"That's their business. Certainly, we're all responsible. But 'all' means each of us. I've always felt that, even when I was a kid; my eyes are sufficient for this boulevard to exist; my voice is sufficient for the world to have a voice. When it is silent, it's my fault."

Hélène turned her head away.

"Do you still not understand?" I said.

"Yes, I understand," she said unwillingly.

"I didn't create the world, but I create it again, by my presence at every instant. And I see everything taking place, as if everything that happens happens through me."

"Yes." Hélène looked down with a worried expression.

"What's wrong?"

"Why, nothing."

"Why do you look so sad?"

She shrugged her shoulders. "There are times when I feel as though I were an atom in your life."

"Don't be silly! Your value has gone up since the days when you used to complain that you only occupied a two-hundred-and-fortieth part of my time."

"You haven't the slightest need of me," she said. "Nothing that is really part of your life has any connection with me."

"It's possible to be very fond of someone without needing them." I pressed her arm against mine, but she stiffened.

"I feel so useless."

I ought to have been able to say to her: "I love you," but I dared not lie to her. I had sworn to leave her free, and to be free she must be able to see clearly. And clearly did she see my tenderness and my indifference, and she dragged along, like a joyless burden, that love which I did not need.

"Are you sure that you don't love her?" Denise would say to me.

"It isn't love."

"But perhaps you can't love in any other way."

"Perhaps, but that makes no difference. It isn't what she calls love."

What Hélène required was that I should have an essential need of her; then she would have existed in her entirety, she would have had a miraculous justification for being what she was, for being what I should have loved.

"You do not *will* to love her," said Denise. She shrugged her shoulders. "You are deliberately spoiling your life as well. A great love is not to be scorned."

She believed that all mankind loved one another spontaneously; she was kindly disposed to everyone; it did not occur to her that anyone might not be so disposed toward her. She would only see in Marcel's harshness an assumed perversity. He did not have to assume it. Marcel hated the state of idyllic brotherhood in which Denise thought she lived, a well-kept human garden of Eden, through which flowed abundant virtues, where worthiness, truth, and beauty hung from the trees like golden fruit. Even I was frequently annoyed by her. I hated to listen to her holding forth on the fate of the world — she tried in this way to escape from her own worries, when the only important thing was the march of history.

"It's not to be scorned, but you must be capable of experiencing it."

"Yes." Denise's laugh was harsh. "I wonder what Marcel is capable of. You at least do things, you have friends. But he — Don't you think he's a little mad?"

She looked at me with anxious suspicion. Marcel no longer did anything; he had even given up carving lumps of sugar and plaiting strings. He spent whole days lying in his damp bed, encased in pullovers; then he came out of his shell and called for his friends. He greeted us so merrily that, had it not been for Denise's accounts, I would never have suspected his daily fits of gloom. I only noticed that he had idiosyncrasies; his hands always had to be busy; either he clutched the arms of his chair, or he held his tobacco pouch, or a vase, or an orange, in the palms of his hands; he sat with his back to the wall. "I hate feeling an empty space behind me," he used to say; and he would laugh. "I loathe emptiness." The floor was covered with rugs, cushions, animal skins, and there was not an inch of bare wall; Marcel had hung them with butter-flies, shells, bawdy pictures, and colored postcards representing St. Theresa of Lisieux, with her arms full of roses.

"He's probably looking for something that isn't possible," I said, "but it doesn't mean that he's mad."

"But what is he looking for?" asked Denise. "Do you know? If I try to ask him, he just grins."

Her eyes already shone with greed; if Marcel disdained love, fortune, and glory, the only remaining hope was that he was holding in reserve for himself something more valuable than all these things, and she wanted her share of it.

"I think it's something that has no meaning for anyone but himself."

She shrugged her shoulders, disappointed.

"Either it has a meaning or it hasn't," she said quite definitely. It was that impartial schoolmarm's voice of hers that sent Marcel raving mad. With Denise, he was always on the defensive; with me, he spoke openly.

[148]

The only thing that worried me was the secret jubilation with which he spied upon all my movements.

"Well, hasn't it? There's something satisfactory about a glass that's being filled?" His eyes followed the rising level of the red liquid.

"And also about a glass that's emptied." I emptied my glass.

"No, what you like is to fill yourself up." He was molding his tobacco pouch with his fingers. "Everyone's seeking after fulfillment. Just look round you; look at the number of people in the street who avoid the middle of the sidewalk and hug the wall so they can feel that there's something solid beside them; some of them let the tips of their fingers brush along the railings, as if they were plucking a guitar." He looked at his fingers. "There's nothing more definite than touching things."

"Have you quite given up creative work?"

"Creating is an impossibility. There's nothing new under the sun."

"That's true on all planes," I said.

Blank pages whose destiny was utterly in my hands — that was only a schoolboy's childish dream. Now I knew: nothing is blank except not being there, that impossibility, not being there. To choose between shameful peace and bloody war? Between murder and slavery? I would first have had to choose the actual circumstances in which the choice was imperative.

"Or else what I create are ideas that do not quite attain a separate entity," Marcel continued. He pointed to the things hung on the wall. "The actual shape should be straw, or the straw should come out of my brain, fiber by fiber."

"Then what are you going to do?" I said.

"Nothing more. Creation is an effort to express one's

[149]

being, but first we must exist. That's a big job. We must find a way of getting in touch with the self." He turned his head from side to side. "Looking, feeling — already that puts us in touch."

"Aren't you afraid of getting bored in the long run?"

He laughed heartily. "I'm quite accustomed to that; being bored isn't so very boring."

Poor Denise! With what a smile he listened to her talking enthusiastically of the Sudetens and Czechoslovakia! That day she had come back thoroughly excited by an anti-Fascist meeting at which she had spoken; there was a brightness in her eye that I had not seen for years.

"She's pleased," said Marcel. "Look at her; she thinks she has *done* something." He good-naturedly put his big paw on Denise's shoulder; Denise shrank away, and the brightness vanished from her eyes.

"You see," she said to me a few moments later, "that's how he always behaves to me, always. I stifle when I'm near him; he stifles me." Her voice was trembling. "From morning to night, his great silent laugh and his eyes that look through me. He'll drive me mad, me too."

"As far as that goes," I said, "I can see that it's not easy to live with him."

Denise stared into the distance at something horrible. "It's hell."

There were days — there were nights. Marcel had often told me that he could not bear to touch a body if he could not see it absolutely as an object. For long stretches at a time he would not touch Denise, and when he did grasp her with his strong stubby hands, it must have been still worse.

"Why don't you try to give up living with him? Perhaps it would work out much better."

"Give up living with him?" Denise looked at me in dismay; she made an effort to summon up a calm and reasonable expression. "But what would become of him without me? No," she said heatedly. "It's from within that I must free myself from him."

"That's much more difficult."

"I'll tell you a secret," she said with an uneasy smile. "I've begun to write a novel."

"Really?" I said.

"A novel about him and about me — very much transposed, of course." She tightened her lips. "Ah, if I could only do it! In one way Marcel is right, you don't really get anywhere in political work. Don't you agree?"

"It depends," I said. Our conversations always started with so many misunderstandings that I was often quite unable to answer her.

"Only, how can I work?" she continued despairingly. "I have to provide food and clothes without a penny. It takes all my time."

"Yes. Marcel doesn't see that."

"It doesn't matter," she said fiercely. "I'll make the time." She could be trusted — she never wasted a minute. She had a well-organized mind.

"What a terrible species!" said Marcel, his eyes goggling at me; he seemed to be really frightened. "They don't want to waste time; they don't want to waste gifts, or money. And never, never do they ask themselves what they stand to gain by never wasting anything."

"All the same, you're a brute to Denise," I said.

"What do you expect? We don't speak the same language. Denise is social-minded. What matters to her is what people think, what they say, and what they approve." He struck his great chest. "And that I, poor little solitary individual, should be worried over my own fate seems to her to be utter madness." He shook his head. "I tell you, it's a dangerous species."

"Let's say she's misguided," I said. "That's no reason for condemning her to a life of misery."

"I'm not condemning anyone."

"You know perfectly well that she's unhappy, and you salve your conscience by telling yourself that she doesn't deserve to be happy. But you, who blame her for holding the scales of good and evil, have no right to weigh her worth. What's more, there's no appropriate scale. I see no connection between Denise's mistakes and the damned lousy time you give her."

"But why is she unhappy?" asked Marcel. "It's possible to do without so many things. I contrive to do without whisky."

"That's your lookout, but you've no right to impose your standards on her. You're trying to find yourself, your own self, not hers. It's an experience that holds good only for you. In short," I said rather angrily, "you can't demand that Denise should spend her days handling inanimate objects." He began to laugh without answering. "I can assure you that you set yourself up as a judge. You may blame Denise, but no one authorized you to punish her."

He was juggling an apple. "Poor unhappy woman," he said. "If I didn't exist, the earth would be a pink sugar castle." He smiled at me. "All the same, I can't remove myself."

"If only you provided her with a little material comfort."

"Earn money? If it would please you, I'm quite willing to earn money. Why not?" He caught the apple in mid-air. "Dresses for Denise, a maid, handsome carpets — why on earth not?"

I had pleaded well: I was very good at giving advice. But what would I have answered had Marcel said to me: "What about yourself? Do you think that you make Hélène happy?" Time had passed; little by little she was becoming a woman; she was no longer content to love without hope of a return. She did not blame me, but she was often sad. There were days when it seemed absurd to me to think of all the joy I could have given her by the one word that I did not vouchsafe her.

"I'm going to tell you something," she said to me, "but promise you won't be angry."

We were sitting by the side of the Seine, our legs hanging over the bank, on the promontory of that little island where there is the dogs' cemetery; it was a place of which Hélène was very fond.

"Go on."

It was a Sunday in August; she was wearing her prettiest dress, a dress of printed crêpe that she had designed herself. It was pink with a variegated shot design of pagodas and Chinese hats. Her face, her neck, and her arms were golden in the sun. She looked at me with a shy smile. "Well, yesterday morning old Ma Grandjouan suggested that I should go with her to America." She looked away. "And I refused."

"Hélène!" I seized her shoulder. "It's too absurd. You've been waiting for that chance for three years: you're going to telephone her tonight without fail."

"No." She looked at me. "Please. I can't accept the offer. I should have to stay over there for at least a year; as a matter of fact, I would even have to settle there. It would mean establishing a branch office and managing it." She shook her head. "I don't want to do it."

"Remember our agreement," I said. "Our affair must never make you lose an opportunity. Go over for at least a year. Just think — you've always longed to travel!"

"A year without you!"

"You'll find me here when you get back."

"I should be too frightened, especially now. Supposing it really ends up by war?"

I held her close to me. I knew quite well that she no longer wanted to travel, or wanted a bicycle, or wanted anything else but me. For two years, with my connivance, she had forged those bonds which fettered her to me. How could she have decided to break them in an instant?

"Are you disappointed?" she asked. "It would have been a good way of getting rid of me?" She smiled sadly.

"I've no wish to see you go. But I'm sorry that I've made you lose such an opportunity."

I was sad. I was the only thing she loved in the whole wide world; the remainder of creation was colorless in her eyes. And I gave her nothing but a wan tenderness. I kept her imprisoned in a poor lonely love.

"When I think!" I said. "You're going to stay in Paris and you're going to go on looking at the same streets, the same faces, you're going on painting in your room, and walking in the Luxembourg — all that monotonous life which so often makes you fed up. And all because of me! . . ."

"If only I could think that you're not positively annoyed that I'm staying," she said in a low voice.

"Hélène, why do you say that? If you left me, I should be like a lost soul."

I held her in my arms; I kissed her sunlit hair, her cheeks, her lips; I kissed her with a kind of passion; I sought the most loving words; I no longer understood why there were some that I never allowed myself to

[154]

speak. I looked at the graves adorned with shells and at the stone poodles: *"To Médor, love eternal."* The gravel crunched under our feet; we walked slowly, side by side; she was beautiful.

"You know," I said, "I've grown fonder of you than I ever thought I could be. I'm extraordinarily pleased that you're not going away."

She bit her lip. Her surprise hurt me. "Is it true?"

"It's quite true."

She looked at me with shining eyes and I was deeply moved as I gazed at this joy which was all my doing. What was actually true? And what did truth matter?

"But why don't you marry her?" my mother had asked. I had introduced Hélène to her, and from time to time they took tea together in my room. Hélène was shy of my mother; my mother considered Hélène "very young," but she thought well of her.

"I love her, but I'm not in love with her."

"Then you ought not to have come into her life in that way."

"She wanted it to be so. She says that it's for her to choose and that she is free."

"Yes, it's all very fine allowing people their freedom," said my mother. She sighed; she had allowed Elisabeth and Suzon the freedom to marry as they pleased; Elisabeth's match was a failure and Suzon's a success, and my mother did not know which of the homes made her feel the sadder.

"It's what you've always done," I said, "and you were right."

"Ah, I wonder! Whatever you do, you are always responsible."

Once again I saw the rosy face, the resolute eyes. "It is for you to choose." But what kind of choice had been given her? Could she choose that I love her? That I should not exist? That she should not have met me? To leave her free was still tantamount to deciding for her; to remain inactive and docile to her will was still to create by my own authority a situation to which she could not but submit. She was there, bound by my docile hands, imprisoned in a joyless love. In spite of herself and in spite of me.

"Then what?" I asked. "She would not agree to my marrying her without love. Must I lie to her?"

"Ah! I can't advise you," said my mother sadly.

When we were small, she had fiercely taught us not to lie, but now even she was no longer convinced of anything; of prudence, charity, or truth. Why not lie? Little by little the idea took hold of me. If I could not leave you free, if the fact of my existence was in itself a restraint, why not at least make myself master of the situation that I imposed on you? I was being obliged to decide for you. Well, I had only to decide according to the dictates of my heart. I wanted to love you; I loved you; I wanted you to be happy; you would be happy through me. After all, a lie was the only weapon that would allow me to defy the arrogant power of reality. Why should I remain in your eyes obstinate, stupid, and stony-hearted, such as I was in spite of myself? I could mold my words and my actions and foil your destiny.

That evening a great wave of rejoicing swept over Paris; people sang and laughed together, lovers clung together; we had handed over Czechoslovakia to Germany and we said that we had declared peace on the world.

"Are you pleased?" Paul asked me. "It's people like you who've made such shameful agreements possible."

I was in the cloakroom with Laurent and Jardinet;

I was washing my hands. Paul and Masson were look-ing us up and down angrily.

"Peace is the result of such agreements," said Laurent, "a peace we have made ourselves. It's because we re-fused to fight that war was impossible." He was young; his enthusiasm made me feel awkward.

"You are playing the game of the bourgeoisie with your pacifism," said Paul. "They use the pretext of avoiding war to make you swallow any kind of peace."

"They use the pretext of a revolution to involve us in any kind of war," said Jardinet.

"Because we're revolutionaries, we are," said Masson. "You're afraid of revolution."

"No," I said, "but we don't want to buy it at the price of a world war. The cost would be too dear."

"The cost will never be too dear." Paul looked at me disdainfully. "You'll never get anywhere, because you aren't prepared to pay."

"It's easy to pay with the blood of others."

"Other people's blood is the same as our own," said Paul.

"The means don't matter if you have the will to achieve an end," said Masson. "We know how to will a thing, we do."

"Perhaps you have the will, but you're not sure of the way," I said. "If you cheapen men's lives, what's the sense in fighting for their happiness and their dignity."

"You're not working-class," said Paul; "that's why you didn't stay in the party, that's why you side with the bourgeois."

I knew that I wasn't a working-class man, but that didn't prevent Paul being wrong. If men were simply material to be wastefully handled, why worry about their future? If massacres and tyranny carried so little weight, how important were justice and prosperity?

[157]

From the depths of my heart I denied their blind war, but the peace in which we were bogged did not appear to my eyes in the light of a victory.

Hélène was waiting for me at the door of the workshop. Her face shone with joy.

"Is it really true?" she asked. "Is it really true? Is it peace?"

"It's peace," I said, "at least for a time."

As she hung on my arm, she was laughing, like all the other women. "Whatever you may say, it would have been too stupid to go and get yourself killed for the sake of the Czechs."

In Vienna, under the amused glances of the passers-by, the Jews were cleaning the pavements with acids that ate into their fingers. We weren't going to get ourselves killed for that; nor to stop, almost every night in Prague, the muffled shots of the suicides; nor to prevent the fires that would soon be lit in the Polish villages. While we were busied in stating reasons why we did not wish to die, did we bother about discovering why we were still alive?

"What? Aren't you pleased?" Hélène said to me. "And yet you weren't for war?"

Neither for war, nor for peace. I wasn't for anything. I was alone. I could neither rejoice nor be indignant. I was anchored to the world by tenacious roots that fed my own sap with a thousand borrowed juices; I was incapable of freeing myself so that I could soar above it, destroy it, remake it; and I was only separated from it by the lonely anguish that bore witness to my own presence.

"I don't know what to want any more," I said vaguely.

"Oh, I'm so happy," said Hélène. "I was so frightened, I feel as if I had risen from the grave." She

[158]

stroked my fingers. "They might have taken you off and dumped you far away, in some hole, in front of guns and rifles. It's worse than protracted death, to go on thinking, minute after minute, that the man you love is in danger." She smiled at me. "But you, do you feel guilty because of the Czechs?"

"It makes me a bit sick to see all those people so pleased at having saved their skins."

"I can quite understand how they feel," said Hélène. "Once you're dead, what's the use of having been generous, heroic, and all the rest? Ugh! I'd hate to die."

"I'd hate to die." You were walking with long supple strides and the hem of your dress lightly brushed your sunburned knees; no one thought that you could die. You pressed close to me. "I should hate it even more if you were to die."

She loved me; she was happy because I was allowed to stay with her. I did not want to spoil her pleasure. I smiled, I spoke cheerfully. We walked right across Paris and ate ices in the Place Médicis. The night air was mild. We sat on the little flight of steps at the corner of the rue Saint-Jacques. She put her head on my shoulder.

"You think I'm too young? That's it, isn't it? I don't really understand you?"

I stroked her hair. I was thinking: "I no longer know what to want. Everything I do turns out badly; in the long run, it's not important to take any special course of action." Since I wanted her to think that she was loved, all I had to do was to say the word she longed to hear.

"You've grown up in the last two years," I said, and added: "My feelings for you have also grown up."

"Yes?" She pressed my hand. "You seem to care more for me than you did."

[159]

"You know, you used to complain that I had no need of you; that was true. But you've created that need. Now I do need you."

"Me? You need me?"

"I need you because I love you," I said.

You were in my arms, and my heart was heavy on account of those cowardly festive echoes and because I was lying to you. Crushed by all those things which existed in spite of me and from which I was separated only by my own anguish. There is nothing left. Nobody on that bed; before me lies a gaping void. And the anguish comes into its own, alone in the void, beyond the vanished things. I am alone. I am that anguish which exists alone, in spite of me; I am merged with that blind existence. In spite of me and yet issuing only from myself. Refuse to exist: I exist. Decide to exist: I exist. Refuse. Decide. I exist. There will be a dawn.

6

A^T the far end of one of these avenues of Spanish chestnuts, guarded by a bronze lion, she knew that he used to sit between his father and mother. His presence flowed back to this clearing, flowed back over the whole world, and the world was forever transfigured by it. It was his world, rich and in harmony, through which surged a great wave of joy.

Hélène picked up her campstool and carried it under her arm with her painting materials. She must not walk too quickly, it would be dreadful if she got there early and came face to face with M. Blomart. Two o'clock. "In a few moments I shall hear his voice: 'Have you done some good work?' And then tomorrow evening. I like Sundays now. Tonight in his arms. He loves me." She glanced at a looking-glass in a shop window and smoothed her fringe coquettishly; the color of her hair, the shape of her nose, everything had become important since it was now the face that he loved.

She reached the house. "Blomart & Sons, Printers." She pressed the bell; there was a buzzing sound and the front door swung open automatically. A musty smell hovered on the staircase. "He used to climb these stairs and breathe in this smell." The smell was still the same, and the blue carpet still there, but the good, rosy little boy was nowhere at all. Yet she had the feeling that the past was existing somewhere not very far away, at about the same distance as Shanghai or Constantinople. He used to open the door of the workshop and go up disgustedly to the apartment. "How well he managed without me! He might never have known me!" Hélène felt despondent; the ground suddenly seemed less firm under her feet. She put her finger on the bell of the apartment.

"Please come this way, mademoiselle." The maid vanished from sight. Hélène went down the steps leading to the big drawing-room. She was suddenly filled with a great joy. He was there, sitting at the tea-table covered with cups, beside his mother. Tulips sprang, massed and waxen, from a crystal vase.

"Good afternoon, madame."

"Good afternoon, Hélène."

Hélène drew back her hand. "I've got paint under my nails, because I worked all this morning." She smiled at Jean. "Good afternoon."

"Here's some good coffee for you." Jean smiled. "Perhaps you'd like a small glass of liqueur brandy?"

"Why not?" said Hélène. She sat down beside Mme Blomart. His mother: it was queer to think that he owed his life to someone. Was it possible that he could not have existed? Mme Blomart was sitting in a basket-work chair, her legs crooked under her, and her hand was round one of her ankles. She still looked very young.

"What's puzzling you so much?" asked Jean.

She laughed rather shyly. She could not get accustomed to his reading her thoughts.

"I can never believe that you're his mother," she said to Mme Blomart.

"It's because he's so big," said Mme Blomart. She looked him over with a kind of happy surprise. That was strange, too — that a particular description could be applied to him. "He is tall, he is dark, he is a little over thirty." Thus he had appeared to Hélène the first time she saw him, at the Port Salut.

"What are you going to do this afternoon?" asked Mme Blomart.

"We're going for a walk with Marcel and Denise," said Jean. "Hélène wants to take us to see the Zoo."

"It's such fun!" said Hélène.

"What won't be so funny is having to tell Denise what I think of her novel," said Jean.

"What exactly are you going to tell her?"

"You've read it. What can I do about it? It's hopeless."

"It's mediocre," said Mme Blomart.

"Mediocre," said Jean gently. "You also described that putrid carp that was served up to us the other day as mediocre!"

"Poor Denise! She was so set on there being a genius in the family," said Hélène.

"Perhaps she'll improve if she works at it," said Mme Blomart.

"She has worked terribly hard," said Jean. "She got up as six o'clock every morning, and she refused to see anyone." He looked rather anxiously at his mother. "Do you think, when she asks me for a frank opinion, it would be honest to allow her to go on?"

"He'd never ask for my advice so seriously," Hélène thought, with a bitter pang.

"Couldn't you get her onto something else?" said Mme Blomart.

"Politics!" said Jean. "But that's not enough for her now. It's a pity she's not gifted; it would have settled everything."

"It is a pity," said Mme Blomart. "She's so plucky."

"She has lots of virtues," said Hélène, "but the sad

thing about it is that no one is grateful to her for them."

"Personally, I like her," said Mme Blomart with some warmth.

"But her novel is so unpleasant," said Hélène. "That woman crushed by her husband's personality — the character of her great negative genius is ridiculous. I wonder if she really sees Marcel like that."

"Marcel is impossible," said Mme Blomart. "The way he behaves! It's senseless."

"He's improving," said Jean. "He's agreed to do the decorations for Schlosberg; he's going to earn some money."

"After all, he only asks to be left alone," said Hélène. "All the same, Denise can't really expect him to act against his conscience."

"His conscience ought to tell him that Denise exists," said Mme Blomart. A little color mounted in her cheeks. "It's all very well having moral anguish, but it's really too convenient if we limit it simply to what suits us."

"But why should other people have rights over us?" Hélène asked. "It's a thing I've been unable to understand."

"It's not a question of rights," said Jean, "they are there."

"Yes," said Mme Blomart. "One must be blind not to see them."

Hélène looked at her, then at Jean. "I must be blind," she thought with annoyance.

Jean rose. "Well, I must go and perform my duty now." He bent over his mother. "What pretty little shoes you've got on!" he said as he took possession of one of her slippers.

"Jean!" exclaimed Mme Blomart in distress.

[164]

He touched the elevator hidden in the heel of her lizard-skin shoe. "You'll never get over not having been a big, tall woman!"

"You're indecent," said Mme Blomart.

"Here," said Jean, "take back your property." He kissed his mother. "I'll see you on Wednesday. I'll talk over our plans with Hélène."

"What plans?" asked Hélène when they were once again in the street.

"I'm going to tell you about them." Jean touched her on the shoulder. "You're very beautiful today."

"What plans?" repeated Hélène.

"You are curious!" said Jean. "Well, here they are. Mother asked me a question that I've been asking myself for some time now: why don't you and I get married?"

"Get married!" echoed Hélène. She ran her tongue over her lips. Every night in his arms; every morning, on awakening, his face! But she did not wish to give vent to a joy that was more indecent than a prayer. "You wouldn't at all like to be married."

"Why not?" Jean smiled. "I wouldn't make you unhappy."

"How sweet you are!" said Hélène.

"I'm not sweet, I love you."

"It's sweet of you to love me." She looked at him uncertainly. He was so tender, so generous. Was he only thinking of her?

"I'm afraid of being rather in your way," she said.

"Little fool," said Jean. "You've become very modest all of a sudden." He caught Hélène's hand in his. "Do you think it's a good idea that we should decide to get married?"

"Let's decide to do it," said Hélène in a spasm of joy. She could not stop her mouth from laughing, or her eyes from shining, and her heart bubbled with burning gold. He was smiling. For a while they walked on without saying a word; they loved each other, and there was nothing to say.

"We're going to give Marcel a great surprise," said Jean.

They went up the stairs. There was a notice on the door: "Knock loudly." The bell was always out of order. Jean knocked and Denise opened the door. She was wearing a little hat with a veil that made her look very ladylike; she was carrying her gloves and her handbag.

"Don't come in," she said. "It's a stinking mess." Her lips curled with nausea. "It's impossible to tidy up this brothel." In her well-bred mouth, the coarse words sounded vulgar and forced.

"Isn't Marcel coming with us?" asked Jean.

"He'll meet us for dinner. He didn't want to miss his game of chess."

"Is he as keen on it as ever?"

"He's set his mind on becoming a champion," said Denise dryly.

They went slowly down the twisting staircase. "That's a bad start," thought Hélène. Under her tulle veil, Denise had two red blotches on her cheekbones, and the corners of her mouth drooped.

"I'm standing the party a taxi!" said Denise. She signaled and a taxi drew up beside the sidewalk. "Could you please take us to the Zoological Gardens at Vincennes?" she said in the singsong tone she used to taxi-drivers and waiters. Her voice grew abrupt again. "Let's take advantage of it, quick, since Marcel has decided to earn some money."

"Is it going on all right?" asked Jean.

"Admirably. He's daubing away at his cartoons as if he were house-painting, and afterward he goes off serenely to push his pieces of wood about."

"But it pays well," said Jean.

"It pays so well that it seems as if I'd never had to complain of poverty," said Denise. A heavy silence fell. Denise stared into space with an absentminded intensity. Hélène remembered that it was horrible to be unhappy, you were so alone in the world.

"I'm going to show you everything," said Hélène as she went through the little entrance gate. "The aquarium, the parrots, the lion house, the kangaroos. Do you want to see them?"

"Of course," said Jean. "I like looking at animals."

Hélène smiled. She had often come here to draw the flamingos, the giraffes, the armadillos, and the anteaters. At noon she would climb to the top of the monkey rock to look over Paris as she ate a slice of bread and potted meat. Those were good days, red-letter days. But at that time there was something missing even in moments of happiness.

"Wait, I'm going to buy some fish for the sea-lions," said Jean. He went up to the saleswoman who was standing behind a counter with a squirming basket on it; he said a few words to her and the woman began to laugh. People always liked him: perhaps it was because of the brotherly way in which he looked at them and spoke to them.

"Would you like some?" he asked Denise.

"No, thank you," said Denise.

Jean seized a small fish by the tail and hung over the cement rim; a large, bewhiskered sea-lion rose up, with his jaws open, and jumped perpendicularly from the water, barking greedily. Jean snatched the fish back.

[167]

"You'll get your fingers bitten off," said Hélène.

"No fear," said Jean. He began the same maneuver again. He looked so carefree, so happy. In the old days he was always so preoccupied. "He loves me," thought Hélène. He let the fish drop and the sea-lion caught it in its mouth.

"Funny animal," he said solemnly.

"All animals are funny," said Hélène.

She smiled at him. He loved her. She no longer had a feeling of emptiness inside her, or of uncertainty. She no longer wondered where she should go or what good it was staying there. It was as if there were a special place assigned to her on earth, and she exactly fitted into it; just this very place by his side, with her head the height of his shoulder, in the middle of this great park full of artificial rocks, where the reek of wild animals mingled with the fresh scent of buds. "We're going to get married."

"Well, you haven't let us off anything!" said Jean.

"But now you know the Zoo as well as I do," said Hélène. They were sitting under an orange-striped tent, near a hut where children were drinking pink and green sodas. Hélène loved this dusty display: the variously shaped marshmallow, the liquorice, the madeleine cakes, and those large jars full of brightly colored liquids, the same colors as the balloons hanging on the end of a stick, like a gigantic bunch of acid drops.

"It would make a pleasant watercolor," she said.

"Yes," said Denise. She was looking right through the jars and the balloons as if they were invisible. Hélène glanced at Jean; he was drinking his coffee in a detached manner, but he too knew that the time had come.

"Do you remember your promise?" asked Denise.

Jean looked at her questioningly. "You were to give me your opinion about my novel. Have you finished reading it?"

"Yes," said Jean.

"Well then?" There was a silence, a very brief one. Denise's smile froze on her lips.

"It's interesting," said Jean. "It's got some good points." His expression was open and frank enough to deceive even Hélène. "Only, as is to be expected, it's the work of a beginner. I suppose that one learns to write novels as one learns to make shoes. You haven't yet got the hang of the trade."

"What exactly do you mean?" said Denise. Her cheekbones were flushed. It was with difficulty that she kept her voice calm.

"You explain too much," said Jean. "You don't paint a picture. You've something to say, but you're not very concerned about the way in which you say it. It reads more like extracts from a personal diary than a novel."

"And yet I show Sabine, I show Eloi — "

"You tell people what they must think about them; you don't draw their characters. They are terribly abstract. And you haven't attempted to construct a story."

Denise lit a cigarette with elaborate care. "What it amounts to is that I must start all over again."

"Frankly, yes; or as near as makes no difference."

"I didn't think it was as awful as that."

"Awful — no. It's a first effort."

"Yes." For a moment she smoked in silence. With Denise, it was not possible to gloss over the truth: she had always faced things.

"Do you think it is worth while beginning all over again? Do you think I shall ever achieve anything?"

"I can't tell you that."

[169]

"I don't ask you to prophesy," said Denise. "Just give me your opinion. . . ."

Jean hesitated. Hélène anxiously watched his lips. He always spoke the truth.

"I think your bent lies more in writing essays," said Jean. "What is important for you is to find the proper form of self-expression."

Denise abruptly pulled down her veil over her face.

"Oh, I think I've understood what suits me," she said. "Many thanks." She rose. "Marcel must be waiting for us, we ought to be going."

"Don't take it like that," said Jean. "It's very seldom that success comes at the first attempt. It's a matter of knowing whether you really want to write. . . ."

Denise did not reply: she was walking quickly and went up to a taxi. "Place Saint-Germain-des-Prés."

She huddled deep in her corner of the cab and stared at the back of the driver's neck; her whole face had collapsed, she was not even trying to assume a conventional expression. She who was always so artificial, so well mannered; she must really be at the end of her tether.

"We're there," said Jean.

She turned her head and looked at him in a kind of amazement.

"You first," said Jean, opening the door.

She got out, paid the driver, and went through the revolving door.

"You struck her!" said Hélène.

"But why did she ask for my advice?" said Jean almost angrily. "It's always the same old story, always. . . ."

They went in. Marcel was sitting at the back of the room, his face wreathed in a smile.

"I've been waiting impatiently for you," he said. "I'm as hungry as a hunter."

"So are we," said Jean. "Hélène drove us mercilessly from the monkeys to the crocodiles and from the crocodiles to the vultures."

"It's a pity you didn't come," said Hélène.

"At least, did you play a good game, may we ask? Did you win?"

Marcel gave a mysterious little laugh. "I'm improving." He handed the menu to Hélène. "What do you want to eat?"

Hélène studied the menu perplexedly; she would have liked to eat the lot.

"I'm going down to wash my hands," said Denise.

"Order something first," said Marcel.

She shrugged her shoulders.

"Order anything for me."

"I'll have some *pâté,*" said Hélène. "After that, I can't make up my mind whether to have beef or pigeon."

"Have both beef and pigeon," said Marcel.

"Oh, no," she said, overcome.

"Why not? You're dying to do so."

"After all, why not?" she said.

She took her handbag and went downstairs to the ladies' room. She pushed open the door. Denise was standing in front of a looking-glass. She had raised her veil and was staring at herself; she seemed petrified for all eternity in a hopeless self-interrogation.

"I look like a Zulu," said Hélène.

Denise's eyelids flickered; she stretched out her hand toward her lipstick and passed it mechanically over her lips; Hélène uneasily began to comb her hair; there did not seem anything that she could say, the very fact

[171]

of speaking would have been an insult, but with every
moment, the silence became more stifling. Hélène was
suddenly panic-stricken, "Bah, it will do like that." She
went upstairs at a run. Behind her, Denise followed
with a measured step.

"Dinner is ready," said Marcel.

The table was covered with a damask cloth; a long-
necked bottle stood in a pail of ice. On Hélène's plate
was a huge slice of pink *foie gras,* marbled with
truffles.

"Oh, *foie gras!*" said Hélène ecstatically.

"It's because we're celebrating tonight," said Marcel.
"Jean has told me the news." He filled the glasses.
"What do you think of it?" he asked Denise. "Do you
think Jean will make a good husband?"

Denise made a kind of grimace. "Perhaps. I believe
that some couples are happy."

Only her lips were stained scarlet, for she had not
made up the rest of her face again; from its yellow
pallor her eyes shone in a stony glare.

"I drink to your future home," said Marcel.

"To your chess championship," replied Jean.

They clinked their glasses. Hélène kept her face
down over her plate; Denise's immobility paralyzed
her.

"Aren't you eating?" asked Marcel.

"It's nauseating," said Denise. She looked distractedly
at Marcel, Jean, and Hélène in turn. "We're here and
we're eating *foie gras.*"

"There are no objections to be made to this *foie gras,*"
said Jean good-naturedly.

"Pass your plate to Hélène, she'll manage it quite
easily," said Marcel.

"She'll make herself ill," said Jean.

"She's tougher than that," said Marcel. He slid the

[172]

slice of *foie gras* onto Hélène's plate. "I adore seeing her eat."

"Thank you," said Hélène with some constraint.

Marcel's laugh contrasted painfully with Denise's face. He appeared quite at ease.

She looked at Jean. He was anxiously watching Denise as well.

"This is a nice place," she said, to break the silence.

"Isn't it? The guy who decorated it knew his job," said Marcel. "He hasn't left an inch untouched."

The walls were covered with blue and yellow mosaics, of fishes, birds, and palm trees.

"I say, I'd like to see your murals," said Jean. "I hear they're going very well."

Marcel began to laugh. "Of course, it's so easy to please them."

"Oh, you think it's easy?" said Denise; she seemed to be coming out of a dream.

"It's too easy to be interesting," said Marcel.

Denise sneered. "But chess is interesting?"

"Passionately interesting," said Marcel. He turned to Jean. "There lies the seat of pure creation." He pointed to his head. "You get everything out of that. The chessboard doesn't exist, it's only a landmark." He smiled mischievously. "Anyhow, I'll soon be able to play with my eyes shut."

Denise was tapping the table with the tips of her fingers. "What exactly did Schlosberg say?"

"He said it was easy to recognize the paw of a painter at a glance," said Marcel, spreading out his big hand with satisfaction.

Denise gave a nasty laugh. "But you're no more a painter than I'm a writer."

"It's fine that Schlosberg is pleased," said Jean to conciliate them.

Denise stared at him. "Yes, you don't care a damn," she said in a loud voice. "You've got your trade-unionism, Marcel has his chess, and Hélène has you. But I —" she said with a kind of sob, "I've got nothing."

There was a silence. Denise looked away and crumbled a piece of bread in her fingers.

"Waiter," said Marcel, "the next course."

"Marcel has his chess and I have Jean," Hélène repeated to herself. She looked at Jean. Only him. Was that enough? Once more she seemed to feel about her a bygone dusk, scented with honey and cocoa; the ancient anguish was there, ready to seize upon her again.

"First, here's the pigeon," said Marcel.

The waiter placed on the table a metal-covered dish. He lifted the cover and Hélène rapturously smelt the aroma of green peas. In a flash the past had faded.

"Eat," said Marcel to Denise. "Your trouble is that you don't eat."

She looked daggers at him. Hélène and Jean exchanged anxious glances.

"But I'm serious," said Marcel. "There's no better way of attaining one's ego than by eating."

With the back of her hand Denise swept her plate away; the pigeon and the green peas were squashed on the tiled floor among the fragments of china.

"I've had enough," said Denise. "Enough! Enough!" she repeated as she rose. She walked to the door.

"I'm going with her," said Hélène.

"Go," said Jean, "and stay as long as necessary. I'll wait for you at my flat, both tonight and tomorrow morning."

Her heart sank as she looked at him. Only one Saturday in the week, one single night. She hurried after Denise and seized her arm.

[174]

"I'm coming with you," she said. "Do you mind?"

Denise went on a few steps without answering.

"That man!" she said. She stopped and leaned against the wall. "I never wish to see him again, never, never."

Hélène felt her swaying on her arm. "Don't let's stay here. Let's go up to your place."

Denise mumbled something unintelligible.

"What? Don't you want to go home?"

"Never," said Denise. Her back was to the wall, and her eyes were staring out of her head. Hélène looked at her, uncertain what to do.

"Then come on," she said of a sudden. "We'll take a room for you in a hotel. You're simply dropping on your feet."

She dragged Denise along and they went across the street. Almost immediately opposite was a hotel; the hall had a red carpet and was furnished with deep leather armchairs; an aspidistra sprouted from a copper pot.

"Have you a room for the night, a single room?"

"Emma, show No. 7 to these ladies," said the proprietress.

The housemaid took the key from the hook and climbed the steps of a wide staircase covered with thick carpeting. She opened a door.

"That will be perfect," said Hélène quickly. She closed the door. "Lie down," she said to Denise, "and rest."

Denise untied her veil; she put her hat carefully on the table. "I'm not ill." She sat on the edge of the bed. "If I were ill, I could be cured. No. But there's something damn wrong about my make-up, and that's incurable." She looked at Hélène with a kind of hatred. "Why don't you tell me what's the matter with me?"

[175]

"But there's nothing the matter with you," said Hélène.

Denise laughed harshly. "You don't want to tell me?"

Hélène's heart began to beat quickly; she was frightened.

"I'll manage to find out what it is," said Denise defiantly.

"Denise, don't be absurd." Hélène placed her hand on Denise's. Denise jerked hers away.

"You do know. You know why Marcel hates me." She began to shake. "At night he sleeps on the floor because he can't bear anything to touch him. He's always so polite; I would rather he beat me. Tell me: why does he hate me?"

"He doesn't hate you," said Hélène.

"Don't lie to me," said Denise violently. She looked round the room. "Why did you bring me here?"

"So that you can rest," said Hélène.

Denise's eyes flashed. "Rest!" She wrinkled her forehead. "Did you come here as my friend or as my enemy?" she said in worried tones.

"You know perfectly well that I am your friend."

"My friend! I have no friend. I hate myself." Suddenly she collapsed on the bed and began to sob. "I'm a failure."

Hélène stroked the luxuriant red hair. "You mustn't upset yourself like this. Success doesn't come at the first attempt."

"I know," said Denise. "I've got nothing to say. I knew it all the time. But then what?" she cried despairingly. "Tell me — what?" She was sobbing, her sobs increased in violence; a long moan escaped from her lips; she was shaking from head to foot. Hélène threw

[176]

herself down beside her and pressed her palm over Denise's mouth.

"Don't scream," she said. "Control yourself."

Denise was silent at once. "I'm so tired."

"Try to sleep," said Hélène. "I'll stay here."

"Thank you," said Denise. "Forgive me."

She closed her eyes. Hélène turned out the light and sat down beside the bed. A yellow light filtered through a slit in the velvet curtains. "So what?" she repeated to herself. "What?" She looked at Denise. Beneath the disordered hair her face was aflame with fever. What was the use of so many tears and struggles, so many desires and regrets? Her heart grew cold. Denise's life. My life. Tiny islands in the midst of a black sea, lost under an empty sky and soon to be submerged by the uniformity of the waters. "I have Jean." But he would die some day; their love would die. Only that empty night would remain which she could not even bear to think about. "I'm blinding myself," thought Hélène. "I, too, am deliberately blinding myself." She wanted to throw herself on the bed, like Denise, and scream.

Denise opened her eyes and suddenly sat up. "What are you doing here?"

"I thought you might need me."

"I need no one," said Denise fiercely. She passed her hand over her forehead. "I've been dreaming."

"Do you want me to go away?"

"Yes," Denise looked at Hélène mistrustfully. "You looked at me while I slept."

"No I didn't."

"You looked at me," said Denise loudly. "I don't need you here."

"Very well, I'll go." Hélène rose. "I'll come back tomorrow morning."

[177]

Denise did not answer.

"I'll see you tomorrow morning," repeated Hélène.

She went out of the room and looked back hesitantly at the door. Then she turned away and went downstairs four steps at a time.

"Taxi! Rue Sauffroy." She curled up on the seat. Only a few more minutes. The face was aflame with fever under the red hair; the voice was saying: "Then what?" In a few minutes the voice would be silent. No matter if I am blinding myself — no matter. That's not to be endured. She leaned forward to look out. Place Clichy. La Fourche. She knocked on the window. "Stop here."

She climbed the stairs and rang the bell three times. The door opened.

"Why, I didn't expect you so soon!" said Jean.

She threw herself into his arms and clung to him in silence.

"What did you do with her?" asked Jean.

"I left her lying on a bed in a hotel. She didn't want to go home." Hélène clung closer to Jean. "It was horrible."

"My poor child!" He stroked her hair. "All the same, Marcel is really terrible. I tried to argue with him. But he says that Denise is human folly personified, and there's no way of making him change his attitude."

"I'm beginning to wonder if she isn't really going mad," said Hélène. "She was behaving very oddly. She more or less drove me from the room."

"It wouldn't suit her at all to be mad."

"Why so?" said Hélène. She broke away from him and began to undress. She was in haste to be lying in bed in the shelter of Jean's arms.

"Because, as Marcel says, she's so social-minded. That novel, for instance — she didn't want to write it; she

[178]

really wanted to be a writer. That's something quite different."

"Social-minded!" said Hélène. "But after all, she's like other people; she tries to be someone, as Marcel says."

"Perhaps," said Jean. "In any case, she tries badly."

"Who tries well?" said Hélène. "Do you think that I try well?"

"At least you're happy."

"Perhaps you're wrong." She slipped between the cool sheets and smiled. He was there. She was happy. She need have no qualms about it. "She knows that Marcel doesn't love her," she continued. "She says she doesn't want to see him again."

"She'll see him again," said Jean.

"She oughtn't to."

"She loves him."

"All the more reason."

Jean smiled. "And you say that?"

"Yes," said Hélène, blushing. "When you didn't love me, I hoped to capture you." She looked at him. "But if you stopped loving me now, it would be different."

"What would you do?"

"Ah, you'll see. I'll go away."

He took her in his arms. "I'll see nothing of the sort."

She kissed him and then freed herself. "Come quick."

"I'm coming," said Jean. "Hide yourself."

She turned toward the wall. She heard the sound of his footsteps crossing the room, the rustling of clothes, the water running. He is coming. She closed her eyes. A burning mist poured through her veins — burning and blinding, a cloud that separated her from her past, from the future and from death.

"Here you are," she said.

She clasped him to her — warm, smooth, supple, and

hard: a body. He was there, entirely self-contained in that male body which she held in her arms. During the whole day he had escaped her; in his past, in his thoughts, near his mother and Denise, scattered throughout the whole world. And now he was there, against her flesh, under her hands, under her mouth; to be with him, she let herself slip without memories, hopes, or thoughts into the depths where time stopped. She was no longer anything but a blind body dimly lit by the sputtering of a million sparks. "Do not betray me. Do not go far away from this body which my body is calling. Do not leave me alone, a prey to the burning night." She moaned. "You are here, as surely as I am. For me, not for you, this flesh quivering; your flesh. You are here. You desire me, you require me. And I too am here, an utterly realized flaming fulfillment against which time is shattered. This minute is forever real, as real as death and eternity."

7

THERE will be a dawn. Four chimes. At the corner of the deserted streets the hands of clocks move round; they move round in the room where Laurent sleeps. And the wound spreads in the lung, the heart is becoming exhausted. She breathes gently and with unconscious effort. Is she going to die without being aware of it? Supposing I wake her up? But even if her eyes remained open until the last minute, her death would escape her. Her death — it is hers, and yet it is forever separated from her; she will not experience her death. There will be no dawn.

There will be no dawn. Silence. Night. Decide to speak; decide to be silent. The tireless whispering has ceased. Anguish has come upon me. Silence reigns. Nothing else exists.

But this dream of death exists. I exist, I who think upon death. It is she who is dying. I am alive. In two hours' time he will say: "Everything is ready." I shall hear him. I shall be there, before him, my whole self confronting him, absorbed in rending anguish, and yet, in my whole self, elsewhere — unable to withdraw myself from the world or to lose myself in it. *To be dead. No longer to know anything. Not to know the weight of my dead body.* But I am alive. I know. Never again shall I cease knowing.

In the apathy, in the miserable routine of that year, I knew. I had felt on my head the weight of the original curse; it was no longer even worth while struggling against it; there was no way of circumventing it. With indifference I allowed myself to be tossed to and fro by all the hazards of fate: the chance hazard of a desire, of a regret, of a revulsion. I went forward blindly; I was going nowhere, I was marking time in the night; an unpredictable fate took pleasure in leading us astray and we waited for the light of day to discover in what mud we were hopelessly bogged.

"You ought to learn to play chess," Marcel said to me. We were leaning on the balcony of his studio; we could see beneath us the roofs shining in the sun and, at a distance, the white mass of the Sacré-Cœur set in a blue haze. He smiled. "It seems to me that it's the only thing left for you."

"I'm getting married," I said.

"That's never saved anyone."

There was a silence.

"How is Denise?" I asked. Denise had gone to the south for a rest. She was nursing her unhappiness as one nurses an illness.

"She's going for long walks, and becoming herself again," said Marcel regretfully.

"Well, that's a good thing!"

"Yes," said Marcel. "Poor Denise! She couldn't be expected to stay mad all her life." He nodded his head. "I should never have thought it of her," he said with admiration.

"When she comes back, try to make life bearable for her," I said. "It's not so very difficult."

He looked at me with interest. "Do you know what really surprised me? It seems easy. I thought she wanted to change me to the very marrow of my bones." He shrugged his shoulders. "Not at all. She actually believes what people say."

"Yes," I said. "That's another piece of luck."

"Don't you feel awkward when you lie?" asked Marcel.

[182]

"It's the only way of protecting yourself, if you can't just be yourself without torturing somebody."

"And that's the spirit in which you're getting married!"

"I'm getting something out of it," I said. "While I'm thinking about Hélène, I'm not thinking about myself."

"And do you think about her a lot?"

"I'd like her to be happy."

"You may get deeply involved."

"I dare say, but what does it matter? I don't know what to do with myself any longer."

"Oh, in that case, you're in safe hands." Marcel laughed sympathetically. "She'll always know what to do with you."

That at least was a tangible certainty — the happiness I gave her. She would smile at me and I'd say: "I love you." The joy that lit up her face called for new lies, but what did it matter, since I was resolved never to unsay them? I loved her; we were going to be married, and she was delighted to see that I no longer measured the time that I spent with her. She kissed me rapturously.

"How sweet you are," she would say.

"I'm not sweet — I love you."

"It's sweet of you to love me."

She did not suspect that every minute wasted was henceforth for me a minute saved; all I hoped for now was to scatter my life to the four winds of heaven, without leaving the slightest trace anywhere.

"You've changed since last year," she said to me.

"Do you think so?"

"Yes; you're less solemn and more carefree. You used to look as if you were being torn in every direction at once; you weren't altogether present when you were with me."

"Perhaps."

We had moored the boat against the river bank; other boats, crammed full of young men with bronzed torsos, glided by on the current; flowered frocks floated in the breeze. On the towpath, bicycles passed by noiselessly.

"How nice it is here," said Hélène. "It's such a lovely day."

The air smelt of leaves and water, with whiffs of fried potatoes. The shadows were already lengthening. A lovely day — a little heap of golden dust, almost impalpable, which the wind would drive into the empty ether. Hélène had placed a huge bunch of mauve flowers in her lap.

"You've picked some pretty flowers."

She began to laugh. "When I was engaged to Paul, I always thought of Sundays in the summer as a big bunch of mauve flowers tied to the handlebars of a bicycle, and I felt sad."

"Because of the bicycle?"

"You brute! Because of Paul."

Happiness made her more lovely. Her features had matured. The glow that lit up her face was gentler than it used to be, more controlled.

"The love he offered me was so dreary," she continued. She skimmed the quiet water with her fingertips.

"He really loved you."

"Yes, but for him love was something natural, like hunger and thirst. Our love was just one case among millions of others." She looked at me hesitantly. "I know quite well that there are other people who love each other. . . ."

"Others live and others die," I said. "But it does not prevent each person's life being unique and each person dying on his own account. You're right. It's absurd to try to see the world as if we were standing on Sirius; we're not on Sirius, but on the earth, each of us in his own skin."

"It's not really so natural to love one another," she continued. "It's even funny to think that you're unique so far as I'm concerned. It isn't an illusion, is it? You are unique."

"Who's to decide that, if not you? That is, indeed, what's so moving about love: we ourselves make its truth."

She looked at me seriously. "But you must love me, so that I too can be unique. Is it really true that you love me?"

"If I don't love you, I wonder what I am doing here."

"Is it true that we'll be married in three months' time?"

"Absolutely true."

She threw herself back, her face turned to the sky. She loved me. I loved her. She asked for nothing more. Yet how could I justify her existence, I who was here for no reason, with no justification, useless? I took up the oars. A lovely day with music, flowers, kisses, fried potatoes, white wine, and the rippling of cool water on sunbaked bodies. Soon it would die on the horizon, and its ashes would be light. My heart was sad. Not so light. The sky was smooth, the light transparent, and yet I had a feeling that an insipid odor hung about me, insistent and clinging, as if, under their shining film, all those instants had been rotten to the core; it was the insipid odor of resignation.

Hélène sat up. "You'd think it absurd for us to have children, wouldn't you?"

I looked at her, surprised. "Do you want to?"

"Yes and no. I wonder whether they don't make life richer."

I smiled. "And you don't want to lose a chance of getting rich?"

"Don't laugh. What do you think?"

"I used to think it madness to bring someone into this world. Wouldn't it frighten you?"

She hesitated. "No. Even if a man is unhappy, can you really say that it would have been better that he'd never existed?"

"Quite!" I said. "But if he causes evil in the world?"

"And if he does good?"

"Oh, you're right. To allow a child to be born, to stop it being born — both are equally absurd. It doesn't matter."

"But if you desire a thing, it does matter. Then it's not absurd to do it?"

"Perhaps my fault lies in not being able to desire anything to start with."

She laughed. "Your fault? I don't think you have so many faults."

I was rowing and the boat glided along without leaving a trace, so quietly. To be nothing but the white ripple rising and disappearing into the even surface of the water. *That voice should be killed. The voice that was saying: "I should like to be that ripple." She said: "That voice should be killed." The ripple was born and died without a voice.*

From the end of a springboard a brown body plunged into the river; lovers strolled along the bank. A peaceful Sunday. The hours sped between our fingers. Far away over there, the hours sank into the earth, in molten lead and steel. Every day new guns and new tanks came out of the German factories.

"I wonder if we're not on the wrong tack," I said to

Gauthier. "Perhaps Fascism can be overcome only by using its own methods." I folded up the number of the *Vie syndicale,* on the front page of which Gauthier's new article on peace was displayed.

"Then I wonder what sense there is in being anti-Fascist," he said.

"I wonder too."

His cold eyes looked at me. "And you're saying that?"

I shrugged my shoulders. What could we do if, by living up to the values in which we believed, we brought about their defeat? Were we to become slaves to remain free, or kill to keep our hands clean? Must we lose our freedom because we refused slavery, and sully ourselves with a thousand crimes because we would not kill? I no longer knew.

"You preach peace at us," I said. "That's all very well. But how so? Supposing we're the only people to want it?"

"That would be enough," said Gauthier. "You can't fight on your own."

"You'd let Fascism dominate the whole of Europe without lifting a finger?"

"Anything is better than war."

"There are plenty of other things as horrible as war."

To me, war was not a supreme sin. It was only one of the forms of conflict in which I had been involved despite myself, through being born on earth. Because we existed for one another and yet each for himself; because I was myself and yet another entity to other people: Old Blomart's son — Paul's rival — a social traitor — a dirty Frenchman — an enemy. The bread I ate had always been somebody else's bread.

"So you're also becoming a warmonger," said Gauthier.

"Of course not. Don't worry; I won't write a line, I won't say a word that might incite anyone to war."

It was warm; we were leaning out of the window of my room in our shirt sleeves; a lamp was lit at the corner of the quiet little street, where children were playing hopscotch.

"I'm neither a warmonger nor a pacifist. I'm nothing at all."

Gauthier was a pacifist. Paul was a Communist. Hélène was in love. Laurent was a working man. And I was nothing. I looked at my room; the walls were whitewashed, but little by little my mother had brought cushions and rugs, she had hung Marcel's pictures on the wall; for eight hours a day I worked in the shops, but I had bourgeois friends; I lived in Clichy, but I often meandered with Hélène along the boulevard Saint-Michel and in the prosperous districts. Paul said that if I was nothing, it was because I was neither bourgeois nor working-class; but it seemed more to me that I was neither bourgeois nor working-class because I could never be anything: neither bourgeois nor working-class; neither warmonger nor pacifist; neither a lover, nor fancy free.

"What are you thinking about?" asked Hélène.

We were sitting in the confectionary shop, on the steps of the little staircase; she had put her head on my shoulder and we were silent. On the other side of the glazed door were noisy streets, open under the sky, but in here silence and shadow. I was stroking Hélène's hair. My fiancée, my wife. An aroma of broth mingled with the scent of honey and chocolate; the sugared almonds gleamed softly in the glass jars, like stones at the bottom of a torrent. Pleasant sugary shell, full of memories and scents, calm and dark as a belly. Tomorrow it will be blown into fragments. Men will lie naked

[188]

among the crushed pralines and the trampled flowers — naked and defenseless under a steely sky.

"What are you thinking about?" she repeated.

"I'm thinking about war."

She raised her head and removed her hand from mine.

"Again?" Her smile was forced. "Do you never think of me?"

"When I think of the war, I think of you." I took her hand again. "You rather frighten me."

"I do?"

"You won't face the situation. I think you'll be badly caught out the day that war is declared."

"But it isn't possible! Such stupidity! Do you really believe in it?"

"You know I do. I've told you a hundred times."

"Yes, you've told me." She looked at me with sudden anxiety. "But still, you're not going to let that happen?"

"What can we do about it?"

"Aren't you going to refuse to go? You used to explain that it would be enough to fold your arms; they couldn't do anything without you."

"But I'm not at all sure that we ought to refuse!"

"What?"

"Do you want Fascism to spread all over Europe? Do you want us to have a *Gauleiter* under Hitler's orders in France?"

"You're talking like Denise. I don't want you to die in a war."

"You're so horrified at the idea that you might only be an ant in an antheap — if Fascism were to triumph, that's just what would happen. There would be no more human beings — just ants."

"I don't care a damn. A live ant is better than a dead man."

"There's one good reason for accepting death, and that is to give a meaning to life."

She did not answer; she was staring, preoccupied, into space. Her face relaxed. "Your father has so many connections. Surely he can have you rejected on medical grounds."

"Are you joking?"

"Yes, you don't care," she said violently. "You'd leave me without a qualm." She looked at me. "Sometimes I wonder if you love me — if it isn't all an act?"

"Do you think that I'd consent to dine with Monsieur and Madame Bertrand if I did not love you?"

She shrugged her shoulders. "If you loved me, you wouldn't be in such a hurry to get bumped off."

"I love you, Hélène, but do try to understand. . . ."

I knew that she did not want to understand and it was difficult for me to find loving words. "You don't want to love her," said Denise; now I was quite ready to want to do so, but in the threatening heat of that month of August it was Hélène who was raising a barrier between the two of us. Often I turned toward her in the hope of sharing my hesitations and my anguish with her; but I was alone; she looked at me suspiciously; she was almost an enemy walking at my side. Alone, in the sickly peace that was dying; alone, in the torture of suspense, having drunk shame to the dregs and longing for the explosion that would at last tear me out of myself.

And suddenly it happened. To want war — not to want it. Henceforth the answer was no longer important: war existed. The time of my departure was settled, I had only to get into the train assigned to me, to put on the khaki uniform, to obey. My thoughts, my desires, were no longer anything more than evanescent bubbles that vanished without leaving their mark on

[190]

*the world, without weighing on my soul. Relieved of
myself. Relieved of the agonizing task of being a man.
Only a soldier, submitting indifferently to the daily
routine. Go. Don't go. It was not for me to speak: someone spoke for me. That inhuman silence. Beyond consent and revolution, that mortal rest. It was easy to be
dead. It would be easy. But how does one become dead!
How kill oneself and yet live? The voice says: "I should
like to be dead" — and that voice is life. I close my eyes,
but in vain. There is no more silence; I cannot be silent.
Go. Don't go. I must speak.*

"Jean."

Someone else has spoken. On the other side of the
door a voice is calling softly: "Jean." That's me. Have
I still got a name?

He turned the handle of the door.

"Paul's here," said Denise.

He blinked. He still lived in the present. The crude
light that fell from the bulb dazzled him. "Paul."

He went forward. Paul was standing near Madeleine's chair, his cap in his hand. His hair was cropped;
his skin was parchment-colored and stuck to his bones.
He shook hands with him.

"Poor old thing," said Madeleine, "he needs feeding
up again."

Paul smiled at Blomart; his eyes had remained blue
and young. "Thanks for getting me out of there."

"I didn't do it."

Paul looked at the door. "How is she?"

"It got the lung."

Madeleine was smoking in front of the grate full of
cinders. Denise had gone into the kitchen; there was a
sound of washing up, a living, everyday sound. The
hand of the alarm clock did not appear to be moving.

"What did the doctor say?"

"He said that she wouldn't live through the night."
Paul bent his head. "Could I see her?"

"Go in. She's asleep."

He sat down. Denise came into the room and set a bowl of coffee before him. "Drink it."

"Thanks. I don't want it."

"You must drink. You've had nothing for twenty-four hours."

He drank. "You must drink." Were they still expecting something more from him? Did he still owe them something? Twenty-four hours. How short are the hours! Dawn came — then night again. Dawn will come. Suddenly he was aware of his body; his limbs were stiff, his head was heavy. He felt cold.

"She was asleep." Paul looked at Blomart. "It was because of me."

"If it's anyone's fault, it's mine," said Blomart. "I ought to have gone myself."

"No, you ought not," said Denise quickly. "You had no right to go."

"Had I a right to kill her?" asked Blomart.

"The first two times I was stuck," said Paul. "I couldn't leave. Yet, ever since getting your message, I've been ready every night."

"It isn't your fault," said Blomart. He thrust his hand into his pocket and took out a cigarette. His hand was shaking. The tobacco had a strange taste, acrid yet sweet.

"You landed at Lheureux's?"

"Yes, I got into Paris without any difficulty, no one asked me anything. In any case, the papers are O. K. The guy took me in like a brother. He gave me a ticket for Sauveterre and all instructions."

"You're out of danger," said Blomart. "Crossing the border is child's play."

[192]

Paul smiled. "I certainly thought I'd never see a pal again."

"We haven't seen each other for two years!" said Blomart.

"You haven't had any trouble?"

"On the contrary — I was approached with a view to eventual collaboration. My record isn't compromising."

"And now?" asked Paul. He looked round the room with curiosity.

"Now I am compromising myself."

"Escape?"

"Other things too."

Paul's eyes shone. "That does please me!"

"Are you astonished? You used to think me a traitor."

"Words used not to have the same meaning as they do today," said Paul. He clapped Blomart on the shoulder. "No, I was sure that you wouldn't go over to them. Only I wouldn't have believed — " He hesitated. "You loathed violence so much."

"I still loathe it."

There was a silence.

"It's unavoidable," said Paul. "If you'd seen the effect it had on us in camp, every time we heard of a new attempt! Only that can give confidence — not words, but deeds. No other form of resistance is possible."

"I know."

"You're working in conjunction with the party?"

"We're an independent organization, but we work together. What do you intend to do over there?"

"Find the leaders and place myself at their disposal."

"Try to convince them that they should contact us and form a single front with us here. Later we may have to fight each other, but not now."

"No," said Paul, "not now."

[193]

"Here," said Blomart; he held out a sheet of paper to Paul. "Here are some addresses. Learn them by heart. They're the pals in the other zone. They're quite ready to join in with you."

Paul took the sheet of paper. "You haven't had too many setbacks?"

"No, we're careful. You see, this is a kind of boarding-house. The most active members of the movement are registered under false names. At the same time, they keep their real identification cards, of course. It blurs the trails."

"I look after the boarding-house," said Madeleine.

"In the last six months," said Denise, "four trainloads of German soldiers have been derailed, three Soldaten-heims and ten requisitioned hotels have been blown up." She looked at Blomart. "Presently one of our lot is going to put a time-bomb in a room of the anti-Bolshevik exhibition."

"That's fine work," said Paul. His eyes were still on the door. "And so Hélène was working with you?"

"Yes," said Blomart.

"She must have changed a lot."

"She had understood."

"That's good," said Paul.

Blomart rose. We are talking — Denise, Madeleine, Paul — and our words and our presences are sufficient to themselves. As if she did not exist. *Tomorrow. Always. As if she had never existed.* Only the words on our lips, a picture in our hearts — a legend.

"You're staying here, aren't you?"

"He'll stay until it's time for his train," said Denise.

"It goes at nine o'clock," said Paul.

"Then we'll meet again later," said Blomart. He walked toward the door. "I'll see you soon."

As if she did not exist. Yet, on that bed, there is still

someone. Someone who no longer exists for herself, yet is there. He drew closer. *That's good. A fine story. A fine death.* We are already telling the tale of your death. And you are dying, Hélène, you who are unique. And I am here. In a lighted room a man spoke words; a man with a face and a name spoke words that everyone uses. But it concerns me. He led me here. All the exits are closed. I can do nothing more for you, nothing more for myself. He was not thinking of us, he was speaking words, he was making gestures; he killed you, my love. Shall I allow him to kill again?

8

HÉLÈNE rushed onto the platform and ran toward a porter. "The express for Pecquigny?"

"Oh, it went an hour ago!" said the man.

"When is there another one?"

"Tomorrow." He was moving away. Tears sprang to Hélène's eyes: Jean would be there waiting for her with the two bicycles; smiling, he would watch the express coming into the station, and then his smile would freeze. She ran after the porter.

"Isn't there a bus?"

"I don't know." He looked at Hélène. "What you can do is to take the seven p.m. express to Revigny. There you'll be only fifteen kilometers away. You might find a conveyance."

"Thanks," said Hélène.

Fifteen kilometers carrying that heavy suitcase. She clenched her teeth. "I want to see him tonight. Not tomorrow; tonight." Perhaps tomorrow would be too late; perhaps when she arrived the old woman would say to her: "They've just left." "I will follow him. I will follow his regiment. I'll slip by night into the camp." She held out her suitcase to the porter at the baggage office. "And supposing he's at the front, huddled at the bottom of a hole with shells bursting round him?" Not tomorrow; tonight.

The sky was gray over gray streets; Hélène turned into a long, narrow avenue. All the shops were shut; there was no one on the sidewalks; not a vehicle on the roadway. It might have been an evacuated town. All the streets crossed at right angles, and the houses looked like barracks. A town of eastern France, barren as the poverty-stricken plains that the train had just passed through. She could sense on the horizon, invisible but already present, the barbed wire, the strong-points, the guns. Hélène jumped. The wail of the sirens tore through the air. Of a sudden vehicles, pedestrians, and soldiers sprang out of the ground. Hélène stared dumb-founded at this unexpected harvest.

"Excuse me, madame. Do you know where I could find a restaurant?"

"At this hour the restaurants are all shut," said the woman; she pointed vaguely into space. "Try at the Brasserie Moderne."

"Was there an air-raid warning?" asked Hélène.

"There are warnings every day," said the woman, shrugging her shoulders.

Hélène went across the square. A waiter was arranging tables on the terrace, protected by evergreens planted in green-painted boxes. Inside, the *brasserie* was empty. Hélène sat down in front of an imitation-marble-topped table.

"Could I have something to eat?"

The waiter looked at her reproachfully. "At this time of night?"

"Eggs? Or cold meat?"

"Not at this hour," said the waiter.

She rose. "All right. I'll try elsewhere."

She recrossed the square; rain was drizzling; she went into the Café du Commerce. The room was huge and empty, as in the café opposite; the shiny seats were split in places and showed their horsehair intestines.

"Could you bring me some food?" asked Hélène. "Eggs? Bread and chocolate?"

"Eggs?" said the waiter. "You won't find a single one in the whole town."

"Haven't you anything at all?"

"We've got beer and coffee."

"Give me some coffee," said Hélène.

She sat down and took some cigarettes out of her bag. Now he was wandering down the village streets, with an anxious heart. And she was here in this lead-colored town where no place was reserved for her. There was no way of letting him know. "There will be no sign, only that endless absence." She drank her cup of coffee at one gulp and threw three francs on the table. Outside it was raining heavily; but never mind, she must walk, walk very fast, throw herself quickly from one minute into the next, so that anguish could never seize upon her. "Tomorrow without fail he'll sign that application. He must sign it." For a moment the vice loosened; he'll be at Chartres, he'll oil airplane engines, he'll run no more risks. I'll be able to see him. She repeated to herself: "He'll sign it." She slackened her pace. Soldiers were strolling about in small groups, waiting for the time to rush into the cafés; some of them were lining up outside a cinema. They will be stretched in the mud, with a hole in their heads, all alone — perhaps at this minute, exactly this minute. She bit her lips; she felt her eyes hard as stone in their sockets, so hard that they hurt her; when she kept her eyes fixed like that, it was more difficult for the pictures to take shape.

"I ought to look for something to eat," she thought. She went up the main street again. Not a fruiterer, not a grocer. She pushed open the door of a pastrycook's; the plates were empty; the soldiers had devoured everything; only three melancholy tartlets remained on a tin plate. Hélène ate them and drank a glass of water.

She set off back to the station. All she could do was to sit in a corner and wait; she had not slept all night and she was so tired that she could no longer stand.

She went into the waiting-room. People were sitting on the seats, on the tables, on the floor, among huge bundles; they were refugees coming from the east. They were waiting, with their hands laid flat on their knees, empty-eyed. Since the beginning of the war everyone had been waiting, endlessly, without knowing why. Hélène sat on the floor, against the door, curled up on herself. The heat and smell of humanity suffocated her.

"They won't say so," said a woman, "but where we come from, a lot have been killed aready."

"And where we come from, they say there're so many telegrams that the mayor doesn't dare take them to the families," said another.

A train passed, whistling. In the first cars were men, soldiers sitting on the steps, with helmets on their heads and beside them their haversacks and their rifles; in the cars at the rear were guns, camouflaged in autumn colors, their muzzles gaping to the sky. The train was speeding toward the east. There at the end of the shining rails, the war was awaiting the guns and the men. There — so near. It was already here, in the depth of hopeless eyes, among the hasty bundles, in the whistling of the trains. Hélène closed her eyes, rested her forehead against her knees, and her head was filled with night.

When she found herself back in the local train with wooden compartments, she was drenched through and stiff. The rain fell in heavy drops on the roof of the car. But hope was reviving. "I'm going to see him." Every revolution of the wheels was taking her nearer to him. "I'll find a conveyance. In a few hours I'll be in his arms. He will agree. He can't refuse," she thought passionately.

Revigny station was pitch-black.

"Where's the baggage office?" asked Hélène.

"Leave your suitcase there," said the porter, pointing to the sentry who was on guard at the door. "We'll keep an eye on it."

"All right," said Hélène; she put down her suitcase and walked toward the exit.

"Your papers?" asked the sentry.

Hélène brought out her pass and her identification card. The pass was quite in order; no reason for her journey was stated.

"Pecquigny. This isn't Pecquigny here."

"But I'm going to look for a car to get there."

"All right — pass," said the soldier.

Hélène carefully put away the precious paper. "So long as nothing happens; so long as I'm not arrested," she thought in agony. The night was as dark as pitch; it was still raining. She tripped in a black puddle and then in another; the water was up to her ankles. Where could she go? The policeman on duty at the crossroads frightened her, she dared not ask him the way. She crossed a bridge and haphazardly followed a street. Garage.

"Can you hire a car here?"

"No," said the man.

"You don't know where I could find one?"

"You should try Mallard's, Place de la Gare."

She retraced her steps. A group of soldiers dawdled past; the cafés were full of soldiers, their laughter could be heard through the hermetically closed doors. She knocked at a little door at the side of the garage.

"Please, I was told that I could hire a car?"

The woman looked at her sulkily. "My husband isn't in."

"You don't know if he is coming back?"

"He won't take the car out at this hour."

Again the black streets, the water splashing underfoot, the water soaking through her coat. A door. "No." Another door. "No." Again another door.

"Go and try the Café des Sports, at the end of the rue de Nancy."

Hélène half opened the door of the café; her heart failed her; the room was full to bursting with soldiers, sitting with glasses of red wine in front of them; their laughter — their looks — she plucked up her courage and walked up to the bar. The owners were joyfully eating a large dish of string beans.

"Please, monsieur," she said; her voice was trembling; at any moment she was going to burst into sobs; "I was told that you had a car."

The man was eating; he was warm in his thick, dry pullover; a good bed was awaiting him.

"I don't drive at night," he said; he shrugged his shoulders. "You're not allowed to use headlights, so you can imagine! No one drives by night now."

Hélène bit her lips; she was beaten. Now there was nothing to do but lie down and forget everything.

"Have you any rooms here?"

"Rooms? My poor lady! You won't find a straw mattress in the whole town. The army's here."

"Thanks," said Hélène.

Her legs were giving way. Not tonight. Her tears flowed. She passed in front of the Hôtel du Lion d'Or. It was not even worth while going in and inquiring. No — always no. The slightest act had become so difficult. She felt she was struggling among suffocating undergrowth. Jean. She would never be able to rejoin him. This night would have no end. This night, this war, this silent and deadly absence.

"In the end, I went back to the station," said Hélène. "A porter took pity on me and showed me a car where I could sleep." She yawned. "But I didn't sleep. I'm dropping with sleep."

"Poor little thing," said Jean. "Was I worried! I was afraid that you'd tried to come without papers and that you'd got into trouble."

"Do you think I could get into trouble?"

"Lots of officers and noncoms have sent for their wives," said Jean. "They're turning a blind eye to it. At the worst you would be sent back to Paris."

"But I don't want to be sent back," said Hélène. She looked at the red-tiled floor, the big country bed with its bouncing eiderdown, the cast-iron stove. "It will be so nice living here, both of us." She opened her suit-case. "Look — all that's for you." She placed on the table a bottle of old brandy, tins of *pâté,* tobacco, wool socks. "Those are presents from your mother. I bought the books." She pointed to five little notebooks bound in black imitation leather. "That's my wartime diary. There are lots of newspaper clippings, accounts of conversations, or articles. I've also written down my intimate thoughts. Will they interest you?"

"Of course," said Jean. "How sweet you are!"

She looked him up and down, in his khaki pullover that molded his torso; he had not changed. Yet during the past two months he had had a number of thoughts in his mind of which she had known nothing. He made her feel shy.

"I've lots of things to tell you," she said.

"I'm looking forward to them." He put on his tunic

and his overcoat. "I shall be back at eleven thirty. I'll lunch with you, and then from half past five until to-morrow morning I shan't have to leave you any more."

"Well done," said Hélène. She threw herself into his arms. "Come back quickly."

"Never fear. I'll bring some grub. Don't show yourself too much in the village; the path in front of the house takes you straight out into the fields." He kissed her and walked to the door. "See you soon."

She ran to the window. Two hens were pecking about in the path. A soldier crossed the square. She knocked gently on the windowpane and Jean turned round and smiled. She let the curtain fall again. For a week or ten days she was going to live beside him as if they had been married. "We would have got married just about this time," she thought. She stretched. She was sleepy, she was hungry, but how happy she was! She took a book and slipped on her mackintosh; the courtyard smelt of damp wood.

"Good morning, madame."

The old woman was drawing water from the pump; she raised her head. "So you found your husband? Was he pleased?"

"Yes, I found him. He was asleep."

Hélène set out along the muddy track and smiled happily. The scenery was rather ugly, a grayish-yellow color and quite flat; here and there was a bare hillock, but she liked grass, the sky, the sun, and an open horizon. She climbed up a hillock and put down the book beside her. A fine autumn day. She suddenly felt a little anxious, "I shall have to speak to him." When she was far away, it seemed quite easy; but she could not any longer do what she liked with him; in this dialogue he would give the answers. "He cannot refuse; if he loves me, he cannot refuse." She turned her head.

Someone was coming up. Two officers holding their canes in their hands. They passed in front of her and then retraced their steps casually.

"Are you going for a walk?"

"Yes," said Hélène.

"Do you live in Pecquigny?"

"No, I come from Paris. I got here this morning."

"Have you got your papers?"

"Here you are!" said Hélène, showing her pass.

The officer lightly stroked his fine leather riding-boots with his cane. "You must get the captain's visa on it."

"Oh, I didn't know, I'll go along soon."

"You ought to have gone at once, when you arrived. Come with us; we've got a car; we'll drive you."

"All right," said Hélène. She followed after them. One of them was tall and white-faced and one of them was short and had a black mustache. She got into the car.

"A fine day," she said.

They did not answer. The car went into the village, passed beyond Mme Moulin's house, and stopped in the main street.

"This way."

The two lieutenants stood aside and Hélène went in alone to a small room in which a stove was burning. Her heart was beating quickly; it was the last formality, after that she would have nothing to worry about, but she wanted everything to be settled as quickly as possible.

The captain raised his head; he was seated at a table littered with papers.

"You're the person who arrived at Pecquigny this morning?"

"Yes."

"Have you got your papers?"

She held out her pass and her identification card. The captain examined them silently.

"What have you come to do here?"

"I've come to see an elderly relative, Mme Moulin."

The captain looked at her. "No, mademoiselle, Madame Moulin is no relative of yours."

"Not exactly," said Hélène.

"You don't know her," said the captain. "When you arrived this morning, you hadn't ever seen her before."

Hélène bent her head. Her life had stopped.

"We know everything," said the captain. "We know the name of the soldier who took a room for you."

"Well, yes," said Hélène defiantly. "I came to see my fiancé. I'm not the only one who's done it, and that you know full well."

"We're quite willing to close our eyes if we're not obliged to open them," said the captain.

"But who obliged you?" Hélène looked at him imploringly. "I beg of you, give me at least a few days. . . ."

"The matter is no longer in our hands," said the captain. "You were reported to the proper authorities."

"I was reported?"

"Ah, our information service is good," said the captain. He rose. "You'll be taken to the station in a moment. You'll go back by the first train."

"At least, let me say good-by to my fiancé," said Hélène. She dug her nails into the palms of her hands, she did not want to cry in front of this man.

The captain hesitated. "Wait here."

He rose and went out of the room. Reported — by whom? How? She remained seated on her chair, thunderstruck. Must not cry. She was so very hungry, so

[205]

very tired, and once again it would be the jolting of the train, an empty stomach, a dry throat, and a crowded car. The train will carry me away, it will carry me far away from Jean. "There's no way out," she thought, sick with despair.

The tall, pale lieutenant pushed open the door; he smiled in a friendly way. "You can go and lunch at your place. I've just convinced the captain that you're not a spy."

"Me, a spy?"

"You oughtn't to have arrived with a huge suitcase full of papers. The stationmaster at Revigny opened it and he thought they were seditious pamphlets. He had you reported by the driver who brought you this morning."

"And I thought you had met me accidentally!"

"Luckily a quick look round was enough to show that you were not a dangerous propagandist."

"You took my papers?"

"Your place was searched while we were looking for you in the countryside. Everything will be returned to you." He bowed to Hélène. "We will come and get you in a moment."

"Is there no hope of my staying?"

"None at present; it's not possible."

Hélène set off at a run toward the house. She threw herself on the bed and burst into sobs. As in her childhood, large strange hands disposed of her happiness, of her life. What on earth could her being here matter? Hypocrites! Words, hollow regulations, and after all that horrible journey she was going to leave Jean almost without having seen him. She turned her head. The old woman came into the room with a distrustful expression.

"Some soldiers came to ask for you."

"I know."

"They said you mustn't stay here."

"I'm leaving at once."

The woman looked at her with no gentleness. "You oblige people, and it only gets you into trouble," she grumbled. She left the room.

"The old louse!" murmured Hélène vindictively. Her tears redoubled. "They've read my notebook. I'm at their mercy."

She jumped to her feet. Jean opened the door and smiled innocently. He held a blood-stained parcel in his hand and was clutching a bottle of white wine to his heart.

"I didn't find any red wine," he said, "but I've brought you back two handsome beefsteaks."

"I shall just have time to eat them," said Hélène. "You don't know what has been happening to me."

"What on earth?"

"Well, I'm sunk."

"It's not true?"

Hélène began to laugh hysterically. "They collected me out in the fields and they took me to the captain. It appears that last night the Revigny stationmaster opened my suitcase and took my notebooks for pacifist pamphlets and reported me as a spy."

"Your defense is easy."

"Yes, only the police have been warned." Hélène stifled a sob. "They're going to oblige me to leave. But I won't go," she said, despairingly. "I'll only pretend. I'll hide, I'll come back at night."

"Poor little wretch." Jean took her in his arms.

"I don't want to leave you."

"I think you will have to go back to Paris. But you'll

only have to apply for another pass, and you can come back and stay somewhere about four or five kilometers away."

"I won't! By then, you'll have left for the front and I shan't see you any more."

"It's not certain that we're leaving so soon. And you know, at present, it's quiet over there."

"No, I can't imagine it! I'll go mad!" She looked at him distractedly. She must speak. Every minute counted. "Every instant I tell myself that you're screaming to death on the barbed wire; you don't realize — " her voice broke.

"I know, it's far worse being in your shoes than in mine."

She looked away. "What would you say to the idea of your going back to the base."

"What do you mean?"

"You would have to apply to be transferred to the air force. Madame Grandjouan is an intimate friend of a general who promised to send you at once to a camp near Chartres."

"Did you ask her to do that?"

Hélène's cheeks flushed. "Yes."

Jean sat down and silently filled two glasses with wine. "You know, airmen run far greater risks than infantrymen in this war."

"But there's no question of flying. Ordinary soldiers don't fly. You would be put in an office or in a quiet corner to oil engines." She touched his hand. "I could go and live near you; we could see each other every day. . . ."

Jean looked into the bottom of his glass without answering. Hélène withdrew her hand.

"Well? What's worrying you?" she asked.

"I don't want to be a slacker."

Hélène's heart turned cold. "You're not going to refuse?" She watched him, terrified. Jean hesitated.

"Listen, I can't answer you just like that. I must think it over."

"Think what over? You're offered a decent way of living; we shall be together again! And you hesitate, because you might be branded!"

"You know it isn't only a question of being branded."

Hélène bit her lips. "The war will be won without you, all right."

"No doubt. But it wouldn't be at all the same thing for me!"

"Yes," said Hélène furiously. "It doesn't matter a damn to you that I should be shaking with misery from morning to night."

"My dear child — try to understand. . . ."

Hélène shook her head. "No, I do not understand," she said in a strangled voice. "Much good it will do you when you're dead."

"But if it were only a question of saving my skin, it wouldn't do me much good either," said Jean gently.

Hélène pushed her hand through her hair. "It's not the four shots you'll fire that'll make any difference."

"Listen, Hélène. Can you imagine that I should stay put in a nice quiet little corner while my pals get killed?"

"I don't care a damn for the others," said Hélène despairingly. "I don't owe anything to anyone." She burst into tears. "I'll kill myself if you die, and I don't want to die."

"Couldn't you try for once to think of something else but yourself?" His voice was stern.

"And you. Aren't you thinking of yourself?" she asked violently. "Do you worry about me?"

"We're not in this."

"But we are." Hélène's hands clawed at the table-cloth. "One always fights for oneself."

"Hélène! There should be no question of our fighting!"

"I'd do anything for you," she said rancorously. I'd steal, I'd murder, I'd betray — "

"But you are not capable of accepting the risk of my death!"

"No," said Hélène, "no. You won't make me do that. You see that we are fighting."

"If there was only a little friendship between us — "

"Friendship. . . . I happen to love you."

"I don't understand that way of loving."

He was judging her; he was judging that burning tornado which dried up the blood in her veins.

"There's no other way," said Hélène. "You — you don't love me." A blinding evidence suddenly struck her. "I've never counted, so far as you're concerned."

"I love you," said Jean, "but love is not the only thing. . . ."

He was there, obstinate, opaque, surrounded with steely ideas; every line on his forehead, every flash of his eyes shouted that he had no need of anyone.

"All right," she said. "I will see that you come back without your being consulted."

"Hélène, I forbid you."

"Oh, you forbid me! And what do you think that matters to me? Each for himself." She sneered. "One fine day you'll find yourself specially assigned to Paris."

"I beg you," said Jean. "We have only a few minutes left; don't let's part in this way."

"Who cares? It doesn't matter, as you'll be back in Clichy in a month's time."

"If you do that — "

"You'll break with me? But let's break it off at once since it's so easy for you."

"Think: you'd kill all my feelings for you. I can't love without respect."

"Well, you won't love me any more. It won't make such a great deal of difference!"

"Hélène!"

She started. Heavy footsteps shook the kitchen floor. There was a knock on the door.

"Come in," she said.

The two lieutenants came in. Jean rose and buckled up his belt.

"Don't be afraid," said the tall white-faced one.

Jean smiled. "What should I be afraid of?"

"Lieutenant Masqueray wishes to see you."

"I'll go at once." Jean took his cap and looked at Hélène undecidedly. She did not move.

"Good-by," he said.

"Good-by," said she, without giving him her hand.

"We won't make things awkward for him, don't worry," said the little lieutenant. "He's a good soldier."

Hélène rose. "I supose I ought to pack?"

"Yes, please. The car is waiting for you." The tall lieutenant smiled. "Allow me to introduce myself: Lieutenant Mulet."

"Lieutenant Bourlat," said the other.

Lieutenant Mulet threw the black notebooks on the table. "Here are the incriminating documents."

She picked up a notebook. Their men's eyes had read. She felt dizzy. The room was suddenly empty; the parcel of meat lay beside the half-empty bottle. It was like memories of another life.

"I'm ready," she said.

They went out and she climbed into the car. Lieutenant Mulet sat beside her.

[211]

"So you're turning me out?" she said.

"Believe me, we're sorry," said Mulet. He smiled with martial magnanimity. In the middle of his chalky face two blue holes opened up over unfathomable depths.

"Try to get another pass and come back without being spotted," said Bourlat.

"And we'll try not to run into you," said Mulet.

"Thanks," she said.

"Oh, we understand," said Mulet. "We're both married."

Hélène gave a cowardly smile. "Their dirty men's thoughts. And I'm smiling. I am at their mercy. One ought not to have to depend on anything. I'd like not to depend on anything."

"Can't you leave me now?" she asked, getting out of the car; she looked at Mulet in supplication.

"We've actually got to see that you really get into the train," said Mulet with a charming smile.

She turned her head away. It was all over; there was no more hope. New formalities — they'd take over a month and it wouldn't work a second time. It was all over. She stared at the empty horizon at the end of the railway tracks. She longed for the train to be there so that she could be alone, so that she could weep and hate them. And hate him.

"Bon voyage," said Mulet.

She climbed the steps without answering and went into the first compartment. They remained on the platform, they were watching her. She put her suitcase in the rack and sat in a corner next to the corridor. It was a fine compartment, with green leather seats. It was hot. Three soldiers were drinking a white liquid in their mugs; they were on leave; they were laughing.

"Have some marc from Alsace?" said one of them. "It's good stuff."

"Don't mind if I do," she said.

The soldier carefully wiped the rim of the mug with a corner of his handkerchief and poured out a bumper.

"What do you think of it?"

"Smashing," said Hélène. She drained the mug. There was a sharp buzzing in her head; everything was burning, flaming; in an instant her heart had become a little heap of ashes.

"She takes it straight," said the soldier in admiration.

"He'll see. I don't care a bit. He'll see," she said to herself. She took off her coat, rolled it into a ball, put her head on it, and lay full length. The soldiers were laughing, the train was rolling on, and it rocked her. Everything was over for today.

9

H E brought me here. And yet he seemed quite harmless, wearing his khaki uniform and his forage cap. It was as if the original curse had been lifted — the curse of existing: did he exist? There was only an anonymous soldier in the barns of Pecquigny and Caumont, in the railroad cars and trucks, on the roads, at the bottom of the freezing hole in which he mounted guard, a soldier free from anxiety and guilt. It was so simple. He did not have to choose to want a thing: he wanted it. He was at one with himself. There were no questions to solve. The goal stood peacefully and clearly before him: victory against Fascism. A merciful necessity regulated every one of his actions.

And suddenly he was again face to face with himself in the midst of shame and anger. He came out of the big building with blue-painted windowpanes, and the lieutenant smiled disdainfully behind his back. He crossed the little square, and the glances of all the soldiers who passed him seemed to burn his cheeks. She had done it, she had dared to do it. They don't know yet, but they will know, they'll have to be told. Boucher, Dubois, and Rivière will have to be told. They will know. They will know that everything has been a lie: the uniform, the tin mug, our drunken laughter, and the communal animal warmth in which our sodden toes gradually unfroze among the straw in the barns. How joyously had he donned the earth-colored overcoat and had had cropped his too thick, too close hair, which he had inherited from his mother. But it was only a fake, I was never one of them; I shall never be like other men, naked and alone without protection and without privileges. . . . . "Specially assigned as proofreader at the Imprimerie Nationale." He had often hated his face, but this aspect of it was the most odious — that of a coward.

"I swear that I shan't stay there long!"

"You'd be a damn fool to come back," said Rivière.

There were six empty bottles on the table and each plate was a miniature ossuary: the taste of the wine had not changed, nor the aroma of the jugged hare, nor their laughter. But everything was different. "I didn't ask for it," I would say, and they would clap me on the shoulder encouragingly. "Go on, we'd do the same in your place." But they weren't in my place, and that they knew well. I was in it; now we were each in his place, and I was all alone. It was I who got into the train, who was running away from the war, who came out of the Gare de l'Est giving a false impression of being on leave, and at whom the women looked with smiles. At Caumont it was still winter; here it was spring, and the women smiled. The Paris women, with very fair or very dark hair, and red lips, smiled at the impostor. Bogus workman, bogus soldier. They will go up to the front line without me; I shall sleep in my room, I shall eat in the restaurants with their paper tablecloths surrounded by old men and women, and I shall be alone. I kept close to the walls as I walked for fear of meeting Laurent or Gauthier or Perrier. The boys would know, they would say: "Blomart got himself assigned to Paris," and even if I should say: "It's not true, I didn't do it," they will look at me coldly. "In any case, you're here." And it's me, it's really me. I choked with anger; I would have liked to wring her neck until there was *nothing* left between my hands.

"Hello, I'd like to speak to Hélène."

"Hello, it's Hélène speaking."

"It's Jean."

There was a muffled exclamation at the other end of the line, "You're in Paris!"

"Do you doubt it?"

"You're angry with me?"

"I've a few things to say to you. When can I come round?"

"I'd rather come round to you myself. Now?"

"If you want to. Shall we say in an hour's time?"

"Jean!"

"Well?"

"Listen, Jean. . . ."

"You can tell me about that presently. . . ."

I hung up. She'd see. I was already breathing more easily. I began to walk down the avenue de Clichy. There I was, going home, just as I used to — the same cafés, the same shops. And yet something had changed since September. Formerly my life seemed to be entirely enclosed between those tall houses; they had always been there, they would always be there; I was only a bird of passage; they would still be standing there, looking just the same, when I had long since vanished from the earth. I looked at them; already they were different. They were no longer an impassive block, but an accumulation of stones whose temporary equilibrium could be destroyed in an instant. In the past, each of those façades had a special character; now they were only shells of friable material supported by iron girders. Twisted iron girders, crumbled walls, lumps of plaster, calcined stones — that is what might perhaps exist tomorrow; and I might still be there, unchanged among those ruins. My fate was no longer intermingled with the fate of those streets. It belonged only to me. I was no longer enclosed. I was nowhere; I was out of reach. Suddenly anything seemed possible.

"I'm going to break with Hélène."

I had thought of beating her, of strangling her, but I was so far away from her that I had not even thought of breaking with her. Now I was going to see her and speak to her: what would I say to her? I looked at the long, straight avenue. So lonely, so free, without a past. I was no longer bound by outworn lies. If I lied to her presently, it would be a new lie. My anger had gone; with a kind of surprise, I thought: "I must break off for good."

Could I lie again, since I knew that my every action would give the lie to my vows? Tomorrow I would have to face death, exile, or revolution; I would face them alone and free, and I would make my own decisions without taking Hélène into consideration. Each time she would hate me and try to circumvent me; we would be two enemies. No, it isn't possible, it cannot go on. And yet could I abandon her? My mother was left alone in the satin-upholstered flat, Hélène would be left alone. Oh, it was easy to be a soldier; it was much less easy to become a man again. Once again everything seemed impossible. And yet I was going to speak. *Something will come into being which, up to that time, existed nowhere.* Slowly I went up the stairs. Usually I felt guilty *after* the crime; this time I was guilty *beforehand.* Lies or unhappiness? I had to choose the evil myself. "I ought not to have come across her. I ought not to have been born." But I had been born.

She held out her hand and looked away. "Good day."

"Good day, sit down."

She stood before me, timid and unhappy, and I felt overwhelmed with sadness.

"Hélène, why did you do it?"

"I don't want you to be killed." She looked at me defiantly. "You can break with me, you can beat me, you can do whatever you like; I prefer that to having your head blown off by a shell."

"Don't think I'm going to stay here for long. This time I intend to use my father's influential friends."

"That much time will have been gained." I was glad to see that arrogant flame in her eyes again.

"Do you understand that you've made any relationship between us impossible?"

The blood rose to her cheeks. "Are you deciding that?"

"I have nothing to decide. You've spoilt everything."

"Oh, you're only too pleased to be able to get rid of me, you're taking advantage of the first excuse."

"It isn't an excuse. You treated me like an enemy."

Her tears flowed. "Yes, I treated you like an enemy. I hate you. You've never loved me. Well! Don't be afraid; I'm going away. I don't care a rap."

She was sobbing convulsively. Her nose and her cheeks had at once become red and swollen. There was a taste of dirty water in my mouth and I wanted to say to her: "All right, don't let's think about it any more," but soon the struggle between us would begin anew just as bitterly.

She looked at me through her tears. "Is it true? Do you want me to go away?"

"I'm fonder of you than I've been of anyone," I said. "But there's too deep a misunderstanding between us. You've never tried to share my life, you've only loved me for your own sake."

"I want to *be* your life," she said despairingly.

"It's impossible. I cannot love you as you would wish."

Her face changed. "You don't love me!" She looked at me silently with dilated eyes; she passed her tongue over her lips. "But then why did you tell me that you loved me?"

"I was so fond of you. I wanted to love you." I hesitated. "I ought to have understood that we were too dissimilar. It's not your fault, but we have nothing in common."

"You don't love me," she said slowly. "That's funny, when I love you so much."

She stared into space. She seemed to be carefully spelling out a difficult book. I had a qualm. Did I not love her? She seemed so near, I would so have liked to comfort her.

"That's funny," she repeated, "although, when you think of it, why should I be loved, after all?"

"Hélène!"

She was already very much alone, very far away from me. And I felt her close against me, intimate and warm.

"What?"

I bent my head. I could say nothing to her. The barren distress that flooded my heart reeked like a swamp.

"Forgive me."

"Oh, I don't blame you. It's better so. Now I can't lie to myself any more." She rose. "I want to go."

"You're not going like that!"

"Why not?" She looked around the room and then at my face, with a kind of astonishment. "You've no idea how I've lived for the past month, you can have no idea. It was — it was abject."

"It's as you wish," I said. If I did not protect myself, tears would rise to my eyes, and it was not for me to weep.

"I prefer never to see you again," she said. She tried to smile. "Good-by."

[219]

It seemed impossible. I looked at her without understanding, as if someone had shown me my own hand in a glass jar, with its scars and the individual shape of the nails.

"Good-by," she said. She walked to the door. A devastating impulse threw me toward her: I loved her. But already the door had slammed and she was going downstairs. I loved her for her sincerity and her courage. I loved her because she was going. I could not call her back. "Hélène!" I dug my hands into the arms of the chair, holding back that barren cry. It was done. Her tears, her suffering, had not previously existed. And now they were there — because of me.

I had done it. Why should I have done that, why that particularly? You were crying and it was purposeless, since I was going to love you tomorrow. *Perhaps your death is purposeless; the yellow posters and the doors that open and shut, and the crack of bullets in the early morning are purposeless, utterly purposeless. He brought me here for nothing. We shall be defeated. They will conquer without us. All those crimes, for nothing. He had not thought of that. He said: "Something must be done." What did he do? Only your death is certain, and this night.*

"I shall not see her again. It's over," he thought in the train that carried him far away from Paris. Slowly, like a wound, the past was closing up. Now the decision was behind him, just like the things that he had not chosen and that existed. *To have decided.* It was no more criminal than to have lived. The break with Hélène weighed on him neither more nor less heavily than the dinner at the Port Salut. *To have decided to kill him, to have killed him, to be dead.* Moreover, he no longer looked behind him. He looked toward the future, yonder at the end of the rails. A single goal, a single road.

He was becoming a soldier again. What wonderful holidays! Now he was alone as in the fields of his childhood, when apples crunched guiltless in his mouth and everything was allowable; he could safely stretch, loll, take, break; his actions no longer threatened anyone; there was no one confronting him; men were only means to an end, or obstacles, or part of the scenery, and all the voices were silent, the whispering voices, the threatening voices, the voices of anxiety and guilt. There were only the rumbling of the guns, the roar of the planes, and the whining of bullets to be heard. As calm as if he were eating an apple, he threw hand-grenades and fired his rifle. The guns fired on the armored cars and trucks; his job was to fire on the men. But cement, steel, and flesh, all came under the category of objects. He was only a cog in a machine of iron and flame that blocked the way of another machine. "It's me," he thought one day, stupefied, as he lay on the edge of a wood with a gun in his hands, and he wanted to laugh; over there, in the middle of a plowed field, men fell under the bullets and his heart felt light. "It's I who am killing them." Even that was allowable, because he knew what he wanted. He was only a soldier and he was laughing because he could no longer do anything wrong. When he felt the pain in his left side, then he knew that he could no longer do anything at all. He was entirely lost and entirely saved, and he felt peace rising within him like a fever.

Lost in the smell of chloroform and in the whiteness of sheets and the silence of the big, light room — his suffering was anonymous. Time no longer flowed. A single moment — always the same: that immaculate pain. He floated alone with his body, he no longer weighed on the earth: a pain without weight. A breath would have sufficed for its extinction, which would have made no difference to anyone, since it gave neither light nor warmth: it was a will-o'-the-wisp.

Presently the world took shape again about him and once more he was back in the world; the wound was healing. "What's happening?" He walked with bare feet on the linoleum and looked out of the window at the red plain and the fields of blue lavender. The French army was retreating back toward the Seine; it was said that the Germans were at Rouen. But he wanted to sleep a little yet.

What an awakening! He had slipped into the little office, he had turned the knob of the radio, and a voice had spoken in French with a guttural accent. "We have entered Orléans. A captain with a few men entered Verdun, and Verdun fell. The French armies, cut into five sections, are flying in disorder; millions of refugees block the roads; the whole of France is falling to pieces." That arrogant, triumphant voice which shouted their victory — our defeat. My defeat. He had bent his head, he had remained motionless for a long while, his mouth filled with an unbearable bitterness that was the taste of his own life. Because we did not dare to will it. He heard Paul's voice. Once more he saw Blumenfeld's eyes. How soft and gentle were the spring evenings! How the flags flapped, red and tricolor, under the sun of the 14th of July! "No political strikes!" That prudence, that senseless prudence! "I will not drive my country into war." And it is war, a lost war. We did not dare to kill, we did not want to die, and those gray-green vermin devour our living bodies. Women and new-born children die in the ditches; on the soil that is already no longer ours, a huge steel net has fallen, caging Frenchmen by the million. Because of me. "Each of us is responsible for everything." One night, under the piano, he had dug his nails into the carpet, and that bitter thing had been in his throat; but he was only a child, he had wept and gone to sleep. One night in the streets he had walked like a madman, his eyes staring at a bleeding face; but he was young, his life was then before him, so that he could try to forget his crime. Now his life was behind him, his wasted life. It was too late, everything was over. Because I wanted to keep myself pure when it was already within me, part of my flesh, my breath, the original rottenness. We are defeated; mankind is defeated. In its place a new race of animals proliferate over the earth; the blind heartbeat of life will no longer be distinguishable from the decomposition of death; life swells, teems, and falls asunder in an even rhythm — muscles, blood, spermatozoa, and writhing heaps of satiated worms. Without a witness. There will be no more men.

The roadway sped on, empty and shining, toward the frontiers of Paris; it seemed disproportionately wide; only a few bicycles disturbed the silence. The rare passers-by all looked utterly alone; they had experienced their loneliness through exile, through misfortune, and through fear, and they had unanimously withdrawn into their own skins and were lost in the heart of the disaster as in a desert. He too was alone; he had been wandering all over Paris since morning, with his demobilization bonus in his pocket; the printing works were closed, his mother was far from Paris. He knew nothing about Hélène. He was alone, but he was there. A complete man. He was walking under the sulky sun. The shops were asleep behind closed iron shutters; through the scaly grilles of the red-painted butcher-shops, bare marble slabs could be seen; in front of the closed door of a grocery, a long black queue stood wearily. "France's turn will come." Vienna. Prague. Paris. On the windows of a hatter was stuck a large yellow butterfly: "Jewish firm." On he went. "I am here. But what can I do?" Alone, like all the others. But others, nevertheless, were advancing in long files along the deserted boulevards, the strong smell of their boots enveloping them like a cloud; trucks carried them in compact masses to the top of Montmartre, with measured step they paraded round the Place du Tertre, and when the blast from a whistle broke up their ranks, they stayed coagulated in dozens to go and photograph the Sacré-Cœur. The sound of their footsteps, the click of their heels, their songs, their uniforms, wove a huge gray-green network between them, so thick, so tangled that it was impossible to pick out any individual face. He bought a newspaper and crumpled it in anger. Our masters. And we bow our heads without speaking, without moving. In Poland the women fired shots from the windows, they poisoned the wells.

"Only by a loyal collaboration can new disasters be avoided," said Gauthier. "Why do you refuse? We have never yet had a chance of being able to give the *Vie syndicale* such a wide scope. And you'll never be forced to write anything but what you think."

"I want to write *everything* I think or nothing."

"But you'll be able to write everything," said Gauthier. "After all, haven't we always hoped for a more equitable organization of Europe?"

He had told me to meet him at a café terrace; a large middle-class café where he seemed quite at ease. It must have been the kind of place that he frequented nowadays. All round us was a swarm of gray-green uniforms, and the yellow leather of the field-glass cases smacked of the tourist. A woman with a basket full of photographs, illustrated papers, and "Souvenirs de Paris" hanging from her neck made her way between the tables. Just like the days of the Americans! They carelessly showered into the basket brand-new paper notes stamped with unknown designs. Nearly all of them had ordered champagne. Beside the ice-bucket they had put down neat little parcels — chocolate, scent, silk underwear. With tender care they were finally stripping the last luxury shops in Paris.

I looked angrily at Gauthier. "Do many of the comrades think like you?"

"A few of them." His eyes were avoiding mine. "None of us wanted this war."

"We didn't want this peace."

"It is peace."

Vienna: peace. Prague: peace. Paris; shall we again say: peace?

I was looking at a young German girl at the next table who, with innumerable instructions, was giving a parcel of tea to the waiter; she placed on the table a small pot of jam, some butter, and sugar. We were drinking barley coffee with saccharin. In our midst they were like a nation of colonizers among a crowd of natives; two worlds that ran parallel with each other without ever intermingling. They lived at the level of motor-cars and planes; we had only our feet, and, at best, our bicycles. Distances did not mean the same for us as for them, nor did the price of a glass of wine.

"Are you really going to agree to sell the paper to them?" I asked.

Gauthier smiled dryly. "Why shouldn't one work under their control? Daladier's control didn't worry you." He shrugged his shoulders. "I should have thought you were more clear-headed."

"I am clear-headed. So are you. You know what you're doing." I rose. "If you can still look at yourself in the glass after that, so much the better for you."

I was shaking with anger. Anger against Gauthier,

[225]

against myself. Had Paul been right? Had we been traitors? With anguish I tried to recall the past; no, we were not cowards; no, we had not betrayed. *Prove it. Prove it. It's up to you to prove it.* But wasn't I being a traitor at that moment? What is the difference between me and Gauthier? He crawls in front of them, he is more open than I am. But I am an accomplice as well. I am walking about in Paris, and every step I take sets a seal upon that complicity; I eat the bread they give me, the bread they refuse to Lina Blumenfeld, to Marcel, to starving Poland; my cage is wide and I docilely walk up and down in my cage. "No," he said. "No." He looked at his trembling hands. It is useless; anger is useless, questions are useless, the past is the past. It is for me to decide if it is a slave's past or the past of a man. *Prove it.* I will prove it.

"What can one do?" But he knew that everything happens through men's actions and each of us is a complete man. He sought out his friends, one after the other. "We are not alone if we unite," he would say. "We are not defeated if we fight. So long as we are here, there will be men." He spoke and his friends went to seek out other friends and spoke to them. And already, because they spoke, they were united, they were fighting; men were not defeated.

"Words are not enough," he said.

The two gentlemen looked at him nervously. Both were growing gray; Leclerc's eyes were gentle and blue in a friendly face; Parmentier's features were sharp and regular; there was a nonconformist air about him.

"I know," said Parmentier. "There's danger ahead of us; lacking definite aims, our meetings are bound to degenerate without doubt into study circles or drawing-room conversations."

"That's why we would be willing to agree to collaborate with you to found a newspaper," said Leclerc, "and also to produce leaflets and distribute them."

"That's not enough, either."

Leclerc stroked his chin in perplexity. No sound could be heard. Curtains, heavy carpets, leather portières, deadened the echoes of the world. On the massive desk were three coffee cups and glasses filled with liquor. Books covered the walls.

"What could we do?" asked Leclerc. He added quickly, as though to prevent an answer: "We could also try to build up an information service."

"All those are only token actions," said Blomart.

Silence fell. A threat now hovered over that civilized, hermetically sealed room. Those men were no cowards; they knew how to dare, to will, but only as far as it enabled them to live at peace with themselves. It was that peace which was suddenly in the balance; they would have prefered any other kind of risk.

Parmentier gathered his courage together. "What have you in mind?"

"Real action," said Blomart.

"Action," said Leclerc. He was not looking at Blomart, he was looking within himself. He had never wanted to ask himself whose hands had made that reassuring barrier that stood across his path: his own hands. He could destroy it. He was afraid of himself.

"If we had money, it would be easy to get weapons," said Blomart. "And I've comrades who are capable of making explosives. We're ready to take all the risks."

"Oh, there's no lack of money," said Leclerc.

"It isn't that I disapprove of violence on principle," said Parmentier, "but I confess that I can't see the use of murdering a few unfortunate, irresponsible soldiers."

"If we want to establish a body capable of rallying the masses, capable of holding out until the end of the

[227]

war and of building the future, we must act," said Blomart. "We only exist if we act."

"We might perhaps undertake sabotage," said Leclerc.

"We require actions that can be clearly seen," said Blomart. "Munition trains exploding, requisitioned hotels blowing up. The French must feel that they are still at war. Do you, yes or no, wish to create a resistance party? You won't keep the country in a state of insurrection by V-signs, crosses of Lorraine, and fishing rods."

"Have you considered the likelihood of frightful reprisals?" asked Parmentier.

"That's the whole point," said Blomart.

"The point?"

Scandalized, Parmentier looked at Blomart. "I know," thought Blomart. Who knew better than he? He was here, with a glass of brandy in his hand, and through his words he was disposing of blood that did not feed his own heart. But it was not a personal matter.

"I'm counting on those reprisals," he said. "French blood must be shed, so that the policy of collaboration may be impossible, so that France shall not slumber in a state of peace."

"So you would allow innocent people to be shot without a qualm?" asked Parmentier.

"I've learned from this war that there's as much guilt in sparing blood as in shedding it," said Blomart. *No political strikes. I will not drive my country into war. And here we are. Enough. Enough. That senseless prudence.* "Think of all those lives which our resistance will perhaps save."

They were silent for a long while.

"But if our attempt fails," said Parmentier, "we shall find ourselves burdened with useless crimes."

"No doubt," said Blomart. Whatever one did, one was always guilty, but those two did not know it; they feared to commit a crime. "But we must presume that we'll succeed. Whatever happens, your partisans risk prison and death. A newspaper, leaflets — these are not safe undertakings."

"It's not the same thing," said Parmentier. "Our members have accepted the risk."

"They accept it in order to achieve certain results. If we endanger their lives in a profitless manner, then we are guilty. No," continued Blomart, "we must only be concerned with the end we have to achieve and do everything necessary to attain it."

"Do you consider that all means are good?" asked Leclerc doubtfully.

"On the contrary: all means are bad," said Blomart.

Once he had also dreamed of ensuring his actions by fine resounding reasons; but it would have been too easy. He had to act without an insurance. It was an impossible undertaking to value human lives, to compare the weight of a tear with the weight of a drop of blood; but he no longer set a value, every coin was current, even this one; the blood of others. The price would never be too high.

"Well, we have the money," he said to his friends.

"You're champion," said Laurent.

"At last we can do some real work," said Berthier.

They were all laughing, but there was anguish on some faces.

"If only we knew whom we're going to work for," said Lenfant. "If it's to bring Raynaud and Daladier back . . ."

"No," said Blomart. "You know perfectly well: we're working to become strong, so that we'll give orders tomorrow."

"Shall we be strong enough?" asked Lenfant.

"That's right," said Berthier. "How are we to be sure that we are not fighting for bourgeois capitalism, for Anglo-Saxon imperialism, for the triumphs of reactionary forces?"

He hesitated. That was right. It was impossible to know in advance what one was actually doing. He hesitated, but he answered in a steady voice: "Anything is better than Fascism." And he said to himself: "At least, it is possible to know what one wants; one must act for what one wants. The rest is no concern of ours."

He was willing it. He was going forward, knowing what he wanted. *Not knowing what he was actually doing.* Treading underfoot the old snares of prudence, thrown blindly toward the future, and refusing to doubt; *perhaps everything has been useless; perhaps I have killed you in vain.*

🌠 10 🌠

Hélène closed her book again; she could not go on reading any longer. She looked up at the black sky over the Pantheon. The weather was stormy, but it was not clouds that veiled the sun; the air was thick with a film of fine black ash. It was said that the oil dumps were burning all around Paris. There were rumblings on the horizon and little white puffs spiraled out against the dark background of the sky. "They" were coming nearer; a leaden threat was hanging over the city; soon the last defenses would give way, "they" would be parading through the streets. All around Hélène, the terrace of the Café Mahieu was deserted. The rue Soufflot was deserted; not a taxi. There was a one-way stream of cars speeding along the boulevard Saint-Michel towards the Orléans Gate. The boulevard had become a highroad cutting across the town from one end to the other, a highroad of escape through which life was pouring out. And yet there was a man in blue overalls, perched on a ladder, carefully cleaning the globe of a street lamp.

"They will be here tomorrow." Hélène peered into the distance with some anxiety. The car was due to arrive at ten o'clock. She did not want to be trapped in this beleaguered city. The streets would be wrapped in silence, spellbound between blind housefronts; each inhabitant would be more alone than a flood victim, forlorn in an inundated countryside. It was hard to believe that the houses would remain solidly ensconced in the earth, that the chestnut trees would throw the same shadows in the Luxembourg Gardens.

[231]

Among this impetuous flow of motor-cars the farm carts of the refugees slowly rolled past, transporting whole villages. Huge wagons, drawn by four or five horses, they were laden with hay covered with tarpaulins; mattresses and bicycles were piled up front and back, and in the middle, as motionless as waxwork figures, the family was grouped under the shade of a big umbrella. It was like a *tableau vivant* staged for a ceremonial procession. Tears rose in Hélène's eyes. "I, too, am going into exile."

She looked round about her. All her past was here, among these islands of stone. She had played hopscotch with Yvonne on that sidewalk, under the kindly eye of God. Paul had kissed her near that street lamp. At the end of this street Jean had said: "I love you." She dried her eyes. God did not exist, and she did not love Paul. Jean did not love her. All promises were false. The future was ebbing, drop by drop, out of the town, and the past was being liquidated; this lifeless shell did not deserve a single regret, it was already crumbling into dust; there was no longer any past, there was no such thing as being exiled. The whole world was nothing but an exile without hope of a return.

The lavatory attendant came out of the café carrying her heavy suitcase. At the same time M. Tellier's car drew up alongside the curb, and Denise's head appeared. "Have you heard?" she shouted. "We've just been told that the Russians and the English have landed at Hamburg!" She seized hold of Hélène's suitcase. There was an accumulation of suitcases inside and on top of the car; a bicycle was lashed in front of the headlights. Hélène sat in the back next to Denise, and the car drove off. The proprietor of the big grocery store was drawing the openwork iron shutters which protected his cans of preserved fruits. All the shops were closed.

"Aren't your parents leaving?" asked Denise.

"They're afraid that the shop will be looted," said Hélène. She added in a louder tone: "It's awfully kind of your father to take me."

"It's only natural," said M. Tellier. "The house is a big one and there's room for everyone in it."

The car passed through the Orléans Gate and turned off the main road. The sky was blue over the shut-up villas and it was just like going off for the week-end. "It's finished," thought Hélène, "forever." Forever must she remain behind in the shadow of the chestnut trees, in the aroma of honey and cocoa, forever in the sunken city; herself sunk with the ghost of her lost love. The woman who leaned out of the window of the car was only one refugee among millions of others.

On the road were to be seen farm carts like those that had just now been rolling along the boulevard; but they had been dismantled; the peasants were walking on foot beside the horses, and the supply of hay was half used up; these people had come from afar and must already have been trudging for some days. From time to time a bottleneck held up the traffic, and the car had to stop behind a long queue of vehicles that dragged slowly along in the dust like a disarticulated caterpillar.

"It will be impossible to move tomorrow," said M. Tellier. He turned his head. "Are you hungry?"

"We could stop at the next village," said Denise.

"Let's stop."

Standing outside their houses, gay with roses and irises, the peasants were looking on. "What about it? Is Paris taken? Is it all over?"

"Paris is not France," said M. Tellier.

They went into a café. Denise unpacked sandwiches, brioches, and fruit and ordered coffee. Seated beside the radio set was a woman listening to the communiqué; tears rose in Hélène's eyes, tears that she did not recognize. She had learned the taste of despair and anger in her own tears during the past months; now they were tepid and barely salt, they rolled painlessly down her cheeks.

A car covered with branches, as if for a village festival, had stopped in front of the door; it had come from Évreux; Évreux was burning, Louviers was burning, Rouen was burning. Throughout the afternoon they passed cars on the roads coming down from Normandy, filled to overflowing with mattresses and camouflaged with branches, which gave them a festive appearance. "Something is happening," thought Hélène. "Not to me, I have no existence. Something is happening to the world." There was no going back, no retreat. In the anxious and reproachful eyes of those who watched the procession of vehicles, on the dusty faces of the fugitives, among the blankets, the crockery, and the chairs piled high on the trucks, was written defeat.

Night fell. The carts were halted beside the hedgegrows, the horses were unharnessed; the people lit fires to make soup and set about preparing a camp for the night. Hélène thought of the pioneers of the wild West films. It seemed as unfamiliar as if she had been in a foreign country, as if time had become a vast unexplored space.

"We'll stop for a moment in Laval to telephone Mother that we're arriving," said M. Tellier.

A gigantic rabble had invaded the quiet little town during the course of the day. The pavements were packed with cars, all open spaces were black with refugees; the richest were sprawling on chairs beside the café tables, which entirely overflowed into the public squares; others lay on the bare ground.

"Stay in the car. I'm going up to the post office with Hélène," said Denise.

She took Hélène's arm and, as soon as they were alone, her expression changed. "We're going to be cut off from everything," she said. "I shall have no more news of Marcel. How shall I live without knowing anything?"

Hélène said nothing. There was nothing to say. "Without knowing." There was nothing to know. Only her tired body, her beating heart, a heart that does not beat for anyone, an anonymous heart. "History unfolds, and I have no future personal history. No more life. No more love."

"It was lucky for Blomart that he was wounded," said Denise. "He'll probably be evacuated south."

"Probably," said Hélène. Mme Blomart had told her of his wound.

They went up to the counter. A harassed crowd was jostling each other amidst the reek of dust and sweat. Tiny and poorly clad, a woman in black raised an imploring face to the telephonist. "Please, madame, will you telephone for me?" The telephonist shrugged her shoulders. "Please, madame!" the woman repeated.

Hélène touched her shoulder. "To whom do you want to telephone?"

"To the village, so that they can tell my husband."

"What village?"

"It's Rougier," said the woman.

"Wait, I'll look it up for you," said Hélène. She thumbed the directory. "Rougier, Maine-et-Loire. Whom do you want to speak to?"

"I don't know," said the woman.

There were ten subscribers in Rougier. "To Boussade?"

"Eh, no. He's left the village."

"Fillonne?"

"Gracious, no! He's in the fields at this time of day!"

"To Mercier?"

"Oh, no!" said the woman looking scared.

She was hopelessly lost in this too vast world. "We are all lost. Shall I ever find myself again?" thought Hélène. "What's the use of it? What's the use of my nails, which catch at things, of my heart, which wants not to want any more and yet which still wants in spite of itself?" Not to want anything. Not to know anything. Just to be there, quite simply, absorbed in listening to the quiet ripple of life, which flows on without going anywhere.

They went back toward the car. M. Tellier was rolling a cigarette as he leaned against the hood.

"The Russians haven't mobilized," he said. "And the Italians have just declared war on us."

Trucks filled with women, children, bedding, and china passed through the village every day. They were coming from Alençon, from Laigle. One evening a driver shouted: "They're at Le Mans." The inhabitants of the house looked at each other — Denise's parents, her grandmother, an aunt, two sisters-in-law. M. Tellier's car was too small to take the whole family away. And no one cared to look like those wan refugees, who paused at dusk to beg a roof for the night.

"We must set an example to the population," said Mme Tellier. "We will stay here."

Next day, at break of dawn, the villagers fled in light trucks, in carts, and on bicycles. Those who could not leave closed their shops and their houses and ran and hid in the depths of the fields. The guns thundered in the distance and the dull sound of an explosion could be heard from time to time: the oil dumps at Angers were blowing up.

"We are going to put up the tent at the bottom of the big field," said Mme Tellier.

"What's the use?" said Denise. She was in the garden with Hélène; she was watching the trucks from Laval pass along the sunlit road. "Thirty kilometers. Barely a few hours. The armistice is being signed. We'll stay quiet. We shan't fight."

"All the same, it's wiser not to show oneself," said the Dutchman who was accommodated with his wife and his mother-in-law in the summer-house.

Mme Tellier went off, her arms laden with blankets; the Dutchman followed after, carrying a basket full of provisions. Denise leaned over the gate.

"I'm sure Marcel is a prisoner," she said in a flat voice. "They were surprised from the rear."

"Perhaps they got orders to retreat in time," said Hélène.

Denise bit her lip. "I shan't see him again for years."

A truck came into sight. A military truck, laden with singing French soldiers. Another truck passed. And another. The men laughed as they waved their hands.

"They are singing!" said Denise.

"The war is over and they've saved their skins," said Hélène.

A car drew up and out of it got four officers. They were just like the officers at Pecquigny, elegant, care-free, with two liquid holes in the middle of their faces. "Is this the right road to Cholet?" asked a young lieu-tenant.

"Yes," said Denise.

"What we ought to know," said the colonel perplexedly, "is whether or not the Germans are at Angers." He looked decisively at Denise. "Where is the post office?"

"I'll take you there," said Denise. She opened the gate. Two soldiers passed by, without caps or rifles, leaning on sticks: prisoners who had escaped from German hands. No one else was in the streets. The picked guard that had marched down the main street on the previous days, so proudly shouldering their rifles, had melted into thin air.

Inside the post office the telephone was ringing. The door was locked.

"Where are the responsible officials?" asked the colonel angrily.

"Somewhere in the fields," said Denise.

"It's crazy!" said the colonel. He beckoned to a lieutenant. "Break this door in for me."

The lieutenant gave the door a violent blow with his shoulder.

"Won't work," he said, "we need an ax."

"I'll go and get one," said Denise.

Now guns and tanks were passing through the village.

"Will they soon be here?" asked Hélène.

"In an hour's time. But don't be frightened. Nothing will happen." The lieutenant smiled self-importantly. "We are going on to the Loire, to try to fight a delaying action."

"Here's the ax," said Denise. The lieutenant smashed the lock. The colonel went in and came out again after a moment.

"Let's go," he said. They made their way to the car.

"Go back to your houses," said the lieutenant.

"We're going back," said Denise. She looked at the car, already speeding on its way toward the Loire. The tanks continued to pass by, their guns turned toward the south, their backs to the enemy.

"Denise!" called Mme Tellier. "Come here at once, both of you."

"I'm staying in the house," said Denise. "I want to watch."

"Your father doesn't want anyone to look out of the window; that's how accidents happen," said Mme Tellier in some agitation. She was wearing her pearls round her neck and all her rings on her fingers; unusual excrescences burgeoned on her stomach and her bosom.

"But I shan't open the shutters." Denise laughed. "Do you think your jewels are safe?"

"They wouldn't dare to take them off my person," said Mme Tellier.

Hélène went up to Denise's room; they went to the window and pushed open the venetian blind a little way. Another tank passed beneath the window. Then the road was deserted. A pang shot through Hélène's heart. Now the village lay abandoned between France and Germany, without a master, without a law, without protection. All the shutters were closed; nothing stirred in the white, sunlit houses. It was like being outside the world, floating suspended in the heart of a mysterious delirium that had neither beginning nor end.

"Ah!" said Denise. She clutched Hélène's hand. Something had exploded at the corner of the street, and the restaurant windows burst into fragments. Then there was a great silence and suddenly a guttural voice rapped out strange words. They appeared. They were all tall and fair, with rosy faces; they marched gravely without looking about them, with steel-heavy tread. Victors. "We are defeated — Who, us?" There were tears in Denise's eyes. "And I?" thought Hélène.

[239]

"France is defeated. Germany is victorious. And I, where am I? There is no place left for me!" With dry eyes she watched the men, the horses, the tanks, the strange guns pass by; she was watching the march of History, which was not her own personal history, which did not belong to anyone.

The Dutchman planted himself firmly in front of the three women who were sitting on the edge of the pavement; he was swinging an empty gasoline can in his hand.

"There was no gas," he said.

The mother-in-law shrugged her shoulders. "Of course."

People were saying that the arrival of a gas truck had been announced for the past week. No one believed in it any longer.

The Dutchman put down the can. "I'd like to eat."

"Me too, I'm hungry — hungry," said the young woman in a childish voice.

"They won't get anything to eat as easily as that," thought Hélène. The shops of Le Mans were more barren than a field after a swarm of locusts. There was not a piece of bread nor any fruit to be had; there was not a place to be had in the restaurants, now teeming with green and gray soldiers. Hélène was no longer hungry; she had no more physical needs; she could remain sitting on these stones indefinitely, in the narrow band of shadow at which the sun was nibbling. All along the road, people were walking from the Prefecture to the main square, where the Kommandantur was installed, carrying empty tins and watering-cans; from time to time they put their receptacles on the ground, to sit down for a short while before starting off again; a little later they were to be seen returning in the opposite di-

rection, sent back from the Kommandantur to the Prefecture, with empty tins and watering-cans in their
hands. Tirelessly. Like Sisyphus, like the Danaïdes. In
the murderous heat of these hells life went round and
round more quickly, like a demented circus. Thousands
of cars stagnated in the square, surrounded by women
and sad-eyed children, who were seated in their shade,
on bundles, on mattresses, on the ground. Other gray
and shining cars, armored cars, sped down the main
street; motorcycles spluttered round the square. The
cafés disgorged even into the middle of the street thousands of young soldiers tightly buttoned into new uniforms; columns of soldiers with heavy tread made their
way through the crowd reduced to pulp by sun and by
hunger. A loudspeaker broadcast military music. And
the fiery voice, the lifeless light, the dense air had been
in existence since the dawn of time, throughout eternity. Hélène had become eternal; the blood had dried
up in her veins; she was here, with no memories, with
no desires, forever.

"Sit down," said the mother-in-law. "Don't stay like
that with your arms hanging."

The Dutchman smiled. He was rosy and fair, his
teeth protruded over his bottom lip in a fixed smile, like
that of a child or of a corpse.

"Mind the sun," said the young woman. Her white
hat had become soiled since yesterday and her frock
was crumpled. She handed her husband a big paper
cornet. "Put that on your head."

He did so obediently and, still smiling, sat down on
the running-board of the car.

"It's really hot," he said.

The mother-in-law looked at him witheringly. "To
think that the day before yesterday, at Angers, you
could have had twenty-five liters."

"The line was so long," he said in apologetic tones. "I thought the Germans would supply us on the way."

When she had accepted a place in the car, Hélène had also thought that the tank was full. In any case, she did not regret having left; in spite of Denise's kindness, she felt herself unwanted in the overcrowded house.

"There are still people in front of the Prefecture," she said.

"Someone ought to go and see what's up," said the mother-in-law.

"It'll be the same as this morning," said the Dutchman.

"Let's go and see. We can't spend another night in the car," said his wife.

She stood up on her slender Louis XV heels. Hélène followed them. Two to three hundred people were pressing against the gates, clutching empty receptacles. Round the base of a statue of a revolutionary wearing a large befeathered hat, women were heating the contents of saucepans; others slept, stretched out on mattresses.

"There are too many people," said the Dutchman.

"Have a little patience, darling," said the woman. She pressed a small lace handkerchief against her nose. "It doesn't smell very nice."

Hélène turned toward a woman. "What exactly are they waiting for?"

"For a serial number. To be given a gas coupon."

"And once they've got the coupon, will they get gas?"

"When the gas comes."

The gate opened and there was a rush. Hélène found herself carried to the end of a long corridor. A man was giving people little squares of paper, and these they carried jealously away. Hélène seized hers and ran toward the Dutchman, who had stayed at the back.

"I've got a number!"

"They say there's a garage at the end of the town that is supplying gas, five liters at a time," said the mother-in-law.

"Yes." The Dutchman was looking stupidly at the piece of cardboard now in the palm of his hand.

"Well, go and see," said the mother-in-law, giving him a shove on the shoulder.

"I'm going for a stroll," said Hélène.

She made her way toward the station. Failing the five liters of gas, a means must be found of getting out of that burning, looted town. The Dutch family could go hang! Perhaps she would manage to get herself on a train. Yonder, at the end of the line, was a clean bed, gingerbread, and hot tea. She went into the ticket office.

"When will there be a train for Paris?"

"We're not accepting any travelers for Paris. Only as far as Chartres," said the clerk.

Hélène hesitated. An inert crowd, lying on the ground among their bundles, were waiting for heaven knows what. Anything was better than that stupid resignation.

"Have you any papers to prove that you live in Chartres?"

Hélène turned on her heel.

"Why do they tell us to go home, if they won't help us to move?" asked a woman who was holding a child on her knees.

"They say there's a famine in Paris," said a man.

"And here?" said the woman. "They'd rather we died on our feet."

Hélène looked at her. It seemed to her that she suddenly felt the weight of the child on her knees and the appeal of its reproachful eyes. With astonishment she heard within her a voice from the past: "The others

[243]

exist. You must be blind not to see them." She paused in front of the woman.

"Are you from Paris?"

"I come from Saint-Denis," said the woman.

"I'm with some people who have a car," said Hélène. "They may find some gas and be able to start off again. Would you like them to take you?"

"They — take me?" said the woman without clearly understanding the words.

"Come with me," said Hélène. "I don't promise anything, but there's a chance."

The woman followed her. A barn to sleep in. The fresh country air. Milk. Eggs. Tomorrow, Paris. "Why I rather than she?" thought Hélène. Hunger and the sun made her head swim, but she had no desire for food or shade. It was queer. She used to want so many things.

The two women were sitting on the running-board of the car, both of them red-haired and dressed in light colors.

"Maurice hasn't come back," said the mother. "Poor boy."

"The nasty Germans," said the daughter. "It's all their fault."

Hélène went back to the woman. "You must wait a little." She leaned against a wall. It was not even a period of waiting; there was nothing to wait for. I am no longer alone; only a little stagnant puddle in which is reflected the inconstant face of the world.

"They've given me ten liters," said the Dutchman.

The two women promptly leaped to their feet.

"Ah," said the younger. "We'll be able to get out of this place."

"I hear that it is easier to get food a little farther on," said the Dutchman. He lifted up the hood. Hélène went up to them.

"Please, would you mind if I gave my place to the young woman who is over there with her child? I can manage, if only you would be kind enough to take my suitcase with you."

"That young woman?" said the Dutchman vaguely. The woman was poor and her hair was unkempt; he looked at her without understanding.

"Yes, that child of hers will drop dead if you don't take it away," said Hélène threateningly.

"But what about you?" said the mother-in-law. "It's impossible to take five people in this car."

"I know," said Hélène. "I told you I'd manage."

"Then she'd better get in," said the Dutchman.

The woman hesitated.

"Get in," said Hélène.

She got in next to the mother-in-law, who looked her up and down grudgingly.

"Aren't you coming?" said the woman.

"No," said Hélène. She smiled at the Dutchman. "Good-by. Thanks."

She made off in the direction of the main square. Behind her she heard the door bang and the car start up. It fled through the empty streets, it would be speeding toward warm shadows scented with new-mown hay. Hélène remained alone in that blazing dust. "Might as well be here as elsewhere," she thought with indifference.

In the square German soldiers were bustling round a truck; the refugees looked at them with faces filled with horror and despair. The victors. The masters. They were young and often handsome; their spotless uniforms showed off their muscular necks; they bent condescendingly over the homeless, heartless flock. One of them held out his hand to a woman who heaved herself into the vehicle.

"Where are they going?" asked Hélène.

"To Paris," said an old woman. "They take people when there's room."

In a few moments the truck was filled with women and children.

"Will there be any others?"

"They don't know. We must wait."

Hélène sat on the ground between the old woman and a dark shock-headed girl.

"Well, I'm going to wait," she said. She leaned her head on her knees and closed her eyes.

When she awoke, the dark girl beside her was biting into a hunk of bread. It was less hot.

"You seem to have slept well," said the girl.

"I was sleepy," said Hélène.

"Haven't you got anything to eat?"

"No, I didn't find a thing."

"Here," she said mysteriously. She held out a slice of bread to her.

"Oh, thank you," said Hélène. She bit hungrily into the bread. It was solid in texture and too salt, and the process of eating was almost painful.

"Look out," said the dark girl. A truck came onto the square. "Come, Granny," she said, taking the old woman's arm. She motioned to Hélène. "Come too." They ran forward.

Nur zwei," said the German, lifting two fingers. He lugged the old woman into the vehicle. The girl clambered over the side of the truck and dragged Hélène up by the hand.

"She's my sister," she said to the soldier. "Get in, do get in." Hélène hung onto the truck. The soldier laughed and held out his hand to her.

Hélène sat right at the back on an empty gas tin. The truck was crammed with people. A thick canvas

covered the whole of the vehicle. At the first jolts, stifled
by the smell of gas and by the heat, Hélène felt her
stomach turn. She looked round inside the truck. It was
impossible to move. She shuddered. Sweat beaded her
forehead. Another woman, at the other end of the vehicle, was calmly vomiting. "Never mind," thought
Hélène. She drew her feet away as far as possible, bent
over, and was sick between the gas tins. She wiped
her mouth and her face. She felt relieved; at her feet
was a kind of white splodge, but no one paid attention to it. "Just as if we couldn't even be ashamed of
our bodies," she thought, "as if even my body was no
longer me."

The truck, bursting with gasoline, was speeding without obstructions along flat roads, pitted here and there
by a shell-hole. As it went along, overturned or burnt-
out cars, and graves with crosses at their heads, could
be seen by the wayside. The endless procession still
went on: in hay-wains, on bicycles, and some on foot.
They passed through a town; bombs had burst open
roofs, two blocks of houses had gone up in flames, and
in front of the scorched bare walls were heaps of
twisted metal. Exodus, misery, and death. And all the
time in their fine steel-gray cars strong young men
passed by, singing.

"Heil!" shouted one of them, cheerfully waving his
hand. He was wearing field-gray, like his comrades,
and they all wore red roses over their hearts.

The truck stopped at the gates of Paris. Hélène
jumped down; she could scarcely stand. In a looking-
glass she caught a glimpse of her face begrimed with
dust and dirt. The avenue de la Grande-Armée was deserted. All the shops were shut. For a moment she remained motionless in the midst of the silence, then
she began to walk toward the Étoile. Everything was

still there: the houses, the shops, the trees. But every human being had been annihilated; there was no one to open the closed shops, no one to walk in the streets, to rebuild a tomorrow, to remember the past. She alone survived by a miracle, intact, and absurd in the center of this lifeless world. But she no longer possessed either body or soul. Only that voice which said: "I am no longer myself."

Denise had put the writing-pad on her knees and was writing in her small, copious hand.

"I've finished," she said. "We can go when you like."

Hélène raised herself on her elbow. The road was still white with heat. Five o'clock. Three o'clock French time. The air was heavy and the Seine flowed slowly under the motionless sky.

"You'd never think it was Sunday," said Hélène. She picked up her bicycle, which lay against the hedgerow. No more cars, no more tandems, no more lovers, no more laughter: the countryside was deserted. Here and there men with bronzed torsos were sitting in the shade; they could be identified by their shaven napes. They were the only people alive on this French Sunday; a Sunday in exile. Out in midstream, in the dreary sparkle of the sun, one of them was all alone in a boat, playing an accordion. Hélène's feet refused to move; time and space had exploded around her; she had suddenly been projected along a mysterious dimension, into the heart of an epoch and of a world in which she had no ties; lost under a strange sky, she was watching a story unfold from which her presence was excluded. "Just as if I were not there. As if I were only here for the purpose of saying: 'I am not there.'" She bent over her handle bars. All the villas were shut up; the sign-boards of the inns were beginning to fade and flake. Sometimes behind an open gateway gray cars were to be seen on the gravel, and raucous voices to be heard echoing in the garden.

"Hélène."

Hélène accelerated. At times she was astonished to find herself plunged in this extraordinary adventure; but at others she was frightened; she had lost the key of the way that led back. "There will never again be anything else!"

"Do you think your German can do anything for Marcel?" said Denise.

"I'll speak to him at dinner," said Hélène. "He has a lot of connections. In any case, when I'm in Berlin I'll see that I get to know useful people."

"Something should be done at once," said Denise. "Three quarters of the camps have been evacuated to Germany." She looked at Hélène. "Are you really going?"

"Why not?" said Hélène; she stiffened; she knew what Denise was thinking, she knew what Jean would think. She stared defiantly at the far horizon. "You were right, we did not have anything in common."

"Don't you mind working with them?"

"What difference does it make," said Hélène.

"That's not the point," said Denise, with a shade of blame in her voice. "I wouldn't do so, for my own sake."

"My own sake." Hélène looked at her hand on the handlebars. "I, Hélène. . . ." On the roads people had lost their cars, their cupboards, their dogs, their children; she had lost herself.

"In short, you have accepted the position?"

"Oh, I'm not converted to Fascism," said Hélène.

"So what? It exists. And after it something else will come." She shrugged her shoulders. "So what can it matter?"

"But what matters for us is the time in which we live."

"It matters if we make it matter," said Hélène. She remembered Jean used to say: "It is we who decide." But that's just the point. Why should I decide if it's my personal fate that matters, or that of France, or of this century in which I happen to have been thrown? She gathered speed down the long, paved avenue, under the fixed and single sun, fleeting as a meteor cleaving the indifferent sky.

They passed through the gates of Paris.

"I'm going round to take my letter to the Red Cross," said Denise.

"I'll go with you," said Hélène.

The sky had clouded over. They were steeped in a damp heat. About ten young women with lifeless eyes shifted from foot to foot in front of the door of the committee rooms. Gray cars were parked all along the sidewalks. At the far end of the avenue the Opéra with its stormy green dome seemed like a monumental totem, witness of a bygone age.

The clerk looked at the envelope and pushed it back at Denise. "We're not accepting any more letters for Baccarat," she said. "The camp has been moved toward Germany."

"Baccarat too!" said Denise.

"Yes, madame, Baccarat too," said the clerk somewhat impatiently. Hélène seized Denise's arm and dragged her toward the exit. Denise had turned so pale that she seemed about to faint.

"They often get their information all wrong," said Hélène.

"In Germany!" said Denise.

A lump rose in Hélène's throat; on Denise's face, in the gray heat of a Sunday evening, she recognized the hated shadow of sorrow.

"People come back even from Germany," she said. "We'll find a way." She took a deep breath. Thank heaven it was not her sorrow; as far as she was concerned, she had finished: no more love, no more life, no more sorrow.

"Just imagine their departure!" said Denise. Her voice broke.

"I'm sure that Marcel contrives not to be unhappy."

"Perhaps *he* does," said Denise. She dropped Hélène's arm. "Excuse me. I must be by myself."

"I understand," said Hélène. She pressed Denise's hand. "I'll telephone you tomorrow morning to tell you Bergmann's answer."

"Thanks, do telephone," said Denise.

Hélène smiled at her and mounted her bicycle. To suffer for someone else: what humbug! They don't care a damn, they make a nice little personal meal out of their own hearts. It's finished; it's quite finished. She crossed the boulevard Saint-Germain. Armored trucks rattled noisily by, followed by armored cars from which emerged coal-black soldiers, wearing large berets that floated in the wind. With all their marveling youth they hailed their victory. Victory. Defeat. He lost his war. She held the handlebars tighter. There is neither victory nor defeat; there is neither thine nor mine; it is just a moment in History.

Hélène stopped in front of the confectionary shop, propped up her bicycle and went upstairs to her room. She put on the pretty printed frock of which she had herself designed the material. In the cupboard a brand-new light-colored coat swung from a coat-hanger beside a handsome sports suit. The German client paid well.

"Good evening, mother: good evening, father."

"Good evening," said Mme Bertrand coldly. M. Bertrand did not raise his eyes from his newspaper. They were attracted by the splendor of the position that was offered their daughter, but they blamed her for compromising herself with the invader. Hélène opened the shop door and the long metal bell-tongues tinkled gaily, as they used to when she went to let in Paul or Jean; she would have liked to tear them out.

The bicycle sped along the boulevard Saint-Michael. It was dirty and rusty; the layers of blue and green paint were coming through the black varnish, but it was still a good machine. "I'll take it out there," thought Hélène. She put on the brake; at the end of the boulevard a mob was crowding in front of a wooden billboard. A yellow placard had been stuck on the boards: "Robert Jardillet, of Lorient, engineer, was condemned to death for an act of sabotage. He was shot this morning." The people stood motionless and silent in front of the piece of paper. Shot. Those bold letters displayed on the yellow background exercised a fascination. Shot. Hélène briskly moved away. "Well, doubtless one has to go through that stage," she thought. She began to pedal furiously. "All that is unimportant. Nothing is important. Nothing!"

She opened the door of the restaurant; among the copper bowls and the strings of onions a profusion of sausage and hams hung from the great beams of the ceiling; each side of the corridor opened up on recesses in which tables had been placed. Herr Bergmann rose, slightly clicked his heels, and bent to kiss Hélène's hand.

"As punctual as a man," he said smiling.

[252]

He wore a smart, dark-colored suit, with a stiff collar; under the auburn hair his face was affable and slightly solemn. He made a sign; the maître d'hôtel, wearing a peasant's smock, signaled in his turn to a waiter.

"Our special dish," he said as the waiter placed on the table a tray covered with *pâtés,* smoked ham, sausage, and potted meat.

"I think one eats fairly well here," said Herr Bergmann.

"So it seems," said Hélène. She helped herself generously. At the next table a large red-faced woman in a satin blouse was devouring a porterhouse steak; the clientele was chiefly made up of German officers dining together or in the company of elegant young women; some of the recesses were shut off by thick red curtains.

"I had a long talk with Madame Grandjouan," said Herr Bergmann. "We ended up by coming to an agreement; moreover, you are not bound by any contract."

"No, but I did all my apprenticeship with her. It's not very gracious to leave her now."

"She ought to have made you a partner," said Herr Bergmann. "To treat you like an ordinary employee was exploitation."

"Once she made me an offer to go and manage a branch in America," said Hélène. "It was I who refused to go."

"Why did you refuse?"

"Oh, then — I wanted to stay in Paris."

"You will not regret it," said Herr Bergmann. "There's no future for you in France. Soon Lyon will no longer exist. We are the masters of the silk trade."

He spoke with a self-satisfied assurance that suddenly connected him to the officers at the neighboring table.

"Wait a little," said Hélène with a light laugh. "Everything isn't over yet."

"No, everything is beginning," said Herr Bergmann. He poured out a little sweet Bordeaux for Hélène. "France and Germany are made to agree. Look at us two, how profitable our collaboration will be. I produce the materials and you bring me what cannot be found in my country — French taste," he ended gallantly.

"Yes," said Hélène.

"The papers are in order," continued Herr Bergmann. "I've reserved our seats for Monday."

"Monday . . ." said Hélène.

"I should have liked to stay longer." He hesitated. "Although it is sad to find Paris again as it is at present. It is no longer a capital. It's a garrison town."

"Had you often been to Paris?"

"I lived near the Parc Monceau for a year," said Herr Bergmann. "In the morning I went for a walk in the gardens and I watched the little children playing."

"I prefer the Luxembourg," said Hélène.

"And also the Luxembourg," he said, "the Latin Quarter, the quays by the Seine. I ate onion soup at Les Halles at five o'clock in the morning with French friends." He sighed. "That restaurant was so interesting; full of typically French faces. Now, at Montmartre, at Montparnasse, you hear only German spoken." He filled Hélène's glass with dry champagne. "I must come back later on."

"The past will never come back again," said Hélène.

"No, but there will be something else. Are you not curious to see the New Europe?"

"Yes, I am curious," said Hélène. "I like novelty." She smiled at him. The past would not come back, it was quite over; she was free. No more dinners at the Port Salut, no more laughter in the snow, no more

[254]

tears on warm evenings scented with violets. Only one future for the whole world: Germans, French, men and women; all were equal. No one would ever again have a distinctive face, an expression like no one else's. This man was a man with head, heart, and hands, just as much as Jean.

"I must ask you a favor," said Hélène.

"With great pleasure."

"Would it be possible to get a prisoner repatriated who has just left for Germany? He's the husband of my best friend."

"I have friends in the Embassy," said Herr Bergmann. "Give me the name and address and I will see if I can do something." He hesitated. "Although I don't think it will do much good."

Hélène's heart was sad. How long would Marcel stay over there? Four years? Five years?

"This question of prisoners is a painful one," said Herr Bergmann. "Friendship between us would be easier if we could give them back to you."

He lifted a large piece of steak to his mouth; he ate quickly. Hélène looked with sudden stupor at his manicured hands, at the big signet ring that ornamented his white fingers. *We* cannot give them back to *you*. He lied; she lied to herself; both of them knew it, not for a minute had they shared the same history.

"You could if you would," she said.

"Not all the French are reliable friends," he said in courteous tones. "You could hardly expect it, these things are the necessities of history."

Hélène put her fork on her plate. She was no longer hungry. She watched the bespectacled officers gorging themselves on rich French food. All this time Mme Bertrand was warming up a dish of leeks, Denise was peeling a boiled potato. Marcel had been a week without eating anything at all. And tomorrow Yvonne, the Jewess, would be out of work and soon have no home. Doubtless these were the necessities of history. But I? Why am I here?

Herr Bergmann held out the menu to her. "Cheese? Fruit?"

"Thanks. I don't want anything else."

"A liqueur?"

"No, thanks."

Herr Bergmann ordered strawberries and cream; he squashed the red berries in the cream with his spoon.

"Do you know a nice place where we could finish the evening?" he asked. "A real French joint, which is not 'for tourists,'" he added guiltily.

"I don't know anything very exciting," said Hélène; she made an effort: "I've heard of a place in the Latin Quarter where one can dance."

"Well, let's go there. I've got my car."

"What am I going to do with my bicycle?"

"Don't worry. It's quite simple. I'll ask that it should be taken back to your home. They are very obliging here."

Hélène drew her compact from her bag. Of course it is simple. Everything is simple. He was talking to the maître d'hôtel in a slow precise voice and he was taking notes out of his wallet. The maître d'hôtel bowed and smiled. I too am smiling. Smile, smile. Those who do not smile are shot. The necessities of history; but who decides for me whether I go on smiling or whether I smile no more?

She got into the car. It was still broad daylight.

"Where must we stop?"

"Stop at the Place Médicis. It's in a little street near by."

The Place Médicis was so quiet that they could hear

the murmur of voices on the terraces of the two big cafés; the boulevard was a deserted highway. But nothing had changed; the fountain, the chestnut trees, and the street lamp that the man was cleaning with such care on the morning of the 10th of June. She thought that everything would have changed, the houses, the faces, even the color of the ground. But there was only silence, the strange light of the sky, and beside Hélène a deferential and pompous man.

"It's here," she said. She opened the door. They went into a very small room draped with red and decorated with evergreen plants. The musicians seemed to be swinging in a gallery between heaven and earth. A few couples were dancing.

"You see, there aren't too many uniforms," said Hélène.

They sat down and Herr Bergmann ordered champagne. He looked about the room thoughtfully. "A pleasant place. But it lacks — what do you call it? — we would say *Stimmung*."

"It's the war," said Hélène.

"Yes, of course." Herr Bergmann nodded. "You did yourselves a lot of harm!"

"Is Berlin more cheerful?"

"You will see Berlin, it's also a fine city."

Hélène watched the couples who were dancing and her heart became heavy. The musicians played a prewar tune and something forgotten awoke in her; it was sweet and warm, and suddenly it tore her with a thousand sharp points. The last days, the last evenings. In a week, at this hour, the people all around me will be speaking an unknown tongue.

"I've never traveled," she said.

"Ah, now you are going to become a European," said Herr Bergmann.

A young woman in a black dress decorated with orange bows came up to the table holding a basket in her hands. "Chocolates? Cigarettes?"

"A box of chocolates," said Herr Bergmann.

Blood colored Hélène's cheeks; she knew those beribboned boxes; a fair young woman, the very image of this one, bought some each week from Mme Bertrand. "I sell them again for four hundred francs to the Fritzes," she would say, laughing.

"No," said Hélène.

"Allow me," said Bergmann.

"No, I don't want any," she said vehemently. She added, "I loathe chocolate."

"Cigarettes?"

"I don't smoke. Please — I don't want anything."

She looked at him resentfully: nothing except Marcel's liberty, and security for Yvonne; except the life of Robert Jardillet, engineer, who was shot this morning. The young woman had moved away. There was an icy silence.

"Will you do me the honor of accepting this dance?" said Herr Bergmann.

"Certainly," said Hélène. She rose. He took me in his arms and we danced, the flags flapped under the blue sky, he was standing on the platform, he spoke and everyone was singing. "That's mine," she thought agonizedly, "that's my past. I shall take it with me to Berlin. I shall go to Berlin with the whole of my past." Herr Bergmann held her solidly against him. He danced correctly, but laboriously. Their steps matched, but each body remained isolated. She thought: "He is holding me in his arms." She glanced in the looking-glass. "In his arms. It's really me." She could see herself. And Denise saw her, Marcel saw her, Yvonne saw her, Jean saw her. "It's me they see."

"Excuse me." She disengaged herself and walked toward the table.

"What's the matter?" asked Herr Bergmann paternally; he added, smiling: "Do I dance so badly?"

"No. I am terribly tired." She sat down and did not try to smile. She did not want to smile any more. They see me, they exist. Jean exists. She put her head in her hands. It was because I didn't want to suffer: I lied; I exist. I have never stopped existing. It is I who will leave for Berlin, with all my past; it is I whom he held in his arms. It is my life that I am actually living.

"Drink a little champagne," said Herr Bergmann solicitously.

"Thank you." She drank a prickly mouthful. "I lied to forget, to revenge myself. I chose to lie, I chose to be there, beside that man." All at once a thousand daggers stabbed her heart: "I exist and I have lost Jean forever."

"Do you feel better?"

"Yes," she said. She was once more aware of her heart's lasting sorrow; she recognized the beating of her heart and the taste of the saliva in her mouth. It is I. It is really me. Our defeat. Their victory. Our prisoners. She looked at Herr Bergmann.

"I do not think I shall be able to leave for Berlin," she said.

11

I HAVE killed you to no purpose, since your death was not necessary; I could have gone myself, or sent Jeanne or Claire; but why Jeanne? Why Claire? Why you? How dared I choose? I remember, he said: "You must act to get what you want." He said that. Ages ago. Now I can no longer say anything. Neither "He was right" nor "He was wrong." But since I cannot say anything, that voice must be silent. My life must be silent.

The voice speaks and the story unfolds. My personal history. And you — you are silent, your eyes remain closed. Soon it will be dawn. You will be silent forever and I shall speak out loud. I shall say to Laurent: "Go," or "Don't go." *I shall not speak.*

He used to speak. He knew what he wanted and he spoke as he was striding along the deserted streets, he spoke in his room, he spoke all over Paris, and on Sundays he spoke at the farms of the Morvan, at the farms of Normandy and Brittany with the peasants who had buried their weapons. The peasants listened to him, and the workmen and the bourgeois; they listened to him in England, and sometimes in the evening the radio answered him: "Poppies will grow on the graves." In the fields of Normandy and Brittany machine-guns and hand-grenades were parachuted by airplane.

"It's really going to begin."

They had rented an isolated old house in a suburb and M. Blomart was agreeable to supplying printing material. A press. An arsenal. We will go and get the weapons in a delivery van. And everything will begin.

Something will happen through me, and no longer in spite of me; because I willed it.

He started; someone knocked at the door.

I didn't recognize him at once. His head was shaved and he had a tufted beard.

"Marcel!"

"Would you believe it!" said Marcel. He was laughing.

"How do you manage to be here? Did you escape?"

"Do you think they gave me a special pass?" said Marcel. He came into my room and looked round him with satisfaction.

"Why! You've still got some of my pictures," he said. He examined them silently for a moment.

I seized him by the shoulder. "I can't believe that you're here."

"It's really me," he said.

I took a loaf of bread and some butter out of the wall cupboard. "You're probably hungry."

"I don't mind if I eat," said Marcel; he sat down. "Is it true that there's a famine in Paris?"

"Not yet." I put a saucepan full of potatoes on the fire. Marcel was here, with his big head, his stocky hands, his mysterious cannibal smile; he filled my room. I was very happy.

"We thought you were already heading for Germany."

"Oh, but that's where they wanted to send me," said Marcel.

"Did you have much trouble in getting away? Was it difficult?"

"No. I like walking," said Marcel. He spread the butter on a hunk of bread. He looked up. "Tell me. How are things going here?"

I shrugged my shoulders.

"The Germans are walking along the boulevards?"
he asked. "You sit beside them in the subway? They
ask you the way in the streets and you answer them?"

"Yes," I said. "It is so, but it may not always be so."

I began to tell him; he listened to me as he ate.

"Here you are at the head of a terrorist movement,"
he said. He began to laugh. "Certainly, one should
never despair of anybody."

"We come across the most unexpected sympathy and
help," I said. "Can you imagine that I've made it up
with my father? The nationalist bourgeoisie offers us
its hand."

"That's good," said Marcel. He was still eating. In
spite of his beard and his convict's skull, he seemed just
like his old self.

"And you, what are you going to do?" I asked. "I'm
going to give you the address of a comrade near Mont-
ceau-les-Mines who'll get you across the line."

"Must I go and get myself demobilized there?"

"If you want everything to be in order."

"Then I'll go."

"And after that? Are you going to start playing chess
again?"

"I played a lot in camp; in the end I reached the
state of playing seven games with my eyes shut."

"What was it like over there?"

"It was quiet!" Marcel took his pipe from his pocket.
"Have you got any tobacco?" I held out my pouch. He
weighed it in his hand appreciatively. "All that!"

"Didn't you get any?"

"Not often." He slowly filled his pipe. "Would you
have a job for me?"

"Do you feel you're the right type to work with us?"

"It all depends. I don't want to scribble or preach."

[262]

"And yet I can't entrust you with throwing bombs and setting fire to garages. You'd blow yourself up the first time!"

"Obviously," said Marcel regretfully.

I was hesitating. There was one thing he could do for us. "Do you really want to come in with us?"

"Are you surprised?" said Marcel. "Do you think that it's possible to go on playing chess whatever the state of affairs?"

"Political indifference wouldn't shock me in your case. You've always put your shirt on humanity."

"And I've lost," said Marcel.

There was a silence.

"I have something to suggest to you," I said.

"Go ahead."

"Well, this old place where we are going to dump the weapons and the printing press hasn't got a tenant. We would want someone who would keep right outside our activities. You're married, and that's all to the good. All that would be asked of you is to spend your days painting or sculpting."

"Where is this house?"

"At Meudon."

"Meudon," he said, as if put out. "Well, you can't have everything."

"Only, you do understand clearly that you're risking both your own skin and Denise's."

He smiled. "Denise will be only too pleased."

"Are you sure that you are not accepting just for my sake?"

"What can it matter to you?" said Marcel. He laughed. "You mustn't take into account any other interest but that of your cause."

"No," I said. Something seemed to move in the

depths of my being. And yet I thought I had muzzled that voice. *First Jacques.* . . . "I wouldn't like to use you as a means to an end."

"You don't yet seem to me to have the stamp of a leader."

"Perhaps." I was not smiling.

He looked at me seriously. "You're just as presumptuous as ever. Do you think that you can treat me as a means to an end? I do just what I like."

"As you will."

But I still felt sad. Why should it be he? To know what one wants and to do it. It seemed simple. I wanted weapons, a house to hide the weapons in, someone to look after the house. But I didn't want it to be precisely Marcel who ran that risk. *And who else? Why not Vignon rather than he?* The goal shone clearly ahead, but it did not light up the uncertain road. *All means are bad. Why should it be you?*

He brought me here. You are there, you are dying and I am looking at you. She tosses from side to side, she moans: "Ruth! Ruth!" Whom is she calling? Who is she? I no longer know. Now the story unfolds very rapidly, as if I were at the bottom of the water and only had enough breath left for a few seconds. At the bottom of the water. In the depths of despair. Delivery vans streak along the roads. There is even a German truck coming into Paris laden with heavy packing cases; the driver thinks he is carrying butter and ham; he was paid a lot of money.

In the old house at Meudon they are unloading furniture, mattresses, and bundles of linen; they are unloading the packing cases. In spite of the cold, Laurent is in his shirt sleeves; sweat has smeared blotches of dust all over his face. He goes down the stairs bent under the weight of the gunpowder, and he is laughing.

[264]

And I am already in the drawing-room, where Denise has installed her carpets and her furniture, the stove is purring, and I am showing Laurent a thin red line that worms its way across the map of Paris.

"You see: the first turning to the right, the second to the left, and we follow the boulevard."

"O.K.," he said. "I've got it."

"The plan's in your head?"

"I can draw it for you from memory."

I crumple the piece of paper and I throw it into the stove. Marcel is sitting in front of a chessboard, he is thinking. Denise passes backwards and forwards through the room.

"I'm glad to start with the Gestapo," says Laurent.

I look at his curly hair, his blue eyes, his brutal mouth; I had never examined him so closely. He does not look like Jacques, but his blood is of the same color.

"Have you emptied your pockets?"

"Never fear." He draws a false identification card from his wallet and looks at it with pleasure. "It's jolly good. Say, is there any news of Perrier?"

"No, nothing at all. He is still in secret custody. As soon as he is transferred to a camp, we'll try to get in touch with him."

"They say that Singer was found strangled in his cell," says Denise, "and the chaplain swears that he never thought of strangling himself."

"That's quite probable."

I look at the clock. Five minutes past ten, it's still too early. I stand up and go over to Marcel.

"So? The king holds his own?"

He raises his head. "My heart's not in it. I can't do two things at once."

"I'm glad you've started to paint again."

"So am I." He smiles at me. He understands that I

want to talk, to talk about something else. "I've been an idiot."

"It no longer seems absurd to you to paint?"

"No," he answers. "In camp I understood. The chaps asked me to do frescoes to decorate the reading-room. If you'd only seen their eyes goggling at them! Real admiration shakes you to your foundations. It upset all my ideas."

"I've always thought that a public was what you chiefly lacked."

"That too is presumption," says Marcel. "I wanted my picture to exist on its own, without requiring an onlooker. The truth is that it's other people who make it exist. But actually it's wildly exciting, because it's I who force them to make the picture exist." His smile is mysterious and rather cruel. "Do you understand? They're free and I come along and I make an assault on their liberty; I assault it while leaving it free. It is much more interesting than making things."

"Yes." I look at him with curiosity. "And that is why you are concerned with what happens around you?"

"Of course. I want to choose my public."

I put my hand on his shoulder. Everything was well where he was concerned. But I had never been very worried about him. I was sure that he never did anything but what he wanted. I look at Denise.

"Is the bald-headed man still hanging about?"

"I haven't seen him for three days." She smiles. "I must have been dreaming; he was not at all interested in us. There's no reason why anyone should be interested in us."

"Certainly not."

Her voice is matter-of-fact; but there are dark circles under her eyes. She has nightmares at night and during the day she watches through the bars of the garden

[266]

gate. I know she will not hesitate, that she will not betray. She will meet all demands made of her. But she did not choose to die, she only chose a certain way of living. She is frightened. And death can come, a death that would only be a stupid accident, like a rope that breaks, or the current that sucks you under. "It's all very well leaving people free." Where is her liberty?

"A little more hot coffee?" she asks.

"Please."

She fills our cups. Twenty past ten. Laurent drinks his coffee, smacking his wet lips. He is placid. He would willingly accept death, but he is convinced that he will not die since he is working with me. Have I really thought of everything? *I had tested the safety-catch, I had thought of everything.* I put down my cup.

"Let's go," I said.

Denise looks at me dumbfounded. "What? You're not going with Laurent?"

"Of course I am."

"But you mustn't," she says. "What would become of the organization if something happened to you?"

"I know. Generals die in their beds. I haven't the soul of a general."

"You'll have to buy one," says Denise. "You know perfectly well that no one is capable of taking your place."

"You want me to send my pals to risk their skins while I stay sipping my coffee? I could hardly bear to live with myself."

Denise looks at me reprovingly. "You're too interested in yourself."

Those words strike home. She is right. It is perhaps because I am bourgeois that I must always be thinking about myself.

"Your personal scruples do not interest us," she continues severely. "We entrusted ourselves to you as a leader who puts the cause first, above everything; you've no right to betray us."

I look at Laurent; he listens unconcernedly; everything I do is right. I look at Marcel. "What do you think about it?"

He laughs. "As you do."

"Yes," I say to Denise. "You are right. I won't do it again. But this time I'm going with Laurent; two people are required and I don't want to put off the expedition." I rise to my feet. "And I want to see once, with my own eyes, how it happens."

"I'll put the question to the committee," says Denise. "I know what their answer will be."

"O.K.," I reply.

We got out. Our bicycles glide through the night, throwing little circles of light in front of them. In my saddlebag, beneath the onions and carrots, there is a harmless-looking sort of box of sardines. To the right of us, in the dark, is a faint dappled glint and a cool scent; the Seine. Sandbags bar our path; we alight and start off again. We are in Paris. The town seems asleep; there is no one in the streets, and the houses are dark masses of stone. They alone scorn to camouflage their windows, and their buildings gleam with light: over there, at the far end of the avenue, a big luminous rectangle can be seen. I thrust my hand into my saddlebag, I grasp the sardine tin. Laurent pedals behind me, and I know that he too tightens his fingers over the hard, cold metal. On the right the rectangle of light comes nearer. On the other side of the windows are men in blue uniform with a yellow armlet; the house is filled with men from roof to basement. A car is parked in front of the door, and German officers stand beside the car. I turn round.

"Foiled this time," I say to Laurent. "Follow me."

We pass by them; they do not see our hands. We go down the avenue and we turn to the right. I slow down.

"It's a damn nuisance," says Laurent.

"They won't stay there all night. Let's go quietly for a few minutes' spin."

I feel disappointed. Yesterday afternoon there was no car in my head, there was no car, and now it is there, so simply, so naturally. In my head we go home merrily to sleep at Madeleine's. And in actual fact? They found him strangled in his cell. . . . We ride haphazardly and in silence for some time.

"Let's go back and see."

Once more we reach the top of the avenue; we don't hurry down it; the roadway is deserted. A lonely policeman paces up and down on the sidewalk; I slow down, I aim at the lighted window, and I throw the box.

"That's done it!" Behind us a sound of broken glass, an explosion, shouts, the blowing of whistles. The avenue slopes gently down, it flashes by at high speed under our wheels. Whistles are blown behind us. First turning to the right. Whistles again. Second turning to the left. We are out of breath with pedaling. When we get our breath back, silence reigns. The streets sleep, the sky sleeps. It is as if nothing ever happened anywhere.

"We got 'em," said Laurent.

"Yes, I think we did."

"It's not sporting; it's too easy."

"They're not accustomed to it yet. Just you wait."

We pedal along as if in no hurry at all. I'm warm, but I feel light as air. It's easy to do what one wants; everything is easy. We'll begin again tomorrow. Other buildings will be blown up; and trains, warehouses, factories. We are at the door of the Pension Colibri; we are drinking punch by the fireside with Madeleine. Over there they are carrying away the dead and the wounded, they are shouting orders, they are firing at us. And we are watching the punch flame up, quiet and remote as though we were in the heart of the wilds.

Next day at noon Madeleine came to get me when I left the workshop.

"Fine work," she said. "Eight dead and I don't know how many wounded. The whole district is seething."

Rejoicing, I walk in the streets of Clichy: those dead do not weigh heavily on me. There is no trace on my face, on my hands; they pass me by, they see me and they do not see: I am a harmless passer-by. In the workshop my comrades look at me without any surprise. We don't look at all like men condemned to death. It is a day like other days. In the evening I was to dine with my parents; at seven o'clock I went into the subway and I saw the red notice against the white tiles.

"Did you see it?" said my mother.

"What?"

"The notices. There was an outrage last night; twelve hostages have been shot as reprisals." She looks at me: her eyes are hollow, her cheeks flushed, she looks like an old woman. She recites in a colorless voice: "If the authors of the outrage are not discovered within three days, twelve other hostages will be shot."

"I know. It's beginning," I said.

"They're promising five hundred thousand francs' reward for any relevant information," said my father in mocking tones.

"Aren't they going to confess?" asked my mother. "Are they going to allow twelve innocent people to be shot?"

My hands are not trembling; I have not blushed. Yet

[270]

there are traces on my hands and on my face, I feel them; my mother sees them and her glance sears me.

"They can't," I say. "If they give themselves up, they will never be able to do it again."

"They owe themselves to the cause," said my father. He is very proud. He threw the bomb and he does not regret his act: he's a strong man.

"Then they shouldn't do what they've done," says my mother. "They've murdered Frenchmen."

"Do you know what is happening in Poland?" I say. "They load Jews into trains, they hermetically close the cars, and they send gas through the whole convoy. Do you want us to become accomplices to these massacres? As things are now, someone is being murdered all the time."

"Did that bomb save the life of a single Pole?" says my mother. "There are twenty-four more dead bodies — that's all."

"Those dead bodies weigh heavily," I say. "Do you think that after this the word collaboration has any sense left in it? Do you think that they can still smile at us like big brothers? Now there is blood, newly shed, between us."

"Let those who want to fight fight, and let them shed their own blood," says my mother. She runs her hand through her hair. "But those men didn't want to die, no one asked them about it." Her voice chokes. "They've no right, it's murder."

I shrug my shoulders impotently. There is a lump in my throat. Luckily my father is talking, explaining. The old smell of ink and dust floats in the gallery; formerly it choked me, and I dug my nails into the carpet under the piano; Louise's baby is dead. Dead without recall, forever. I have taken their life forever, their own life, which no one will live for them. They did not even know me and I took their life. Someone knocks. *Marcel was reading in the studio, with his feet on the table, and I knocked at the door.* Enough. Enough. I knew it. I willed it. We will begin again tomorrow.

The maid brings in the soup. I am not hungry, but I must eat. My mother does not eat; she is looking at me. She must not know. *She knows. I know she knows. She will never forgive me.*

I eat. I drink the barley coffee. And if I said to her: "Good, I'll give myself up, what would she do?" But I do not say anything and she has nothing to do but to hate me passionately. She does not listen to my father; she stares into the distance, fierce and aloof, and my father talks and I answer him.

We talk and the hand of the clock moves round. Eleven o'clock. A pang shoots through me; suddenly I'm five years old, I'm frightened and I'm cold, I would like my mother to tuck me up in my bed and give me a long kiss; I would like to stay here; I would lie down in my old room, snug in my past, and perhaps I would sleep.

"I must go."

I get up; my legs are heavy; I cannot stay; her glance drives me out; when I bend to kiss her, she tightens her lips and stiffens. "You did it. Now bear the burden." She is silent, but I hear her hard voice. She will die without forgiving me.

I plunged into the night, I walked straight ahead, criminal and resigned to my crime. I would have liked to walk until morning. At midnight I went back up into my room and I sat by the empty hearth. Alone. Shut in alone with my crime. I watched old newspapers flare up in the grate. "And if it were all useless? If I had killed them to no purpose?" At dawn I awoke beside the hearth, frozen, a bitter taste in my mouth, and

[272]

thinking: "We must begin again. Otherwise everything will have been useless. I should have killed them to no purpose."

I have no strength left. I cannot go on; tonight, on that bed, it is you who are dying. I want to stop. Can't I stop myself? I will press the revolver against my temple. And afterward? What will they do *afterward*? I shall no longer be there. But I am here, and so long as I am here, the future exists, beyond my death. I think of dying, I think of it as a living man. Decide to die, decide once more, decide alone. And afterward? Afterward?

12

Hélène laid the nail-file down on the night table
and put her left hand to soak in the basin of soapy
water. She was half-lying on the divan; she had drawn
the curtains and lit the bedside lamp; in this way she
could believe that the day would soon come to an end,
but she knew perfectly well that it was not true. Behind
the window she could guess that there was a blue sky
and the whole of an aimless Sunday in May. Downstairs the door of the confectionary shop was open and
the children were eating pink ices in cardboard cups.
Hélène removed her hand from the basin and took an
orange stick wrapped with cotton, which she dipped
into a white liquid; she began to push back the dead
skin round the moons of her nails. So many hours to
kill, every day, and for how many years? "And even if
he had loved me, would that have made any difference?" Two oysters in a shell. There would always
have been that silence and the nondescript blue lapping
of water. . . . She pulled her skirt down over her legs.
Someone was knocking at the door.

"Come in."

It was Yvonne. She held a bunch of violets in her
hands and there was a queer look about her.

"Well, it's begun!" she said. She was smiling a waver-
ing, forced smile, as if she was playing a good joke on
Hélène.

"What's begun? What's happened?"

"They're in our house. They're carting off all the
Jews."

"It can't be true?" Hélène looked at Yvonne in perplexity; her lips continued to smile, but her face was contracted.

"It's true." The smile came unstuck and her cheeks began to tremble. "What am I going to do? I don't want them to take me to Poland."

"What precisely is happening?"

"I don't exactly know. I had gone out to get a breath of air. On my way back I bought some violets from the flower-woman, who told me to escape at once."

Hélène jumped to her feet. "Don't be frightened. They won't take you away."

"But I'm frightened about my mother," said Yvonne. "If I don't go home, they'll hurt her. Perhaps they're already beating her up."

"You mustn't stay here," said Hélène. "It's the first place she'll send them to. Come on, let's get out of here."

"Hélène, I can't leave her like that, without knowing. . . ." She looked timidly at Hélène. "Would you mind going there? If I must return, you can tell me and I will go back."

"I'll go at once," said Hélène. She put on her coat. "Where can I find you again?"

"I thought of hiding myself in Saint-Étienne-du-Mont. They are raiding the whole district, but I don't think they'll look in the churches."

They went down the stairs two at a time.

"They're carting away the Jews! I can't believe it!" said Hélène. Yvonne looked at her; there was a kind of sad irony in her eyes.

"I can. I knew it would happen." She touched Hélène's shoulder. "Go quickly. I'll be in the chapel of the Virgin."

Hélène went off at a run; however hard she ran, she was aware of Yvonne's look fixed upon her and she was horrified with shame. "I didn't believe in it, I wasn't thinking of it, I was sleeping; and all night she must have kept on tossing in her bed without being able to sleep, waiting. I was varnishing my nails, and all the time they were carting off the Jews! Shut up in my room, heavy with sleep and silence and boredom; while outside it is broad daylight, and people live and suffer." She slackened her pace, she was out of breath. The streets looked as they always looked; a Sunday like all other Sundays, one of those long Sundays when nothing happens.

She went through the main door; there were two policemen under the archway, and all through the house she could hear a sound of noisy argument; doors slammed, heavy objects fell crashing to the floor; a woman shouted in a raucous voice in some unknown language. Halfway up the staircase, Hélène passed another policeman with a tiny baby in his arms; he looked awkward and ashamed. She stopped on the second-floor landing; the door was open and men's voices were audible in the little apartment. Hélène went in.

"Yvonne!"

A policeman came out of the back room. "Oh, there you are," he said.

"I'm not Yvonne," said Hélène.

"We'll see about that. Go in there."

Hélène hesitated for a moment. The forbidden room, full of darkness, nightmares, and the odor of madness, was wide open; the electric light was on and two policemen stood at the foot of the bed. Mme Kotz was buried under the covers, only her head emerged, a head with cropped hair and bulging cheeks covered with soft black hair.

"Where is Yvonne?"

"Have you got your papers?" asked the policeman.

Hélène took out her identification card and her ration cards from her bag. "What's happening?"

"Where is Yvonne?" repeated Mme Kotz. "She's not in the habit of staying out so long."

The policeman was examining the papers and making entries in a notebook.

"They're in order," he said in disappointed tones. "What are you doing here?"

"I came to see my friend."

"Don't you know where she is?"

"No."

"She's sure to be back in a moment," said Mme Kotz in a pleading voice.

"Well, you would do well to tell her not to try to get away," said the policeman. "The Germans will be coming tomorrow to get her, and if they don't find her, they're not always patient."

The two men left the room and the apartment door slammed.

"She'll kill me!" said Mme Kotz. She closed her eyes. "Ah, I'm going," she said, "I'm going. Quick give me my medicine."

Hélène seized at random one of the bottles that stood on the bedside table and filled a spoon.

"Thanks," said Mme Kotz; she inhaled deeply. "Tell her to come back quickly. They'll kill me!"

"I don't think they'll kill you," said Hélène. "Don't be frightened. I'll come back and see you this evening. I'll look after you."

"But Yvonne? Where's Yvonne?"

"I haven't the slightest idea," said Hélène. "I'll be back soon."

She closed the door again behind her. On Yvonne's

table, beside an empty vase, were scissors, pins, and spools of thread. A blue woollen frock, tacked with white, hung on the catch of the french window; it was as though she were going to be back in five minutes. She had bought some violets. And the vase would stay empty, she would not come back. On the shelf where she kept her books, there was a little plush bear which Hélène had stolen for her ten years ago; it already had the look of an orphan. Hélène took it and put it in her bag.

There were no longer any arguments to be heard on the staircase; the whole house might have been empty. Hélène went back up the street; the flower-seller was sitting on a campstool beside her green cart. Yvonne would buy no more flowers from her, she would no longer go into the bakery. What would become of her? Alone, lost, and friendless. . . . "And I had drawn the curtains, and I was doing my nails!"

She stopped dead. Four buses were parked along the curbs of the Place de la Contrescarpe; the two on the left were empty; the right-hand ones were full of children. Policemen stood guard on the bus platform. A long file of women, between other policemen, was coming out of the Rue Mouffetard. They walked in pairs and carried small bundles in their hands. The little square was as silent as a village square. Through the windows of the big buses could be seen dark, hunted little faces. All round the square, people were watching, motionless.

The women crossed the center of the square and went toward the empty buses. One of them held a little girl by the hand, a tiny little girl, with brown plaits tied with red ribbons. A policeman came up to them and said a few words that Hélène did not catch.

"No," said the woman. "No."

"Come," said the policeman, "don't make a fuss. They'll give her back to you later." He picked up the child in his arms.

"No, no," said the woman. She clung to the policeman's arms with both hands. Her voice swelled. "Leave her with me. Ruth, my little Ruth!" The child began to howl. Hélène clenched her fists and tears rose to her eyes. Can we do nothing? If we all rushed upon the man! If we tore the child from him. But no one moved. The policeman put Ruth down on the platform of one of the buses on the right. She was screaming. Inside, several children began to scream with her.

The woman was standing motionless in the middle of the square. The bus moved off heavily.

"Ruth! Ruth!" She stretched our her hands and started to run after the bus. She was wearing sandals with high, worn heels and she ran in clumsy jerks. A policeman followed her with great masculine strides, in no apparent hurry. She shouted: "Ruth!" once more, a strident, despairing cry. Then she stopped at the corner of the street and put her head in her hands. The little square was quite quiet, and she was there, in the middle of a blue Sunday, her head in her hands, and her heart breaking. The policeman put his hand on her shoulder.

"Oh, why? Why?" thought Hélène with despair. She was weeping but she remained motionless like the others and she was watching. She was there and her presence made no difference. She crossed the square. "As if I did not exist. And yet I exist. I exist in my locked room, I exist in space. I do not matter. Is it my fault?" In front of the Pantheon, some German soldiers were getting out of a touring car; they looked somewhat tired, they did not resemble those spirited victors who shouted *"Heil?"* on the roads. "I was watching the

[279]

march of History! It was my personal history. All that is happening to me."

She went into the church. The notes of the organ were echoing under the stone vaulting; the nave was full of people; they were praying, the little children beside their mothers, a family group, their hearts full of music, light, and a smell of incense. At the back of a chapel, behind the curtain of vapor that rose from the candles, the Holy Virgin smiled inconsequentially. Hélène touched Yvonne's shoulder.

"Oh, you're here already! Well?"

"I saw your mother," said Hélène; she knelt down beside Yvonne. "The policemen were very nice; they understood that she was ill and they'll leave her alone. She said you were not to worry about her."

"Did she say that?" asked Yvonne, surprised.

"Yes, she behaved very well." She opened her bag. "Here, I brought you your bear; he seemed to be missing you."

"How sweet your are!" said Yvonne.

"Now we'll look after you. I'm going to see Jean. It appears that he could get you across the line."

"You are going to see Jean?"

"Denise told me to get in touch with him in case of need."

"But don't you mind?"

"No. Why?" Hélène rose. "Stay here. I'll come back as soon as possible."

"Here," said Yvonne "Take these." She thrust the bunch of violets into Hélène's hands. "Thanks," she said in choking tones.

"Don't be silly," said Hélène.

She walked back down the church. The organ was silent. Frail in the silence a bell rang, and the officiating priest raised above his head the gold monstrance. Hélène went down the rue Soufflot, took out her bicycle, and mounted it. "I am going to see Jean." It had no meaning, it was natural. She was not afraid, she expected nothing from him. "Ruth, my little Ruth!" He could not blot out that cry, that cry which she would nevermore cease to hear. And nothing else mattered. "Ruth! Ruth!" In the streets it was the end of a Sunday, Sunday in the church, Sunday round the tea-tables and in tired hearts. "My personal history; and it is being lived without me. I sleep and sometimes I look on; and everything is happening without me."

She went up the stairs and listened for a moment, her ear glued to the door. A kind of scraping could be heard. He was there. She rang the bell.

"Good evening," she said. Her voice stopped in her throat. She had not thought he would look at her with those eyes. He was not smiling. She made an effort and was the first to smile. "Can I speak to you for five minutes?"

"Of course. Come in."

She sat down and said very quickly: "You remember my friend Yvonne? They're looking for her to send her off to Germany. Denise told me that you would be able to get her through into the free zone."

"It can be done," said Jean. "Has she any money?"

"No," said Hélène; she thought of her light-colored coat, of the beautiful coat and skirt hanging in her cupboard. "She'll get hold of some, but not at once."

"It doesn't matter. Tell her to go along at about five o'clock to Monsieur Lenfant, 12 rue d'Orsel. He'll be expecting her."

"Lenfant, 12 rue d'Orsel," Hélène repeated.

Abruptly, words rose to her lips; she had not thought of saying them, but they thrust themselves on her so forcibly that it seemed to her that she had come there on purpose to say them. "Jean, I want to work with you."

"You?"

"Haven't you any work for me?"

Jean stared at her. "Do you know what we are doing?"

"I know you help people. I know you're doing something. Give me something to do!"

"Wait," he said. "Let me think."

"You don't trust me?"

"I? Not trust you?"

"You must have been told that I had considered going to Berlin." She smiled. "But I didn't go."

"Why do you want to work with us?"

"Don't worry," she said, "it isn't because of you."

"I don't think that."

"You might." She looked round the room. Nothing had changed. My love has not changed. "No, it isn't so that I may be once more mixed up in your life."

"It's dangerous work," said Jean.

"I don't mind." Those words, too, she had not thought of beforehand, and yet they were there, all ready to be formulated. "I am no longer alive; I'm like a dead woman. Do you remember, you told me once that one could accept to risk death so that life should keep some meaning? I think you were right."

"Is it really you who are saying this?"

"Do you think I've changed?"

"No. You had to get to that point." He thought a moment. "Do you know how to drive a car?"

"I'm a good driver. My reflexes are good."

"Then you could be extremely valuable to us." There was a pause. "You're quite sure of yourself?" asked Jean. "Will you remain mum if you're arrested? You must know that if ever we're found out, we shall all be shot immediately."

"Yes," said Hélène. She hesitated. "You help people, And — is that all?"

"That isn't all."

"Ah! You too have changed."

"Not as much as that," he said. He stared sadly in front of him. "He's worried, he's alone. . . . I did not know how to love him," thought Hélène. She thought: "It isn't too late. I shall always love him." She rose.

"You'll let me know as soon as you can make use of me."

"In two or three days." He looked at her; he smiled. "I'm so glad to have seen you again," he said.

Hélène ran her tongue over her lips; she was afraid she was going to begin to cry.

"You know, I have understood," she said. "I oughtn't to have done what I did. I — I was filthy."

"Oh, I was to blame, too," said Jean.

They looked at each other for a moment, silent and undecided.

"Good-by," she said. "I would like you not to hate me any more." She opened the door and went down the stairs without waiting for his answer.

Hélène opened the french window. The gravel crunched under her feet. The night was warm; a fresh scent of growing things rose toward the black sky. She sat down on a little wooden bench against the wall. "After all, nothing has ever happened," she thought. At the far end of the valley a train whistled; it trundled along with all the shades down, invisible. "I mustn't think like that. Each time it could happen." She picked a laurel leaf and crushed it in her fingers. "I'm no

[283]

longer afraid." She felt light and fully herself as on the finest evenings of her childhood, when she rested in the arms of a paternal God. To be dead; one *is* never dead. There is no one left to be dead. I am alive. I shall always be alive. She felt her life beat in her breast and that moment was eternal.

"Hélène!"

The red glow of a cigarette burnt a hole in the darkness. She recognized Jean.

"Hélène, I beg of you," he said. "Don't go tonight!"

"It's no good," she said. "I'm going."

"If the first attempt fails, one ought never to start again. You may have been noticed on the road. Wait a few days."

"They won't wait. Tomorrow they may take him to another camp. There's no time to lose."

Jean sat down beside her. "If it weren't Paul, would you do it?"

"It is Paul."

"Paul is nothing to Denise."

"She agrees to do it. We work together." She thought it over. "But I'm going to suggest something to you: this time I'll go alone."

"No. The slightest accident, if you're alone, and you're done for." He crushed his cigarette under his heel. "I'll go with you."

"You? You've no right to take part in any expedition; it's a strict rule."

"I know," said Jean. "I send people to get killed, and I don't even share their lot."

"Even if you shared it, it wouldn't make any difference," she said.

There was a silence.

"You'll be in danger and I shan't be near you; I cannot bear that," he said.

"You will be near me," she said. "Distance doesn't matter; you are always near me."

He put his arm round her shoulders and she laid her cheek against his.

"You're right," he said. "Now nothing will separate us, ever."

"You know," said Hélène. "I was frightened during the first trips. Now I'm so happy that I can't be frightened any more."

"My dear love," he said.

At the other end of the garden a voice called: "Hélène."

Hélène rose. "I'll see you tomorrow. Telephone and tell Lamy that he can give the signal. We'll be there in an hour."

"Take great care of yourself," said Jean. "And come back quickly." He took her in his arms. "Come back to me."

He let her go and she hurried toward the garage.

"Here I am. I'm ready," she said.

Denise lowered the hood of the delivery van, in which were piled bundles of dirty linen. A scarf hid her hair.

"Everything is in order," she said.

Hélène knotted a silk handkerchief under her chin. "Have you got the suit and the papers?"

"I've got everything we shall need."

They got into the van. Hélène took the wheel.

"Jean didn't want us to go. He says it's unwise."

"He said the same to me. But Paul is certainly counting on us. And soon the nights will not be so dark."

Hélène let in the clutch. Somewhere over there, crouching behind a hut, Paul was listening in the silence. Lamy had jumped on his bicycle, and he would be singing as he went past the camp. Jean was going down toward the station; she had not left him. Now she was no longer ever alone, no longer useless and lost under the empty sky. She existed with him, with Marcel, with Madeleine, Laurent, Yvonne, with all the unknown human beings who slept in wooden huts and who had never heard her name, with all those who longed for a different tomorrow, even with those who did not know how to long for anything. The shell had burst open; she existed for something, for someone. The whole earth was one fraternal unity.

"What a lovely night!" she said.

₪ 13 ₪

A RAY of light filters through the venetian blinds.
Five o'clock. The first doors are opening. The doctor and the midwife hasten to the bedside of the sick
and of the expectant mother. The clandestine dance
halls are emptying into the deserted streets. Round the
railway stations, lights go up in some of the cafés. *They
are putting them against the wall*. He thrust his hand
into his pocket. Hard and cold. A toy. "One would
never think that it could kill." It kills. He went up to
the bed. She will not last the night. And the night is
almost over. Shall I still be there to say: "I have killed
her"? To say: "You must kill again." That voice . . .
it speaks for me; for me it must be silent. What does it
matter to them that my silence is still a voice? Nothing
will save me. But I can go to sleep, sink myself in those
guilty waters. Anguish rends and tears me; it tears me
from myself. Let that tearing cease. . . .

"Jean."

He turned round. She had opened her eyes. She was
looking at him. "Did Paul come?"

"Yes, he's here. All is well."

"Oh, I am glad," she said. That voice was weak, but
clear. He sat down on the edge of the bed.

"How do you feel?"

"I'm comfortable." She took his hands between her
own. "You know, don't be sad. I don't mind dying."

"You are not going to die."

"Do you think so?"

She looked at him; her same old look, suspicious, exacting. "What did the doctor say?"

[287]

This time he could not hesitate; he did not doubt; despite the sweat on her temples and her halting voice, this was no poor fleshly object; she saw, she was free; her last moments belonged only to her.

"He didn't give much hope."

"Ah," she said. "I thought so." She was silent for an instant. "I don't mind," she repeated.

He bent and his lips touched the mauve cheek.

"Hélène, you know I love you."

"Yes, now you love me," she said. She pressed his hand. "I'm happy that you are here; you'll think of me."

"My only love," he said. "You are here, and through my fault."

"Wherein lies the fault?" she said. "It was I who wanted to go."

"But I could have forbidden you."

She smiled. "You had no right to decide for me."

The same words. He looked at her. It is indeed her. She used to say: "It is for me to decide." Then her dull hair used to shine, her hollow cheeks were brilliant with life; it was still she. The same liberty. Then I have not betrayed anyone? Is it indeed you to whom I spoke, to you, and you only in the unique truth of your life? In that gasping breath, in those blue lids, do you still recognize your will?

"That is what you used to say; I let you choose, but did you know what you chose?"

"I chose you. I would make the same choice over again." She shook her head. "I would not have wished to have had any other life."

He did not yet dare to believe in these words which he heard; but the vice about his heart was loosened, and hope rose in the night.

"You hadn't chosen to meet me," he said. "You

stumbled against me as you stumbled against a stone. And now —"

"Now," she said. "But what is there to regret? Was it really so necessary for me to grow old?"

The words scarcely passed her lips. But her eyes were watching. Living, present. It seemed suddenly that time had no more importance, all that time when she would be no more, since at this minute she existed, free and limitless.

"Is it true that you regret nothing?" he said.

"No. Why?"

"Why?" he repeated.

"And, above all, don't feel guilty," she said.

"I'll try."

"You mustn't feel guilty." She smiled weakly. "I did what I wanted. You were just a stone. Stones are necessary to make roads, otherwise how could one choose a way for oneself?"

"If it were true," he said.

"But it is true. I'm certain of it. What would I have been if nothing had ever happened to me?"

"Ah! I wish I could believe you," he said.

"Whom will you believe?"

"When I look at you, I believe you."

"Look at me." She closed her eyes. "I'm going to sleep for a little longer. I'm tired."

He was looking at her. *"It is well!"* Perhaps Paul was right to say "it is well." She was breathing softly and he was looking at her. It seemed to him that he could not have invented any other death, any other life for her. "I believe you, I must believe you. No harm came to you through me. Under your feet I was an innocent stone. As innocent as the stones, as that piece of steel that tore your lung. He did not kill you; it was not I who killed you, my dear love."

[289]

"Hélène!"

He choked back a cry. The veins are swollen and the mouth is half-open. She is sleeping; she has forgotten that she is going to die. A moment ago she knew it; now she is dying and she does not know it. "Do not sleep, wake up." He bent over her. He would have liked to take her by the shoulders to shake her, to implore her; by blowing with all his strength on a dying flame he could manage to revive it. But there is no passage from my mouth to her life; she alone could make herself flame up again toward the light. Hélène! She still has a name, can I no longer call her by it? Her breath is rising with effort from her lungs to her lips; it goes back, grinding from her lips to her lungs; life gasps and labors, and yet she is still complete; she will be complete until the last moment; won't you use it for some other purpose than to die? Each beat of her heart brings her nearer to death. Stop. Inexorably, her heart continues to beat; when it no longer beats, she will already be dead, it will be too late. Stop at once, stop dying.

She opened her eyes and he took her in his arms. Those open eyes no longer saw. Hélène! She no longer heard. Something remains that is not yet absent to itself, but is already absent from the earth, absent from me. Those eyes still have a look, a frozen look, a look that no longer sees anything. The breathing stops. She has said: "I am glad that you are here; but I am not here; I know that something is happening, but I cannot watch it; it is not happening here or elsewhere, but beyond all presence." She breathes once more, the eyes cloud over; the world detaches itself from her, it crumbles; and yet she does not slide out of the world; it is in the heart of the world that she becomes the dead woman that I hold in my arms. A spasm draws down the corner of her lips. Her eyes see no more. He closes the lids over the lifeless eyes. Dear face, dear body. This was your forehead, these were your lips. You have left me; but I can still cherish your absence; it keeps your features; it is there, present in that motionless form. Stay, stay with me. . . .

He raised his head again. He must have remained for a long time with his forehead resting against her silent heart. That flesh which was you. He looked with anguish at the motionless face. It had not changed, but already it was no longer she. A relict, an effigy, no longer anyone. Now her absence has lost its shape, now she has finally glided out of the world. And the world is as full as yesterday; nothing is missing: there is no flaw. It does not seem possible. As if she had been nothing on this earth.

As if I were nothing. Nothing and everything; present to all mankind throughout the entire world, yet separated from them forever; as guilty and innocent as the pebble on the road. So heavy and yet so light.

He started. Someone was knocking. He walked toward the door.

"What is it?"

"I want your answer," said Laurent. He took a step forward and looked at the bed.

"Yes," said Blomart. "It is over."

"Did she suffer much?"

"No."

He looked at the window. The day had dawned. The minutes were calling the minutes, chasing, driving one another forward, without end. Go on, go on. Decide. Once more the bell tolls, it will toll until my death.

"The time-bomb can be laid within an hour from now," said Laurent. "Do you agree or not?"

He looked at the bed. For you, only an innocent

stone — you had chosen. Those who will be shot tomorrow have not chosen; I am the rock that crushes them; I shall not escape the curse; forever I shall be to them another being, forever I shall be to them the blind force of fate, forever separated from them. But if only I use myself to defend that supreme good which makes innocent and vain all the stones and all the rocks, that good which saves each man from all the others and from myself — Liberty — then my passion will not have been in vain. You have not given me peace; but why should I desire peace? You have given me the courage to accept forever the risk and the anguish, to bear my crimes and my guilt, which will rend me eternally. There is no other way.

"Don't you agree?" said Laurent.

"Yes," he said. "I agree."

INDIANA STATE T.C. LIBRARY

PRINTER'S NOTE

This book was set on the Linotype in GRANJON, *a type named in compliment to Robert Granjon, type-cutter and printer — 1523–1590, Antwerp, Lyons, Rome, Paris. Granjon, the boldest and most original designer of his time, was one of the first to practice the trade of type-founder apart from that of printer.*

Linotype GRANJON *was designed by George W. Jones, who based his drawings upon a face used by Claude Garamond (1510–1561) in his beautiful French books.* GRANJON *more closely resembles Garamond's own type than do any of the various modern faces that bear his name.*

The book was composed, printed, and bound by The Plimpton Press, Norwood, Massachusetts. The typography and binding are by W. A. Dwiggins.